DON'T TOUCH THE BLUE STUFF!

WHERE THE HELL IS TESLA? BOOK 2

ROB DIRCKS

GOLDFINCH  PUBLISHING

Published by Goldfinch Publishing
An Imprint of SARK Industries, Inc.
www.goldfinchpublishing.com

Publisher's Note:
This is a work of fiction. Names, characters, places, and incidents either are the product of the author's imagination or are used fictitiously. Any resemblance to actual persons, living or dead, events, or locales is entirely coincidental. Use of Nikola Tesla as historical figure and character have been approved by William Terbo, grand nephew and last living relative of Tesla.

Library of Congress Cataloging-in-Publication Data
Rob Dircks, 1967-
Don't Touch the Blue Stuff! (Where the Hell is Tesla? Book 2) / by Rob Dircks
p. cm.
ISBN 978-0692935293

PRAISE FOR DON'T TOUCH THE BLUE STUFF! (WHERE THE HELL IS TESLA? BOOK 2)

"★★★★★ An amusing and unexpectedly crazy ride - a perfect and hilarious follow-up to *Where the Hell is Tesla?*" – *AudiobookReviewer.com*

"So damn funny and insanely entertaining! Loved the first one and this was just as fun."– *Dan Bova, Entrepreneur.com*

"Chip's at it again! He was very fun in *Where the Hell Is Tesla?* and he's just as fun in this book. And Dircks continues to impress me with his narrating abilities." – *Dab of Darkness Reviews*

"★★★★★ **An incredible, madcap adventure that only Dircks could deliver.** The "Tesla" books are living proof that original stories are still out there waiting to be discovered."

"★★★★★ **I love this series!** It gets better and better. Love wins! If you haven't read *Where the Hell is a Tesla?*, you must. You'll love both. I promise. Thank you Mr. Dircks!"

"★★★★★ **So damn funny and insanely entertaining!** Loved the first one and this was just as fun."

"★★★★★ **You never know with sequels... Fortunately, you don't have to worry about this one.** Dircks' second in the *Tesla* series delivers every bit as well as the first - in the same balls-to-the-wall writing style that made the first book so entertaining."

"★★★★★ There isn't another writer like Rob Dircks in the entire multiverse."

"★★★★★ **SHEER EXUBERANCE** - The sheer exuberance displayed by Chip, his damn-the-torpedoes-full-speed-ahead approach to plot twists (plus the crying, cussing, vomiting that accompany it), carry me along like a tidal wave. I never tire of Pete, Tesla, Gina, Bobo, and other fellow travelers as they courageously forge ahead (or bumble ahead) of troubles and catastrophes."

"★★★★ **More fun than the original!** - There are a fair number of scifi based humorous buddy adventures out there, and lots of them are entertaining enough. But, this book, (and the series), strikes me as just right. The energy, cheerfulness, and clever humor was as fresh and engaging as before."

To Dad

It wasn't perfect.
But it was.
As I find myself walking in your footsteps,
I understand more.
Thanks.

NOTICE:

Posted by Special Agent Gina Phillips
United States Federal Bureau of Investigation

The United States Federal Bureau of Investigation disavows the following collection of documents, composed by one Clarence "Chip" Collins. It is a work of fiction. As you read its pages, you will likely exclaim "That's absurd! Completely implausible!" This is good. Keep repeating these phrases to yourself. This is what you should believe. Trust us. We're the FBI.

Additionally, for those repeatedly requesting Room 3327 in the New Yorker Hotel in New York City, also known as the "Nikola Tesla Room" – that room is no longer available. Not because it's been commandeered by the FBI for national security reasons, but because, um, they found rats in that room. Just that one room. Lots of rats. Huge ones. The room will be sealed until further notice. It had a terrible view anyway. The rest of the hotel is perfectly clean, no rats, and has much better views.

Finally, this fabricated document also contains a portrayal of me as a cold, angry agent with a hair-trigger temper. This couldn't be further from the truth. In reality, I am sweet, kind, patient, and rarely discharge my firearm at deserving punk perps. Semi-rarely. Okay, yes, it happens. But like I said, they deserve it.

Please enjoy this fictional document, which spins tales of imaginary events that could never, ever happen.

Ever.

PART ONE: ALL THE PETES

1. MR. PRESIDENT

"Mr. President. We need you to come with us."

Don't you hate when you're having breakfast in the Oval Office, a nice fresh waffle with an egg on top, right there at the Resolute Desk, and a bunch of Secret Service agents crash in, all guns and sunglasses, and ruin it?

"President Collins. The bunker is ready."

"It's Chip. Come on, Artie. Just call me Chip. You want a waffle?"

"Sir. Ah, Chip, sir. We don't have long. The Blue Juice is coming."

The Blue Juice. Those stupid terrorists couldn't figure out a nuclear weapon, so they stole a missile containing some Extraterrestrial Plasma Consciousness – not the catchiest name, so I've been calling it "Blue Juice" – and have it ready to launch from a sub heading towards the coast of Virginia. Assholes.

"Yeah, yeah. I know all about it, Artie. We're not leaving."

"Sir?"

"Look. I might just be your stand-in President, but I know a thing or two about fighting the Blue Juice."

"Sir. With all due respect…"

"Artie. I like you. You're the best Chief of Staff a guy could ask for. And I get the continuity of government thing. I do. But do you really think I'm going to save my own ass when millions of people in D.C. could die?"

Artie rolls his eyes. He knows I love an audience, and that I can't resist a dramatic moment.

"No, sir. Of course I don't."

"Good. Then get a hold of Pete. Pete Turner. And hand me that journal."

"Sir. Chip, sir. The regulations state–"

I grab the journal from his hand, slam it down on to the desk, and open it to a blank page.

"It's time to call Nikola Tesla."

2. WOAH

Dear reader person,

Woah.

Normally, I'd say "Shit's crazy, don't ask," and just move on. Because you know how it goes in the INTERDIMENSIONAL TRANSFER APPARATUS. But you're literally one page into reading this book, so I appreciate that you're totally fucking lost.

So let me back up.

Way up.

Like all the way back to the end of the last book, when I get this email from Pete:

From: Pete Turner
To: Chip Collins
Date: October 23, 2016 1:04am
Subject: Dude

Dude,

You still have your Awesome Man cape laying around? I could use a hand.

- Pete

Now, the first time I got this email I was genuinely concerned. I mean, he's my best friend and he's in trouble, right? And if anything ever happened to him I'd be a basket case. But fast forward a couple of months, and it turns out he keeps sending me the same email every week, and the FBI has to forward it to me with a note that says "your friend is annoying," because, as you know, email doesn't work for shit in the ITA. And every time I go, all worried about him, he's just sitting in his living room with Meg, having a beer. And he says, "Made you look." And we get in a professional-wrestler-style brawl and he throws me out the window.

Uh-oh.

I just thought of something else.

Maybe I should back up even further.

It might have been a while since you read *Where the Hell is Tesla?*, or – horror of horrors – you might not have even read the first book. So you might be like, "What the hell is this guy talking about? And what kind of dickhead best friend throws you out a window?"

So you know what? I've got something special for you:

Chip's Official Summary Of
The Entire First Book In One Breath

Yes, that's right. I'm going to attempt, in *Guinness Book of World Records* fashion, to distill a fifty-three-thousand word novel into a single thought for you, requiring just one breath. First, a little dramatic hyperventilating… in… out… in… out… in… out… in… ready?

Okay, when we first met out heroes (that would be me and Pete), Chip Collins (me) was a security guard at a mothballed FBI research building, where I found the lost journal of Nikola Tesla, the amazing inventor of alternating current electricity, among lots of other amazing things, who also created something called the INTERDIMENSIONAL TRANSFER APPARATUS, or ITA, a portal which allowed a person possessing its lock combination (zero-zero-zero-zero) to travel through a (boring looking) hallway into all the infinite dimensions that make up the multiverse oh my god I'm getting dizzy

…GASP…

Woah, I almost blacked out. Guess I'm not going for the world record. Oh well. Send the *World Records* people home. Anyway, moving on, I talked Pete Turner (my best friend since college) into taking a little trip into this ITA thing. And you can guess what happened:

Shit instantly turned upside down.

We got stuck inside, unable to find our way home, got attacked by – and then BFFd – a furry alien we named Bobo, contacted Tesla through his copy of the lost journal (shit's crazy, don't ask, it just works), who was being held in a prison by an evil being named WHO, who was bent on collapsing all the infinite possible universes into a single one that he could rule with impunity, then we became superheroes in a lighter-gravity dimension where we met Meg (Pete's fiancé, more on that later), Bobo died and was resurrected (not a Jesus metaphor, it just happened that way), we met our Alternates – versions of ourselves from other dimensions – a bunch of times, and fought alongside them in the Epic Battle For The Multiverse. Which – of course – we won.

The end.

Wow. So not in one breath, but only two paragraphs. The whole book. *Boom.*

• • •

Anyway, Pete and Meg now live in her dimension, they've reached some kind of agreement with the feds and the military, they're engaged too, and that dimension as I said has lighter gravity, so Pete throwing me out the window is actually a total pisser. It's like we're in a superhero movie every time we get together – me as Awesome Man (of course) and Pete as The Brute. Like that time last month we saved the people on the plane after it skidded off the runway at LaGuardia Airport into the East River, and I was like "Damn, this dimension is cool. I think I want to live in this dimension."

"Nah. It's kind of a pain in the ass to do it full time, dude. Like you get asked for your autograph every five second– oh wait, you would love that shit."

"Round-the-clock public adoration? Yes, I would love that shit very much."

"Bad example. Whatever. Trust me, it's not all roses. Now shut up and keep pulling, or this thing's gonna sink."

"You think they'll give me another key to the city for this?"

"Don't be an idiot. There's only one key."

"Dude. They gave us each one. That's two keys right there. They probably have a stock room full of them."

"I meant you already got your one key. One key per hero."

"And who made that rule?"

"God, you're such a pain in the ass."

So yeah, it's mostly a blast, but there's also the breaking stuff. We try not to, but we're always breaking expensive stuff. Like the Statue of Liberty. Do you have any idea how much new copper panels cost for that thing?

Oh, and speaking of expensive shit I can't afford, even though the first book did okay, I didn't see any royalties from it. Nada. Zilch. The FBI wouldn't let me make money off of it. Can you believe that? Some bullshit national security excuse. So they put me on salary instead, I guess to throw me a bone – or more likely to keep a leash on me.

Yeah.

Me. Salaried. FBI.

I know, impossible. But true. Chip Collins, former low-end security guard and subsequent Master of Interdimensional Travel, is technically (though they definitely don't like to admit it) an agent of the United States Federal Bureau of Investigation. You should see them when I flash my badge (literally every single time I pass one of them in the halls, it's so badass). Rolling their eyes like I'm the biggest embarrassment to the Bureau ever. Which is total horse shit of course, seeing as I pretty much single-handedly saved the multiverse. (Okay, okay, yes, I got a ton of help. A ton.) Pete got to be an agent too, but also continue his double life as part time superhero and part time hedge fund market options risk wealth something-or-other (I never could understand in all those years what the hell he does for a living).

And then of course there's what happened with me and Julie.

3. THE ROMANTIC PART

Yeah, don't worry, Julie's fine, it's all good. I just like telling the story, because it's so freaking romantic. You're like the millionth person I've told. People cross to the other side of Second Avenue now when they see me coming because they know they're going to hear it again. Here's how it goes:

So the whole time I was trying to save the multiverse and get home, I was also writing Julie – my ex-girlfriend – on my cell phone, because I finally realized that I fucked up, and really, truly did love her. And in the end, after punching me in the face for sending her 3,612 emails at once, she gave me a break, heard me out, and we did other stuff. You know. Don't make me explain. Use your imagination.

Anyway, after a little pizza dinner one night at our apartment (God, I'll take a slice of New York pizza over an Epic Battle For The Multiverse any day), this is our conversation:

"Marry me."

Julie spits out her wine. "Excuse me?"

I start mopping the wine off my shirt. Red wine. White shirt. Yeah, that's not coming out. "Marry me. I mean it."

She hops onto my lap, helping me dab my shirt with some water. "Marry you? Are you drunk?"

"It takes a lot more than half a box of wine to get me drunk." I reach up and kiss her.

She pulls back. "Wait a second… did you find out about my trust fund? Is that what this is about?"

"You have a trust fund? Why are we drinking merlot out of a box?"

"Hey, Mister Fancypants. Look here." She points to the box. "It's got a gold medal."

I pick up the box. "It's a sticker. And it says 'Voted Best Value by Bob's Discount Shoppers.' The salad dressing over there has the same sticker. Now stop stalling. Answer the question."

She squishes my cheeks, puckering my lips, and plants a wet one on me. "Well, since I don't have a trust fund, you must be serious. And you are super adorable. And you treat me like a goddess now. Finally. Hmmm… I don't know…"

I lift her from my lap, making her squeak, and carry her towards the bedroom. "Let's make this more interesting. I've got something to show you. Close your eyes."

She scrunches up her face, shutting her eyes tight, points up at me, wagging her finger. "If it's a thousand candles and rose petals all over the bed, you're cleaning it up."

I gently carry her through the doorway to our bedroom, careful not to hit her head, and dim the lights. My playlist, *Soft Music for Lovemaking*, starts.

"Okay. Now… you can look."

Julie, a blissful smile on her face, opens her eyes.

"Awww, you bought me a stuffed animal. It's cute."

And then the small, furry alien, furrier than you can imagine, sitting on the edge of the bed, wiggles his toes, turns his head, and looks up at her with his huge, black, Bambi eyes.

Blink. Blink.

"BEEZNEEZ."

"WHAT THE FUCK?!?!"

. . .

Julie screams, flailing in my arms, her body spasming and kicking in terror. I'm trying to shush her by putting my hand over her mouth, which just makes it all worse, because now there's spit everywhere and I have teeth marks in my palm. In her frenzy of thrashing around, she slams a flip-flop right in my crotch, and – as happens when your junk is suddenly traumatized – I instinctively let her drop to the ground. She twists her ankle and shrieks in pain.

Then I watch, numb, through the dim light and soft music, as the love of my life limps/runs out of the bedroom, screaming bloody murder. I can still hear her outside the apartment, down the stairs, and outside down Second Avenue. I wonder how long it'll take for the cops to show up.

I let myself crumple to the floor in a fetal position, rocking back and forth, waiting for the pain to subside, although I'm pretty sure it never will.

The furry alien hops off the bed, sits down next to me, and rocks on his little butt to the same rhythm as me. Pats me on the head.

I look up at him. "Oh well, Bobo. Not exactly the marriage proposal I imagined."

4. WAIT, THIS IS THE ROMANTIC PART

There's a knock at the door.

I rush out to answer, ready to flash my FBI badge and let the cops know it was all a big misunderstanding, but I can't really say more, because, you know, national security. I stop mid-step and shout-whisper back to the bedroom. "Bobo! Back in the cubby, dude!"

I can hear Bobo clambering back into his hiding spot behind my shoes in the closet as I peer through the peephole. Uh-oh. The SWAT team is avoiding my view, I can't see anything. I try to sound official. "Officers, I'm sorry to take your valuable time, I'm sure you'll understand–"

"Shut up. Just shut up."

I look back through the hole. It's Julie. "Oh. It's you."

The door won't open. She's holding it closed from the outside. "No. We can talk through the door."

"Um, okay. Listen, Julie, I know I'm an idiot. I was just–"

"I'll do the talking. Julie ask. Chip answer."

I instinctively salute. I don't know why. "Chip understand Julie."

"First, I assume that was the Bobo thing you've been telling me about."

"Yes."

"Second, what the fuck?"

"Okay, here's the story: I love you, and I don't ever want to lie to you, so when this happened, I wanted to share it with you in the right way, maybe even make it part of something special, which of course was very poorly thought out, I realize now, but at the time it seemed–"

"No. I don't need the Chip ten-minute version. Just the normal person five-second version. Just tell me what happened."

"Sorry. Okay, when I came back through the ITA, I must've had a little Bobo matter, maybe just the tiniest smear or something inside my pocket, from when he exploded himself all over the place in the Epic Battle for the Multiverse. I threw the pants in the hamper, and I saw the pocket moving, and I was like 'either those pants are so nasty they're trying to walk themselves to the cleaners, or something is in there.' And sure enough – there was the teeniest little Bobo in the pocket! I didn't know what the hell to do, this dimension's never seen anything like him, and I was scared to tell the FBI, they keep denying he even exists, so I hid him. And of course within a few hours he grew to his normal height, so–"

"So you thought he would make a good wedding present?"

"Yeah. No. Well. Now I see how going for the two-fer probably wasn't very smart. I just, I just finally had you back, and then Bobo came back, and it was all so perfect, I wanted to grab the brass ring. I thought we could all live together like when people get a dog before they get married and start having kids or something. I want nothing more than that. To start something like that with you. To share everything with you – the good, the bad, even the crazy. I love you, Julie. I'm more certain than ever." I move closer to where I think her ear is. "And I'm sorry."

Silence.

She lets the door crack open. An inch. "Two more questions." Another salute. "Chip understand Julie."

"An alien sitting on the bed and *Soft Music for Lovemaking* is playing? What the hell? I can't unexperience that, Chip. Gross."

"Sorry. He likes that playlist."

"Yeah, well. Gross. It's officially retired. Time for a new playlist."

"Of course." I lean down closer to the eye I can see through the door crack, her beautiful green eye. "Now what's your last question?"

The eye squints a little. I can tell she's smiling. "I think you know what the last question is."

I reach into my pocket. Pull out the smallest diamond ring you've ever seen, like something you'd buy for your American Girl doll, she deserves so much more, but it's all I've got, and I pass it through the thin opening. I feel her finger slip into the ring. Perfect fit.

The door opens.

"Yes."

She limps and falls into my arms, and I swing her around, and she's laughing, and her red hair is all over the place, and in my head *Soft Music for Lovemaking* starts playing again, and I still don't know whether Bobo's telepathic or not, but he comes jogging out from his hiding place, doing a little jig, and Julie looks down at him and laughs. So I pick him up too, and I swing both of them around and it's a great, big, beautiful ball of love. It lasts forever.

I told you it was romantic, right?

Oh, that's also the exact moment our neighbor, Mrs. Rosen, shuffles through the open door, looking down at her walker, fumbling through her housecoat pockets to find her cat-lady glasses. "I hope it's okay dears, I heard some screaming, and naturally I want to make sure my favorite neighbors are all right, and–" she looks up, sees me and Julie and Bobo spinning like a whirling dervish, and her eyes roll back into her head and she passes out. Boom.

We stop.

"Is she dead?"

Bobo tentatively approaches her still form.

"Bobo. Don't you DARE hump her leg."

5. MY CITY HALL WEDDING

Fast forward a week. I look down at my ticket: C676. My new favorite number. Well, letter-number combination.

We're here in City Hall, down on Park Row and Broadway, Room 212, sitting on a surprisingly nice yellow couch by the window. It's sunny out, no humidity, and the leaves are still falling in the park outside. Sometimes New York City startles you, how beautiful it can be. And it smells nice in here, like they just washed the floors. Anyway, it's me and Julie. We're getting married. I even rented a tux. It's happening right now. Whenever they're done with couple C675.

We brought my mom and Mrs. Rosen with us – as witnesses, but also to make sure we hadn't caused Mrs. Rosen any permanent physical or psychological damage with our little Bobo surprise dance party, and to make sure she had fully bought into the *Bobo-is-just-a-stuffed-animal* story. But with Bobo's ability to sit perfectly still for her – and I mean *perfectly still* – and Mrs. Rosen's *iffy-at-best* memory, I think we're in the clear. She bought it. Needless to say, Bobo's not with us. We left him at home. Don't want people passing out and shitting themselves at my wedding.

We also decided against having Pete and Meg. Man, *that* was a tough call. He's going to be pissed. But he's been impossible to get in touch with for a couple of weeks, and the FBI's not letting me use the ITA at the moment, and seriously, once Julie found her perfect dress (yes, the one she always insisted was ugly but secretly loved), she started trying it on constantly around the apartment, and we figured we better get this over with before she spilled some box merlot on it or something.

"Okay, kiddos. You're number's up! Let's get you hitched!" My mom points up to the monitor, nudges me and winks. Damn, I love my mom. Moms are the best.

We all get up and shuffle – I swear if Mrs. Rosen walked any slower we'd be going backwards – down the hall into the little chapel. Wait – *chapel?* Who am I kidding? They might as well put a cash register on the lectern. Like "One wedding? That'll be a hundred and four dollars, thank you very much. You get two side salads with that. What dressings would you like? This one here was voted Best Value by Bob's Discount Shoppers."

Anyway, this guy Mr. Patel greets us, seems nice enough, and guides us through the forms. Then I hand him my credit card, he swipes it, and like a carnival fortune telling machine that just got its quarter, he automatically launches into his memorized wedding ceremony spiel.

And you guessed it, tears start streaming down my face immediately. I'm such a sap. Julie's just so beautiful. Like a dream. Holding her little bouquet of daisies, standing there all awkward in her off-white dress with the fancy stitching, sniffing a little. Smiling her mysterious Mona Lisa smile, a couple of tears making their way down her chin. Wow, I don't think I've ever seen her look so radiant. This is going to be great.

I'm in sort of a trance by the time Mr. Patel gets to "… if any party has reason why these two should not be married, speak now or forever hold your peace…" But that line wakes me the hell up. My eyes dart around the room, looking for something stupid to happen. Come on, something stupid, show your stupid face.

Nothing?

Good.

I've sort of developed this *if-something-can-go-wrong-it-will* sixth sense, but apparently it's a false alarm. It's just us. Me and Julie. In love. About to be bound forever. From this moment forward, nothing will ever come between us. Smooth sailing from here on out. I'm certain of it. More certain than I've ever been of anything. Uninterrupted bliss.

And somebody bursts through the doors.

Gina.

Agent Gina Phillips.

Of course.

The FBI agent who hired me as a security guard. Then had Ted fire me. Then was forced to hire me again as an *agent*, against her very vocal objections. The most by-the-book, wound up, terminally-irritated person I've ever met in my entire life, who detests everything I stand for: lounging, skirting rules, having fun at the expense of just about anything, and generally not getting worked up about much. Why am I not surprised that Gina Phillips is here ruining my wedding?

"Gina. Get out of here. I'm getting married."

"Collins. Come with me. Emergency."

"Dude. You ever hear of a phone?"

"For the last time, I'm not a dude. And NOW, Collins."

"No. Whatever this is it can wait. Five minutes. Get out. In the hall. Or I'm going to sick Mrs. Rosen on you." And wouldn't you know, little old Mrs. Rosen nods and hikes up her sleeves. I swear to God. I almost laugh.

But Gina's not having it. She marches over and grabs my arm. "National Security. We're leaving. Now." She tugs me, and Julie starts beating her with her daisies, petals flying all over the place. "Get the fuck off him, Phillips, you big meanie!" Mrs. Rosen shuffles over too, smacking her in the shins with her walker. Good for you, Mrs. Rosen. My mom just sits there rolling her eyes and face-palming, like of course my wedding would turn into chaos, like was there ever really a doubt? Ever since I was a little kid I can remember her just rolling her eyes every time I got myself into something stupid, which was pretty much constant. But she loved me anyway, and even in this chaos I spy her wink at me. She knows I got this. Thanks, Mom.

I rip my arm free from Gina. "STOP!!" And for the next five seconds, you can hear a pin drop. Everyone's frozen. I turn to Mr. Patel. "Look. If you wouldn't mind getting to the important thing, that'd be great."

But Mr. Patel is paralyzed by this extraordinary breach of quickie wedding protocol. "Uh... um.. I don't... where..."

Gina starts pulling me out of the room. She's really strong.

I scream back over my shoulder, "Say the thing, man. SAY THE THING!"

And Mr. Patel, realizing the gravity of the situation, or more likely realizing this union's already been paid in full, cuts to the chase: "By-the-power-vested-in-me-by-the-State-of-New-York-I-now-pronounce-you-husband-and-wife!" And he stamps our certificate like he just finished the hundred meter dash, like a boss, with a sneer at Gina, like "Take THAT, you interloper!"

Julie grabs the paper and rushes in front of Gina, blocking her path, thrusting the empty daisy stems up to her nose. "Now you listen here, Phillips. If you don't give me five minutes with my new husband, I'm calling *Mister* Phillips." She grabs Gina's hand and points to the wedding ring on it. "Yeah. *Your* husband. I think he'd like to hear how his wife kicked Love in the balls. That should make for some nice dinner talk tonight."

Their eyes are locked. Yikes. I'm scared. Of both of them.

Gina flinches. Looks down (oh, did I mention she's at least six inches taller than everyone else in the room?) and gives Julie a weird look, very un-Gina-like. "Three minutes. I'll be outside." She storms out and slams the door in her wake.

Julie turns on me. Uh-oh.

"Now you listen, too, mister..." the tears are really coming now, mine and hers, and she throws her arms around my neck, and whispers in my ear, "...I will not lose you again. You can't do this. Let's sneak out the back. Run away."

I hold her face in my hands, smoothing her loose hair behind her ears. "No. I've stopped running away from things, babe. I ran away from you once, and it was the dumbest thing I've ever done. Now I've got you, you're mine forever, I'm yours forever, and I've got a real job, a job I actually like, that I think I might be good at. Let me check this out, I'm sure everything's fine. You know these people, they get wound up about every little thing. And no matter what, even if I have to do a little dimension hopping, I'll be home tonight in time to grab us some takeout from Wong's. Just watch Bobo– *I mean our stuffed animal, wink, wink* – until I get back." I raise my ring finger and wiggle it. "Now I just need something to remind me of today. Got any ideas?"

She laughs through her tears, unties my new ring from one of the remaining limp daisy stems. Slides it onto my finger.

I smile. "I do."

"I do too."

We kiss.

And on cue, my mom, Mr. Patel, and Mrs. Rosen applaud like a hundred thousand fans at a Barry Manilow concert. (Well, that's what it sounds like to me anyway.) And Mr. Patel pumps his fists into the air and shouts, "LOVE WINS!" Aww, he's probably been waiting to shout that for twenty-three years.

I turn to leave, and Julie grabs my hand. *"Wait!"*

"Come on, Julie, it's just one day. I'll be back tonight." But she's got this weird look on her face, like there's a thought trying to make it out of her mouth but it won't budge. She points down to her stomach.

"Oooh. Stomach ache? Okay, no Wong's tonight, I'll make you pasta with butter. And tea. And I'll pick up a roll of TUMS on the way home. Gotta go."

She clutches me tighter. "No, you idiot." And she points down to her belly again, this time twice for emphasis.

"Cramps? Julie, look, Gina's going to be back in here in thirty seconds. I'll rub your feet later."

And she grabs my face and smushes her lips to my ear and in the faintest whisper possible, I can barely make it out, she says…

"… i think i'm pregnant."

6. HOLY SHIT

Holy shit.

Did I just hear that right? *I think I'm pregnant?*

As I walk out with Gina, I'm stunned silent. (Yes. Silent. Me. I agree: that might be a first.)

Holy shit.

Pregnant.

But… there's no way!

I mean, there were obviously a whole *lot of ways* it could have happened, but I thought we were waiting, being patient, being (for the most part) careful, all that grown-up stuff. Like there was some maturation process that would happen naturally. Somehow we'd both get our shit together first.

But I guess that's not how life works. I should know by now. You don't get your shit together first. Life happens to you first, and then you get your shit together.

Wow.

I'm going to be a dad.

Okay, Chip. Don't jump to conclusions. She said *I think* I'm pregnant. Not *I am* pregnant. Breathe. Breathe again. You're not a dad. Maybe. Just maybe you're a dad. Don't say anything to anyone until you know for sure, after you get home tonight. Zip those lips. Mum's the word. Not a peep. Silence is golden.

"Why are you smiling like a goofball, Collins?"

"I'M GOING TO BE A DAD!"

Whoops. So much for keeping my giant mouth shut.

"Wonderful. You can celebrate in nine months. Now wipe that smirk off and get in the car. They're waiting for us."

Actually saying the word "dad" out loud stops me short, and does, in fact, wipe the smirk off my face. "Wait, Gina. I would make a good dad, right?"

"No."

"Wow. Quick answer. Like you were waiting for me to ask. No hesitation."

"None at all."

"Really? What makes you so sure?"

"I don't have time to list all the reasons, Collins."

Yikes. I mean, I don't really care what Gina Phillips thinks, do I? But it's bugging me now. I know I'm not quite ready, maybe less ready than I should be, but what the hell does she know? "Come on. One reason. Give me one."

"One: you're immature. Two: you have zero discipline. Three: you're a slob. Four: you're the worst role model for-"

"Okay, jeez. I asked for *one* reason."

"Good. Get in the car." And she unceremoniously stuffs me into her *yeah-this-doesn't-look-too-much-like-a-cop-car* Chevy Suburban SUV with the black windows. For one of those forever moments, I'm mulling over what she just said, God, she sounded like she could have gone on with that list forever. But then I snap out of it and look around. "Dude. We're going to work? It's literally four blocks to Federal Plaza. I could beat you to the office walking. In fact, that's what I'm going to do. Ready, set, go." I start to exit the monster truck, and Gina reaches past me and slams the door shut.

"Stop calling me dude. And we're not going to the office."

"Shake Shack?"

"No, we're not going to Shake Shack. We're going right to the ITA." She starts heading uptown to the New Yorker Hotel. Gee. It really must be an emergency. The Bureau hasn't let me use the ITA for a month, said they had a few tweaks in the works. Suddenly they want me there in five minutes? And I didn't tell any of them about my impromptu wedding, but they found me anyway. They're jumpy. "So what's all the hubbub about then?"

"Picked up a spike on the MRM."

"MRM…"

"Collins, do you read any of the briefs? Any of them?"

"Uh, yeah. Of course. I got that one about the golf outing from Keith. I don't think I can make it. Honeymoon, you know. The 'MRM' brief, I'm positive I read it, just a little sketchy on the details…"

Gina squints at me, knowing full well that "just a little sketchy on the details" is code for "I hit delete on every single email you send me, Gina," so she just keeps squinting at me for a while and lets her burning hot laser eyes drill into my soul. While she's driving uptown. Pretty impressive, actually.

She finally speaks. "You listening? Good. MRM stands for MULTIVERSE RESONANCE MONITOR." (Yes. All caps.)

"Oooh. Sounds shiny."

"Tesla invented it for us. Apparently, the multiverse resonates at a specific frequency, with normal variations based on event outcomes. The MRM keeps track of it. They've been picking up spikes. They call them anomalies. Then this morning we got another anomaly. A huge one."

"Wait – Tesla invented something else for you guys? I've been asking him for an AUTOMATIC FURRY FOOT SHAVER – an AFFS, if you will – and he totally blew me off." For emphasis, I slip my shoe off and pull down my sock, revealing my five-day foot stubble, and too many razor nicks to count. "I mean, look at this."

Gina recoils, swerves the truck, almost hits a cab. "Put that thing away! You want to get us killed? What the hell?" And she shudders, obviously trying to destroy the memory of ever seeing my poorly-groomed furry foot.

I'm hurt. "Hey. Gotta make sacrifices when you're saving the multiverse, Gina."

"Fine. Just don't ever show that thing to me again."

I don't know why Gina cops so much attitude with me. I never did anything to her. I mean, that's not totally true. I bailed on the security guard job she hired me for. And I called her that one time at three in the morning asking what happens when an agent – not me, I was asking for a friend – accidentally discharges his firearm into the East River. (Answer: "Tell your 'friend' if you ever do that again, I don't care how many multiverses you save, you're fired. Again.") And I'm pretty much the opposite of everything she holds dear: order, discipline, physical stamina, work ethic, following orders, etc. Whatever. That doesn't excuse her for crashing my wedding. "Hey, by the way. You showed up at my wedding without a present."

Silence. I hate silence. (In case you haven't noticed.) I look down at her wedding ring. "How long have you been married? Ever think about kids?"

Gina screeches into a parking spot, and I practically go through the windshield. She mutters, "We're here."

Oh well. I guess she's done with the small talk. I'll ask her later. Anyway, we're now parked in the small garage under the New Yorker Hotel. They've got five spots – tucked away where no one would notice – reserved for the FBI. (I guess management doesn't exactly want to broadcast that you, enthusiastic New York City Tourist, are staying in a luxurious hotel room right next door to the INTERDIMENSIONAL TRANSFER APPARATUS – an experimental and unpredictable portal that could destroy the multiverse.)

So I put my best swagger on as we walk to the secret entrance (a.k.a the kitchen staff door), me and Gina, yeah that's right we're two badass FBI agents, and she's trying to stay ahead of me, but I'm catching up. "So Gina, why me on this thing? I mean, of course I know what I'm doing in the ITA, and it's flattering, but it's just a spike. Send somebody else in. I've got… you know… important stuff to get back to. Like that thing I told yo-"

She stops short and cuts me off.

"It's not just a spike. This time it's Pete."

7. FOR PETE'S SAKE

Pete?

Yikes.

No wonder he didn't get back to me about the wedding. Something's up. But I swear to God, if I jump into the ITA and find him and he says "Made you look," I'm going to kick his ass. (Well, I'll try to kick his ass while he laughs at my complete and utter lack of ass-kicking ability.)

Anyway, while I'm thinking all this, me and Gina march through the lobby – I must look like her teenage son, that's how much taller than me she is – and as we pass the concierge, Miss Barber, she gives me a little conspiratorial nod and a half smile. Miss Barber digs the cloak and dagger thing, even though she has no clue what's really up there in Room 3327.

We step out of the elevator, walk down the hall. "Hey, speaking of Room 3327, what have you guys been up to in here for the past month? New drapes?"

"You'll see." Gina waves the new schnazzy-looking room badge they gave us and the sound of a hundred (I'm guessing, could be even more) deadbolts retracting lets us know we're good to enter.

I open the door.

Woah.

I swing the door back closed for a second to double-check the room number plate. Yup. It says 3327. But there's *no way* this is Room 3327.

This is the bridge from the Starship Enterprise.

Seriously – there are enough flashing lights and smooth, metallic surfaces to send every single fanboy down at NYC Comic Con into a breathless tizzy. (That would include me. I'm giddy like that kid who won a trip to the set of *Star Wars VII*.) I don't even know where to look, there's nothing even remotely resembling a hotel room left. No windows, no beds, no doorways. No coffee table with the *Big Book of Things to Do in New York City* or the room service menu. Just a bunch of guys in those white clean room suits milling around.

Oh, and Fred.

Fred's the FBI guy who took over the ITA project once I brought it to their attention, when I 1) discovered the journal they lost and 2) saved the multiverse. He's maybe four steps down from the Director. Nice guy, really nice, but not the guy you want to put in charge of something as powerful as the ITA. An example: one time I had him to my apartment – he's cool like that, doesn't shy away from accepting invitations from lowly agents sometimes – and as he was talking to Julie, he backed up and leaned against what he thought was a closed window.

Yeah. He fell out.

Luckily, the fire escape caught him – but you've never seen so many guns get whipped out for no good reason. Like dudes, how are bullets supposed to stop your boss from falling out a window?

Anyway, Fred's now sitting here at the big lab table in the middle of the room, with Tesla's journal right in the center. I go over to pick it up.

He smacks my hand. "Get. Get. Put on a suit first. Sorry, new rules. Everything in and out of the ITA has to be sanitized. You put one on too, Phillips."

Gina gives him the *who-me* look. It's kind of cute. Wait – I can't believe I just said that. But it was cute. A little. Anyway, she hesitates. "Sir, I'm just here to drop off Collins. I'll be leaving now."

"Phillips. Put on the suit. You can leave the hood off for the moment."

She eyes Fred suspiciously, but it's an order, and since she's programmed to never disobey, she grabs a suit from the rack and slips it on over her regular FBI *don't-mess-with-me* duds. I snicker a little bit – I can't help it. The clean suit is way too short on her. The pants are like six inches short of meeting the little white booties.

"Funny, Collins. Yours looks nice, too. Wouldn't want to get blood all over it."

Damn. When Gina wants to scare the piss out of you, she doesn't fool around. I turn to Fred. "Hey Fred. Can I keep this suit when we're done? For Halloween? I can go as that guy from *Outbreak*. Consider it a wedding present."

Fred leaps up and shakes my hand, only now noticing the strange sight of Chip Collins in a clean suit with a tuxedo peeking out underneath. "Wedding? Chip! You got married?"

I show him my ring. "Yeah. An hour ago. And guess what else? I might be a dad."

"*You?* A *dad?*"

Gina snorts. "See?"

I give them both my best hurt look. "Hey!"

Fred backs up. "That's, uh, not what I meant. Not at all. I'm sure you'll be a, uh, wonderful husband and father. And I'm sorry I had to take you away. Very sorry."

"Nah, don't worry about it Fred. Just get me back pronto, I've obviously got some stuff to get back to, and we'll call it even."

"Yes, yes, of course. Now, the reason you're here – there's been an anomaly-"

"Yeah, yeah, blah, blah anomaly whatever. Pete. Just tell me the Pete part. He's fine, right? This'll be over quick."

"Well, we don't know. We haven't heard from Pete in about a

week, after the first anomaly, pretty unusual for him, and then last night there was a tremendous spike on the MRM. We're afraid there might be a correlation, and Pete might have gotten himself into something serious. That's why we rushed over to get you. We need you and Phillips to get in there now."

I point at Gina. *"Her?"*

Gina points at herself. *"ME?!"*

I put my arm around Fred's shoulders. "Listen, there's obviously been some kind of paperwork mistake. Agent Gina Phillips in the ITA? That hallway requires a certain *roll-with-it* attitude. Not exactly her strong point." I turn to her. "No offense."

Gina glares at me. Doesn't even bother to quip "No offense taken." She marches up to Fred, towering over both of us. "Sir. There must be another agent you can send in. I've never even been in the ITA. I'm not authorized. And Collins, sir, I just… I just… I just…"

Cool. I think Gina's head is going to explode. "C'mon, Gina. It's okay. You can say it."

I've given her permission. She can't hold back. "Sir. Collins is an idiot."

I smile and nod. I kind of feel bad for Gina, she doesn't know I've heard variations of that phrase my entire adult life – wait, my entire *entire* life – and I keep coming out unscathed somehow, so by now I've actually equated *idiot* with *lucky*. And I know it's not advisable to goose Gina when she's pissed, but I can't help myself. "See what I mean, Fred? No *roll-with-it*. I know you've got orders and stuff, but maybe she's right. She should stay home. Can't you see she's scared?"

Holy cow, that gets a reaction. Laser Eyes Gina is back. I swear to God the only thing holding her back from killing me is that she can't reach her handgun through the fabric of the clean suit. Her glare now is like the blinding light of a thousand supernovas. "Yeah, Collins. I'm scared of your little ITA." She whips her eyes back to Fred, now resolute. "Sir. I withdraw my request for deferment. I'm ready to 'roll-with-it.' Now." And she gives me one of those classic sideways sneers from the movies, like "I'll show you, idiot."

Whatever.

So the whole time Fred's been sitting there, just enjoying this moment. This was obviously his idea, and it was going to happen no matter how much we argued against it. And it's clear he likes both of us a lot. But it's also clear he thinks putting gunpowder and a lit match together on a mission is a brilliant idea. Yeah. That's Fred.

He turns and straightens my bow tie. "Now go. Both of you. Phillips, you've been authorized as of last night. Chip, you've got one of the best sharpshooters on the East Coast, first-in-class hand-to-hand fighter, and linguist as your partner. You're welcome. Here are your backpacks. Instructions are: find Pete, identify and neutralize anomaly, back by dinner. Easy peasy."

So we walk twelve feet into the other room and I'm like "Hey, wait, where'd the ITA go?"

One of the dudes in the white suits points to this contraption that takes up the whole wall where the closet used to be. There's something enclosing the door to the INTERDIMENSIONAL TRANSFER APPARATUS. It's like the closet version of StarGate, I guess – dials and lights, conduits running all over the place, little jets of steam or some shit coming out little vents, and of course, a hand scanner.

"Guys. It's a door. With a luggage lock. Zero-zero-zero-zero. Why'd you have to go all space age on this thing?"

The guy shrugs. Points to the hand scanner. Self explanatory.

I put my hand on. Blinkety-blink-whoosh with the lights. Green. Okay to go. Then Gina, same routine, green light go.

But then there's a *"clank"* and a little *"fzzzt."* Then nothing.

"Hey dude. Is it supposed to clank and fzzzt like that?"

The guy shrugs again. Wow, he really likes shrugging. I yell back into the other room. "Hey Fred! Having some issues with your StarCloset thing over here!"

I can hear him pound his fist on the table. "Goddammit! I'll be right there!" He rushes in, punches a few buttons. Slams his hand on the side of the StarCloset. "Eighty million dollars, and it's a total piece of shit. Uh, don't tell anyone I said that."

"You paid EIGHTY MILLION DOLLARS for this thing? Dude, I would have built you a nice little cedar linen closet with a padlock for fifteen bucks. Maybe twenty." I look around at the dimensions of the StarCloset. "Gina, what do you think?"

Gina nods. "If we each got twenty I'd throw in a tricycle bell."

Wow. Agent Gina Phillips just went along with a joke. That's gotta be the first time. I grin and put my fist out for a fist bump. She just leaves me hanging, my fist stuck out in midair like the loneliest fist ever. But she's got a little half-smile on, she's trying to hide it but it's there. *Boom*. I mean, being Master of Interdimensional Travel is impressive, and getting married this morning was amazing, and possibly being a dad is incomparable, but add to all that making Agent Gina Phillips half-smile? Like a cherry on top of the best day ever.

Fred's just cranky now. "Okay, listen, guys. We don't have time for the repair crew, it'll take a month, I'm not kidding. So bear with me..." he shouts to the five or six clean suit guys, "OKAY, LISTEN UP. I NEED A, UH, CUP OF COFFEE. EVERYONE. OUT."

The guy nearest me looks at him for a second, like "you need six of us to get you a cup of coffee?" but then he takes the hint and – yes, you guessed it – shrugs. They all peel off their clean suits and make their way out of the hotel room/starship bridge. Fred goes into the bathroom and comes back with a crowbar.

"Hey, dude, do I want to know how much that crowbar cost?"

"Don't ask." Fred looks around, quietly flips a switch which I assume turns off the security cameras, knowing he could get way worse than fired for doing something like this to their eighty-million dollar StarCloset, and starts yanking at the corner, prying open a little hatch.

Gina's head is practically spinning around on her shoulders, she's never seen rules being broken like this I guess. "Wait! Sir. Can't we just hold up and do this properly? Protocol-"

"Protocol? We're talking about an anomaly we know nothing about, and Pete, agent Phillips. Pete Turner. He helped Chip save us, and he could be in danger. We've got to get you two in there, for his sake,…"

…*wait for it*…

"…for Pete's sake."

Me and Gina both groan, but it's kind of funny because Fred's more serious than I've ever seen him and he didn't even hear himself say it. He's digging around inside the little access panel, tearing out wires and shit.

"Fred. You just said 'for Pete's sake' without even a little irony."

"Fine. Whatever. Chip, now you're just pissing me off." He's flustered. He connects a bunch of wires and taps a code or something on a little pad. The StarCloset door and the ITA door both open, with the familiar whoosh sound. "Okay, get in there with your packs now. It's going to close in a few seconds."

I jump in, ducking to make sure I clear my head on the mini-door Tesla designed for a stooped-over old inventor. Before I can turn to warn Gina, she bonks her forehead. I resist the urge to laugh. I point to my forehead. "Gina, I've been there more times than you know."

This apparently does nothing to make her feel better, because she growls *"Move!"* as she pushes me aside to get in.

From behind us, as the door starts closing, I see Fred practically wrapped up in wires, cursing to himself, and little sparks are flying around, and lights are blinking. I want to chuckle, because Fred looks like he's hanging Christmas lights and not having much luck, but something tells me chuckling isn't the appropriate response. That something is telling me loudly I SHOULD BE TAKING STOCK OF SHIT. RIGHT NOW.

"Gina – inventory your pack. Quick!"

List of Stuff in Our Backpacks

1. First aid kits
2. iPad (the proprietary ones that only have boring FBI apps on them. Ho-hum.)
3. Rope
4. Toolkits – knives, screwdrivers, pliers, flint for starting fires, other tools I've never used in my entire life, etc.
5. A comb?
6. Sealed color coded mystery bags that contain either food, or chemical weapons, or dark matter or something, I have no idea. (The writing on them is just more indecipherable FBI code bullshit.)

List of Stuff NOT in Our Backpacks

1. *The Lost Journal of Nikola Tesla, 1941 –*
2. The INTERDIMENSIONAL NAVIGATION CONTROLLER

Great. Fucking great. While Fred was concentrating on fixing my bow tie, he neglected to pack the two things we actually need in our lunchboxes – a way to communicate and a way to find our way around infinity – before we got on the bus for school.

I lunge for the closing door. "FRED! The journal! The InController!"

And as Fred's eyes bulge with the awareness of his massive screwup, he says "Oh." Yep. That's right. He just says "Oh."

And the door clamps shut with a clink.

8. FZZZZT

"Fuck."

The door responds: *"Fzzzzt."*

I bang on it. Gina leans down, sniffs the lock. "Smells burnt. Is that supposed to happen?"

"No. Their stupid multimillion-dollar Rube Goldberg StarCloset machine just fried the lock, I'm guessing. Here, let me check." I rotate the dials to zero-zero-zero-… and the last dial gets stuck between two and three. Harder. Nothing. I put my back into it. Nothing. "Something's jammed. I can't get the last dial to zero. Here, you try."

Gina, who could probably break my femur between two knuckles of her little pinky, applies some of her massive strength to the lock dial.

It grudgingly moves. Now it's on two.

"Keep going, Gina! It's working!"

She leans in, starts turning red from the effort, veins popping in her arms. "MOVE DAMMIT!"

It moves to one.

"Gina! Dude! One more! Go girl!"

She takes a moment to glare at me – "if you say 'dude' or 'go girl' to me ever again…" – and returns to doing her Wonder Woman impression. "MOVE!"

Nothing. Still stuck on one.

Then, as if to give her a raspberry, the lock speaks again: "*Fzzzzzt!*" And this time it shoots out a little spark, in lieu of giving us the finger.

Gina's pissed. Hopping pissed. Before she can regain her composure, she rips her handgun out straight through the clean suit and points it at the lock.

"GINA! NO!"

I move to stop her, but she unloads two shots. *Bang! Bang!* They miss the lock, and ricochet off the walls, bullets narrowly missing my face and careening down the infinite hallway.

"Dude! You can't just do shit like that! Those bullets could go anywhere! This hallway is crazy – they could kill somebody a thousand years from now!"

"I'm… I'm… I'll file a report when we get back inside." Her hand is shaking a little. And I remember. This is her first time in the ITA. I pissed my pants the first time. She's freaked. I should take it down a notch.

"Whatever, Gina. I'm sure it'll be fine. Calm down. Don't worry. We'll just wait here for a few minutes for Fred and the Shrug Team to fix it up and let us back in. And no worries about the bullets." I look down the hallway. "But not for nothing, I thought you were a sharpshooter."

Gina doesn't even know what to say. She's just staring at the lock.

So.

Here we are.

In the INTERDIMENSIONAL TRANSFER APPARATUS, where time doesn't exist, but the infinite possibilities of the multiverse do, behind every door, six feet apart, forever. As I peer down the familiar way-too-gray hallway, how it goes on and on and on and on, I realize I'm once again stuck, without a map, looking for somebody so I can go home to be with the girl I love.

And then this thought hits me like a giant plumber's wrench on the head:

I'm in a sequel.

9. I'M IN A SEQUEL

From: Chip Collins
To: Julie Taylor
Date: November 19, 2017 11:43am
Subject: I'm in a sequel.

Hey Julie,

Yeah.
It's me. Chip. Your brand new husband.
I'm stuck again.

I should've known, as soon as I started telling the story about you and me (which was awesome and romantic, btw), that something like this would happen. I should've known that Murphy's Law, maybe the only law that remains constant through all the insane shit I've seen, would kick in, and the nice tidy life we were building would begin to unravel and become a giant, sloppy, diarrhea mess that needed to be cleaned up.

I should never have stepped back into the ITA. I know it's for Pete's sake *(get it?)*, but still. I'm such an idiot.

Well, for the moment, though, I've decided (against my

instincts) to assume (remember what happens when you assume, Chip!) that this is just a little glitch, and that Fred will fix the stupid lock, we'll hop in for the journal and the InController, and I'll be skipping into our apartment with sesame chicken before you can say "hey, you forgot to get chopsticks again!"

You'll never see this email, this time I know better, but to pass the hopefully few minutes until this all gets cleared up, I've decided to pull out the FBiPad and speculate – using the exacting science of science fiction – a few different ways this sequel thing might work out in the case it goes longer than a half hour. Hey, silver lining: at least I get to do a list!

Top Five Things That Might Happen If This Sloppy, Diarrhea Mess Turns Out To Be A Sequel
By Chip Collins

1. I meet my father. And he's some evil dude that breathes heavy and wears a black mask, and wants to either kill me or recruit me to rule the galaxy by his side with an iron fist. But my dad died when I was eleven, so that's imposs- *wait*. There are infinite possibilities in here. So there's at least one possible outcome of events where he *didn't* die. Oh man, no, no, no, conflicting feelings. I'd love to see my dad, maybe ask some parenting advice in case it's true and I'm actually having a kid, although really I probably wouldn't even listen to him, as usual, and he'd get pissed, as usual, and then maybe he'd kill me with his light saber, or at least slice off my hand. So no, that's definitely not going to happen. Let's just get that out the way right now. Not happening. Not in this sequel. *Or is it?* No. Cut that shit out, Chip. Off limits. *Or is it?* No. Stop. No dad shit. I'm serious.

2. The whole thing is a flashback. I wind up sitting here in the hallway for a couple of hours waiting for Fred, telling Gina about when I was a young boy in Sicily who eventually immigrates to America to build my organized crime empire. I stuff horses heads in beds, perforate people with tommy guns, eat cannolis, and listen to mandolin music. People kiss my ring for fear I may whack them at any moment.

3. I start year two at my magical school of witchcraft. Dumbleface warns me about some evil warlock whose name he can't even remember, but I'm too busy working on my quidditch game to pay attention, and shit goes south fast. In the end I save everybody, as usual, but my joy is tinged with a little foreboding. Must be puberty. Cue ten more books.

4. The Capitol sends some goons down to my District to burn the whole fucking thing down. I get really good at archery and start whooping some serious ass, but then find that I – once again – am the pawn in the middle of a game (of hunger) that's bigger than me. Ends in a cliffhanger. Sorry, folks. You'll have to wait for yet another two-part sequel-sequel.

5. The robot from the future that tried to kill me last time becomes my savior. And the new T-eight-million robot from the future is made out of liquid metal and is scary as holy hell. I live through it, but because this is a time-travel scenario, the evil robot corporation keeps sending shit back, treating us to eleven more sequels of diminishing quality. Sorry about that, humans – but you asked for it!

Gina must be over her shock at this point I guess, because she gets to her feet. "Collins. Stop wasting time writing love letters."

"Okay, first, it's not a love letter. It's just a letter to the woman I love. Oh. I see your point. Anyway, second, this is not only relevant, but helpful. The muckety mucks in the Bureau love this shit, they get to publish it as science fiction to throw people off the trail of the truth. Didn't you read the first one? *Where the Hell is Tesla?*"

"No. I have better things to do."

"Like what?"

"Like not having this conversation."

"Like oh yes we are having this conversation. Come on, Gina.

What do you read, or watch? *CSI Miami*? *NCIS New York*? *AACS*? That stands for *Another Acronym Cop Show*, by the way."

She's looking around the hallway, assessing, half paying attention. "Nothing."

"You watch nothing. I don't believe it. Let's say you're home from work late, don't have the oomph to go out, or even read, just want to pop something on the tube, veg out a little, maybe heat up that leftover pizza, maybe it's that thick crust one from Franco's, with the mushrooms and the onions, and you sit down with a beer, and maybe-"

"*Downton Abbey*! Okay? You happy? Now shut the hell up!"

Woah. Agent Gina Phillips likes a British period drama series set in the early 1900s? I did NOT see that one coming. Interesting. "Wow. So, is Violet Crawley your thing? Or-"

"Shut up. I said shut up. I'm formulating a plan."

I stand up. "Uh, yeah, sure. While you 'formulate,' I'm shedding this getup." I tear off the clean suit, revealing my tuxedo. "Hey! Cool! Gina, check this out, I'm like James Bond." I slide the torn pieces of the clean suit back on and tear them off again. "That's like a classic James Bond reveal, right? Like I'm casually slipping from the deadly virus lab into the casino next door. I just need a martini. You got a martini glass in your backpack?"

She's not even rolling her eyes. Just ignoring me. *Formulating*, I guess. Whatever. I start walking down the hallway. Strutting a little, actually. The tux makes me want to strut.

She rushes up behind me and grabs the back of my jacket. "Where do you think you're going?"

"Listen, you can *formulate* all you want. I'm going to get Pete and get home for dinner."

"No you're not."

"Not Pete? Or not dinner?"

"Not Pete. Or dinner."

"I think it would be 'nor.' Not Pete. Nor dinner."

"Whatever, Grammar Man. You're staying put. We're waiting for Fred."

I jerk my jacket from her grip. "Look, Gina. I don't want us to be against each other or anything, okay? But as soon as we stepped into the ITA, you stopped being my boss." I lean in a little closer (although getting nose-to-nose is pretty impossible, I'd have to get a little step stool). "And I know where Pete lives. You don't. I know how we can get our hands on another copy of the journal and an InController. You don't. I've seen the crazy shit that can happen in here. You haven't. And I know Fred's not coming back in ten minutes, as much as I might secretly hope he is. And I'll bet you a billion dollars you haven't *formulated* shit. Am I right?"

She clenches her teeth. Finally relents. "Fine, Collins. You lead the way. But anything – ANYTHING – that has FBI jurisdiction is my call. And if there's any gray area, I'm the boss. You got that?"

I salute. "Yeah. Gray area. Whatever."

I try to remember the twists and turns to Meg's dimension, I think I've got it pretty down pat, I've been there a bunch of times. But I can't use the notes we've scratched into the doors. You know why? Because every month or so, the ITA automatically resets to its original state. Resets all the locks to random digits, cleans up any messes, and wipes the slate clean. Which makes it impossible to leave clues to where you're going. I was actually in here one time when the reset happened. Remember that time, Julie? When I got home that night you actually said "Hey, you using a new soap or something? You smell clean."

"What, I don't normally smell clean?"

"No. You're fine. Usually. I don't know, you're just..." you sniffed me, "...cleaner than usual."

I raised an eyebrow, and of course you knew what I was thinking, and you beat me to it: "Hmm. Maybe a little too clean. Let's go fix that."

Man, it's been an hour and I miss you already, Mrs. Collins.

"Collins. COLLINS!"

Oh shit. Got a little lost there for a second. Gina's looming over me, poking my shoulder. "Sorry Gina. Well, here we are. There's a copy of the journal and an InController on the other side of this door. It's Meg and Pete's dimension."

"You're sure."

I give her my best *trust-me* look, confidently enter zero-zero-zero-zero on the lock, and pull open the door.

And a huge two-headed, eight-armed, purple reptilian thing leaps out and attacks us.

"Whoops. Wrong door."

10. SHIT STARTS EXPLODING

From: Chip Collins
To: Julie Taylor
Date: November 19, 2017 11:43am
Subject: Shit Starts Exploding

Hey Julie,

AAAAAAAAAAHHHHHHGHGHGHGHGHH!!!!!

Holy shit. This thing is out of a nightmare. Like a cross between a velociraptor and a seven-foot-tall squid. But with two heads. And yeah, it's purple, which was my favorite color until about two seconds ago. Before we can run, it grabs Gina with some of its arms. (I escape because I know how to run away from things better than her. Not sure if that's something to be proud of.) She tries to pull her gun, but the thing smacks her hand and the gun goes skidding down the hallway out of reach.

Then it sucks her inside its dimension and starts slithering away.

I'm so ashamed to admit this, but for a solid couple of seconds I just stand there and consider shutting the door and walking away. I mean, if anyone can take care of a Purple People Eater, it's Agent Gina Phillips, right? She'll be fine.

Right?

Ah, shit.

No she won't. I'm just being a cowardly weenie. Nah. It's time for Courageous Chip. So I jump in after her – hitting my head, GODDAMMIT TESLA WHY ARE THESE DOORS SO SHORT?! – and start running after them. I can't even see them through the brush, the jungle this thing lives in is so dense. It's like the steamiest, densest jungle on Earth – and everything's a shade of purple. EVERYTHING. Like you gave a kid a box of crayons but she's right in the middle of her kindergarten purple obsession, so she drew it all purple: the leaves, the ground, the sky, the sun. Purple, purple, purple.

So of course I'm not going to be able to make out a Purple People Eater, I'd have to literally bump int–

BUMP!

"Sorry."

Yes. I literally bump into the monster thing, and yes, I instinctively say "sorry." Like it's going to curtsy and say "Oh dear me, sir, I shouldn't have been standing in your way. Please, be on your way, young man." Well, Mom, you definitely drilled those manners into me, so there's another silver lining.

Anyway, I must have momentarily stunned the thing, because it drops Gina.

"GINA! RUN!"

"NO SHIT, COLLINS!"

And we make like a couple of inmates escaping the asylum, screaming and falling and getting up and screaming some more, heading for the ITA door. We lunge into the hallway (ladies first of course, wow, I'm just Mister Manners today!) and as I reach for the door to slam it shut I shout, "Hey! We did i–"

And the thing sprouts like four more arms and grabs both of us and tackles us to the floor. Then its two faces hover over us, working its jaws to see if it can accommodate both of us in its gaping mouths. Wow. Purple People Eater's got about a zillion teeth. And Christ, some nasty breath. But I guess I can understand, you know how much work it would be brushing all those teeth? It snaps at us and tightens its grip.

This is, of course, when I start crying.

"Gina! Make it stop! Make the bad thing go away!" Oh well. So much for Courageous Chip from five seconds ago. And even though we're mere moments from being eaten alive, I can see out of the corner of my eye – Gina's smiling? What the fuck?

She twists to look at me while she's wrestling with Purple Thing, squishing around, flinging sticky glue all over the place. "Okay, Collins. Say it."

"Say WHAT?!"

"You know."

Damn. She's good. We're about to be eaten and she's working her angle. "Okay! Okay! This is one of those gray areas! You're the boss! You're the boss!"

She tears her arms free for a second and twists the right head with a jerk. Instantly, it drops like a dead fish.

"Damn right. That's more like it. One down, one to go!"

But Purple Thing's left head looks over at the right head, then back down at us. Now it's SUPER PISSED. It tightens its grip even stronger around us. We're trapped. Gina can't even move her arms now. Not even an inch. We're done.

And then the strangest thing happens. Out of nowhere I blurt out, "CHUCK!"

Wow.

I haven't thought about Chuck in years. You probably don't even know about him, do you? Chuck was my dog when I was a little kid. A mutt. His real name was Charlie's Angel – My dad's name was Charles and my mom and me were fans of the show, I mean who wasn't? – but I called him Chuck. No matter how much crap I got him into, he never complained. He went along with anything. Goofy. Fun. Loyal. Anyway, when he got old and blind and too tired to give a shit, I told him if I ever had a kid, I'd name him Chuck. I don't know if you're supposed to name a kid after your old blind incontinent dog, but I promised.

Anyway, now I can't get it out of my head. I might die in the next few seconds, and never get to see a little Chuck sitting on your knee, giggling while I play peek-a-boo with him, wearing that little sweater with the hood and the teddy bear ears, and those Timberland boots that are totally ridiculous – I mean, how much construction and hiking is a five-month-old doing? – but they're perfectly adorable, just like him. We'll never get to turn to each other, and smile that smile that knows: that this kid, Chuck, is the manifestation of all the love we've shared, all the love in the world smashed together into one giggling little baby. A love that'll outlive us and shine on into the future.

Wait – are we even ready for that?

Shhhplllrrt!

A blob of snot drips down from Purple Thing's nose right into my mouth. That definitely snaps me back to reality. "Oh fuck that's *gross!*" I look over at Gina, and I guess she must've been having her final thoughts too, because she's got a little tear running from the corner of her eye down into her ear.

It's getting tough to breathe. We're being crushed. Maybe that's how it works, like a python. Suffocates us and swallows us whole. Fascinating thought. With my last breath, I wheeze, "... gina...sorry I got you into this..."

And two bullets come out of nowhere and shatter Purple Thing's skull.

It slumps down on top of us, brains oozing out from where the top of its head used to be. (Guess what color.) *Ick.*

Gina's in shock. She looks in the direction of where the bullets came from. "How...? How...?"

"Holy shit. Remember when you tried to shoot the lock at the home door? Those were the two bullets. Wow. You actually are a sharpshooter. Thanks dude."

She sighs, lets out a laugh. "Consider it my wedding present. Dude."

And we start laughing together, that laugh when you just barely escape the literal jaws of death, that huge relief wave of laughter that gives you hope that shit might work out. Just maybe. Probably not, but maybe.

Gina gets up, shoves the dead monster back into its dimension, and shuts the door before any more Purple People Eaters can leap out at us. She peels off her guts-covered clean suit. "Um. Listen. I'm sorry about screwing up your wedding."

I wipe my tux as best I can. "Nah. Weddings are blah. You made ours unforgettable. In fact, if we had a deejay I would've had him play that for you." I start singing, *"Unforgettable.... In every way... unforgettable..."*

"Stop. Shut up. You took a nice moment and murdered it."

Okay, so I start redoing the directions in my head – walk ten minutes, take a right, one elevator, left twenty minutes, one passthrough, another left around the corner, twelve doors in. "Whoops. The door I picked was eleven in from the corner. It was supposed to be door twelve. It's this one." I reach out for the door handle.

Gina grabs my hand. "Wait!" She walks back over to the gun on the floor, picks it up, and holds it all FBI-style, aiming it right at whatever might attack us next. "What makes you so sure of yourself this time?"

"Come on. Trust me." I dial in zero-zero-zero-zero, pull the latch, and swoosh.

No monsters? Good.

And then something lunges out from the doorway and jumps on me. I open my mouth to scream, to tell Gina to shoot it, but it's got its mouth over mine. Man, I JUST escaped death like two minutes ago! This is bullshit!

Wait.

It's not attacking me.

It's kissing me.

11. THE THING THAT KISSED ME

From: Chip Collins
To: Julie Taylor
Date: November 19, 2017 11:43am
Subject: The Thing That Kissed Me

Hi Julie,

God, it's all over me. The thing.

"Pete! Oh, Pete!" Smoochy-smoochy, slobber-slobber, "I was so worried about you! Pete!" Then suddenly it opens its eyes. Stares down at me in horror.

"You're not Pete!"

The thing is Meg.

She jumps up and starts spitting, wiping her tongue on her shirt sleeve, even gagging a little. She won't stop gagging. "Come on, Meg, it wasn't that bad. And that's what you get for not looking before you go attacking people with your tongue. By the way, I used mouthwash this morning – it could've been way worse."

She looks at me with this weird mix of disgust, anger,

embarrassment, and – fear? Yikes. I'm not sure I've ever seen her afraid. "Hey, Meg. I'm sorry. You okay?"

She's either going to cry, or rip my face off. I look to Gina for help. She shrugs her shoulders, whispers, "Not FBI jurisdiction."

"Excuse me. Who's this?" Meg points at Gina. "Is she on the clearance list?"

"Her name's Gina. Phillips. She's an agent. Fred put her on the list last night. She's… my boss."

Meg's scowl immediately softens, and her fear disappears for a moment, and she actually laughs. "Oh, dear. You're Chip's *boss*? You have to manage *Chip*? Then you've been through a lot already. Come in, come in, Gina. Oh, we're going to get along just fine."

She guides Gina gently through the door, shielding her head to make sure she doesn't bonk it.

And yeah, there I am, still standing outside the door in my tuxedo like a groom left at the altar. "Hey!"

They look back at me, together, like sisters or something. "You coming?" And I swear to God it sounds like they let out a little giggle.

Great. The annoying sisters I never had.

From: Chip Collins
To: Julie Taylor
Date: November 19, 2017 11:43am
Subject: Re: The Thing That Kissed Me

Hi Julie,

In a very un-Meg-like move, I guess she assumed Gina knew, she forgets to warn her about the lighter gravity on her way in, so on her first step through the doorway Gina goes shooting up to the ceiling. I'm waiting for the "bonk!" I'd really like to see her bonk her head again. Not in a sadistic way or anything. I've just done it so many times I'd like to see someone else take some lumps for a change. But sure as shit, Gina rolls like a cat, landing on the ceiling on all fours, then tumbles down, again like a cat, landing on her feet. *Damn. She's good.*

Gina's flustered. "Okay. What the hell was that?"

I stroll in, by now I'm finally used to the gravity change. "It's your first time, Gina. A LOT of shit is different, it's going to take getting used to. This dimension has lighter gravity, for whatever reason, so it's like walking on the moon."

Meg holds her down by her shoulders. "Yes. Sorry, Gina. I'm a little preoccupied, to put it mildly. I should've warned you. You see, the mass of Earth in this dimension is closer to Mars in your dimension, approximately 6.42×10^{23} kg, resulting in a gravity that's approximately 0.38 times your normal perceived gravity, or 3.72 m/s^2. Thus, the gravitational force exerted…"

Gina's eyes start glazing over. Now it's her turn to look to me for help. I whisper, "Don't look at me. You're her new pal."

I take the opportunity to saunter away (trust me, this will be at least a ten minute lecture on gravity and density and quantum whatever bullshit) and check out the updated hotel room. Apparently the FBI in this dimension did pretty much the same thing as ours – they got a hold of the set designers from Star Trek and gave them a wheelbarrow full of money to go crazy. Even the Shrug Team is the same, with the clean suits, except everyone here is around forty pounds and skinny as hell, also because of the lighter gravity. And they left the actual ITA doorway alone. No StarCloset to mess with. Smart. Good.

I get right to business and take one of Meg's InControllers and her copy of the journal and put it in my backpack for the trip. One of the clean suit dudes watches me – and shrugs.

Finally, at the end of Meg's riveting symposium on gravity, as I make my way back over to them, she takes her first good look at me since we arrived. "Excuse me, Chip. Why are you wearing a tuxedo?"

I fiddle with my bow tie. "Um…"

But she already knows. You can't put anything past Meg. She's so smart. (Although I guess the tux makes it a little obvious, too.)

"Chip! You didn't invite us?"

"It's kind of a long story, Meg. Shorter than your epic story about gravity just now, but still pretty long. Here's the nutshell: I asked Julie. She said yes. She started wearing her wedding dress around the apartment. It had to happen quick. Then I couldn't get in touch with Pete at all, so-"

There it is. The word. *Pete.* The look of fear strikes Meg's face again. She whimpers, "Pete."

I put my arm around her. "Hey. It's okay. We're here to help. What's got you so freaked out? Pete's a big boy. He's fine. He's probably just out having some adventure or something."

"No. I know it sounds foolish, like I'm some damsel in distress, which I assure you I'm not, but… there's something different about him being gone this time. He's never been gone this long, and whenever he's away, he sends me a message."

"How does he send a message? Emails and phones don't work in the ITA."

"He sends another Pete."

. . .

Me and Gina both do the double-take thing. "Another *wha?*"

"Another Pete. He has several Alternate Petes, a team of Petes with simple personal ITA lock combinations of say one-one-one-one, or two-four-six-eight, from other dimensions. They share reconnaissance responsibilities. If one is out on a longer task, the others help report back. It's ingenious, actually."

Pete. Wow. Never underestimate that guy. He's got an Alternate Pete Posse! I make a mental note to form my own Alternate Chip Posse. How cool would that be? *Wait.* Don't answer that. You're right. We'd get nothing done. We'd wind up playing *League of Legends* twenty-four hours a day. Forget it. "Okay, so, it's only been a week. We just wait a little longer for one of the Petes to report back. Right?"

"We can't."

"Why not?"

"Because they're *all* gone."

12. ALL THE PETES

From: Chip Collins
To: Julie Taylor
Date: November 19, 2017 11:43am
Subject: All the Petes

Hi Julie,

So I can't believe I'm doing this, but I'm arguing with Meg about science. "That's impossible."

Meg nods. "I know."

"Impossible. There are infinite dimensions. Infinite Petes. They can't *all* be gone."

"I know."

"We're talking about infinity, Meg."

"I know."

"Please say something other than 'I know.'"

"Sorry, Chip. It's just that I can usually get my head around pretty complex problems…"

"No shit."

"…but this one escapes me. Frightens me. Pete investigates an anomaly on the MRM last week, which on its own is not an alarming occurrence. But then absolute silence since. Not one of Pete's alternates has reported in. Do you know what that means?"

"That's rhetorical, right? Like you're going to explain it to the two cro-magnons in the room."

Gina sneers. "Speak for yourself, Collins."

"Oh. I see. Genius Gina. Why don't you do the explaining then?"

"Um, I think Meg could, ah, put it in terms you can understand. I wouldn't want to steal her thunder."

Meg ignores our little squabble, turns the nearest whiteboard over to a cleanish side and starts drawing. "The multiverse is made up of infinite universes, as we now know, each spawned by a new outcome to a new event. But other than being connected through the ITA hallway, there is no interaction between universes." She draws separate circles, not touching. "They are discreet. They don't touch. Like soap bubbles floating in the air. They go forth and keep multiplying into infinity." She keeps drawing more and more circles, still not touching. "They don't affect each other. At all."

"Okay…"

"But I believe now, something, somehow, is interacting across universes. Affecting them." She draws arrows intersecting all the big and little circles, all over the place. It's a mess. "As far as I know, it shouldn't be possible. But something's using the ITA to grab pieces of different universes. Specifically, those pieces may be Pete Turner."

"Come on, Meg. You're telling me that ALL the Pete Turners, every one of them, is being collected?"

"I don't know if I'd call it collected, but yes. It's just a theory. Pete somehow interacted with the anomaly the MRM started picking up a couple of weeks ago, and it created some connection or something. And that massive anomaly this morning? I think it's accelerating. I think the Petes are disappearing. Rapidly."

"I'm sorry. I'm not buying it. Pete's been in worse binds. He – they – probably just needed to unplug. He'll be back. I promise." I tap my backpack. "In the meantime, instead of arguing about theories, now we've got an InController and a journal. Let's roll." I march over to the ITA door and dial in zero-zero-zero-zero. I push the door open.

And Pete falls in.

"Pete!"

I start to say "See? I told you he'd be back," but the words get caught in my throat.

Something is radically wrong.

He's on the floor, barely breathing, covered in some kind of blue goop or something. We rush over, but he's putting his hands out, waving them wildly, trying to keep us away. His eyes are wild, and his mouth is moving, but nothing's coming out.

"Pete! Come on dude! Say something! What's with this blue stuff?" God, he looks terrified.

A sound finally makes its way through his clenched teeth. "触らないでください! 触らないでください! (Sawaranaide kudasai! Sawaranaide kudasai!)"

Great. It's an Alternate Pete. One that speaks Chinese. I couldn't even get through two semesters of Spanish – how the hell am I supposed to know what he's saying? "Hey Meg, I know it's a long shot, but you're the smart one – you know Chinese? All I know is 'Xingyun bing' which is 'Can you throw in an extra fortune cookie?'"

Gina pushes past me, leaning over Alternate Pete on the floor. "It's not Chinese. It's Japanese. He's saying 'Don't touch me.'"

While I'm super-impressed with linguist Gina over here, I could care less that she knows what language it is. Good for her. I want to talk to Alternate Pete myself. "Pete. Speak to me. In English. English, dude. Eeeennnngggglllliiiissssshhh."

He groans in pain, but almost half-laughs. "Yā, watashi wa anata ga baka ni naru koto ga dekirunara."

"What? What did he say?"

"He said 'Dude, I'd be speaking English if I could, you idiot." Gina physically hands me over to Meg. "Now keep Collins quiet." And she turns back to Alternate Pete, careful not to touch the blue stuff all over him. "Pete. Can you tell us what happened? The anomaly? Um, nani ga okotta no ka oshiete itadakemasu ka?"

You can see he's using the last of his energy to talk to Gina. His face is stricken again with terror. He whispers, "Sore ga kuru no… Sore ga kuru no…"

She doesn't bother to look back to us, just translates out loud. "It's spreading… it's spreading… Pete, what's spreading? What is it? How do we stop it? Um, dare? Dōshite? Sore o tomeru hōhō?"

He just shakes his head. "Watashi o sukuwanaide kudasai… anata jishin o sukuu…"

And at that exact moment, an alarm blares in the main room. (Holy shit, Julie – it's even louder than that ancient dryer at the laundromat when it goes on the fritz and sounds like it's going to blow up the whole building.) The three of us instinctively rush in to see what the hell is going on.

Meg points to a meter on the wall. "It's the MRM. There's another spike! It's off the scale!"

We gape at each other.

Run back into the ITA room.

Pete's gone.

Alternate Japanese-speaking Pete, and every last drop of that blue stuff, has disappeared. Gone.

Meg, I guess finally tired of being the strong, smart one, crumples. I catch her. And she sobs in my arms.

I look up at Gina. "What was that last thing he said?"

She shakes her head. Doesn't want to tell me.

"Come on, Gina."

Shakes her head again. I kick her foot. "Come on."

Her voice halts. But she gets it out. "He said, 'Don't touch the door. Don't save me. Stay away. Save yourselves.'"

From: Chip Collins
To: Pete Turner
Date: November 19, 2017 11:43am
Subject: Dude

Hey Pete,

Dude... I'm sorry.

Here I am thinking you're fine, because you're always fine, and I'm actually a little pissed that you stole me away from my new bride and maybe a baby on the way... and then I see you writhing on the floor in pain, covered in some kind of blue stuff, more afraid than I've ever seen you. I'm sorry I wasn't more worried.

But now I'm fucking petrified, too – how the hell am I going to be able to help you?

This isn't like that time in the auditorium, when you fell through the trap door in the stage, and broke your ankle, and you were screaming, and I was the only one there that knew how to get to you. You were more pissed than afraid, I remember, like "who the fuck puts a trap door in a stage?" and I was like "uh, actually it's kind of standard. Shakespeare's theater even had them-" and you were like "Okay, Hamlet, thanks for the teaching moment. Can we get the hell out of here now?"

Or that time we skidded halfway down Mount Snow in your car after that ice storm. I was whimpering and practically crapping my pants, and damn, I noticed your hands shaking on the wheel. Your hands never shake. So I distracted you, telling you all about my fantasy football team, how I got all the worst players just to see how bad I could do, and you laughed, and calmed down a little, and somehow we made it off route 580 alive that night, and you said "thanks," like my constant jabbering actually helped. Who knows. Maybe it did.

But this time? I don't think even my best asinine commentary is going to do the trick. I'm way out of my comfort zone on this, dude. I mean, WHO was scary, that evil douche, but he was a man. Skin and bones. Breakable. Defeatable. This thing? This blue stuff? I have no idea what it even is. It's just fucking weird.

I'm scared, man.

Wait. You know what you would say? You'd say that the fear is going to be there, it's part of being human, but that if you can tap your inner courage, just a little, and keep putting one foot in front of the other in spite of the fear, push along in the face of fear, that's what matters. (Of course, you'd be saying all this after a number of beers, maybe while we're peeing in the alley next to the bar.)

And that's what I'm going to do. Just put one foot in front of the other until I get to you, and figure out how to get you home. And who knows? Maybe some day, some little Chuck will even look up at me and say "Cool. I wouldn't mind being like you when I grow up." (Or he'd tell me to look over there, and when I do he steals my phone and disappears down the alley next to the bar. Punk kid.)

Anyway, thanks for the lesson, dude. I'll see you soon.
   - Chip

P.S. It was kind of hilarious listening to you speak Japanese. God, when this is all over we HAVE to make a martial arts movie with Japanese Pete. We'll call it *Dragon Pete*. Get it? Instead of *Pete's Dragon*? Yeah. Stop pretending to gag, you know you like it. And we'll put Tesla in a Godzilla suit or something, it'll be awesome.

13. I MAY HAVE TO CHANGE MY PANTS.

From: Chip Collins
To: Julie Taylor
Date: November 19, 2017 11:43am
Subject: I may have to change my pants.

Hi Julie,

We were all pretty rattled by Pete's appearance, and disappearance, but Meg looks the worst. "Hey, Meg."

She sniffs.

"Look, I know it looks bad. That was some scary shit. I may even have to change my pants."

She laughs grimly. "You always know exactly what to say to make me feel better, Chip."

"No. Listen. It looks bad. I'll admit it. But you know they call him The Brute, right?"

Her laugh is a little less grim this time.

"And you know Awesome Man is on the trail now too, right?"

Now she starts rolling her eyes. Good. I'm getting normal Meg back.

"That means we've got the combined Wonder Twin Powers of

two superheroes going for us. It's going to turn out all right. I promise. But just to make sure – not that I'm in any way doubtful or secretly completely unsure of myself – I think we should call in backup."

Gina's looking more and more lost by the minute. She likes answers, not this constant swirl of unknowns. Her frustration is obvious. "Backup?"

"Yeah. Nikola Tesla."

So I grab the *The Lost Journal of Nikola Tesla, 1941* - from my backpack and start scribbling to Tesla:

"Hi, Nikola. Listen, we've got a problem."

It takes a while, I mean you just never know where Tesla is, he could be off feeding his pigeons for a week sometimes, or taking a nap, or sometimes he just ignores the journal altogether. And he's eighty-six, for Christ's sake, so he could even be… I hate to think about it. But eventually I hear the scratching on the pages, and see the words appear out of nowhere:

"Master Chip! It is wonderful to hear from you again! However, I am just about to step into the bath, where a small glass of whiskey and the newly released book *Being and Nothingness* by Jean-Paul Sartre await me. Don't tell me how it ends, I want to find out myself. Check back in perhaps a week. Until then, farewell, Chip."

"Nikola. Didn't you read my message? *Problem,* dude."

"Hmmm. Two things. First, please refrain from the term 'dude,' as I've said several times before. I understand its central nature to your vocabulary, and appreciate the affection, but it is just not 'my thing,' as you might say.

Second, is this problem more important than a warm bath, whiskey, and a good book? Now be honest, Chip."

"Honest. It's about Pete."

The empty page of the journal stares back at me. It's brutal. Then this:

"Oh dear. Pete? I shall be right there! Let me put on a robe."

Several minutes pass. I'm not sure what to do. Is that it? Is he just going to show up at Meg's dimension in a few minutes half naked with a fresh copy of *Being and Nothingness* under his arm? But then I hear some furious scratching coming from the journal. Something's wrong.

"Problem, you say? I should say you have a problem! You've broken the lock on the INTERDIMENSIONAL TRANSFER APPARATUS for dimension #234,698,594,394,683! I can't get out!"

"Hey! I didn't break it! Fred did. With his stupid StarCloset thing."

"*Fred!* And to think I built him a MULTIVERSE RESONANCE MONITOR! Why is he touching my lock?"

"Long story. And it gets longer when I start telling it. You really want to hear it?"

"No. No Chip soliloquies right now, please. As much as I enjoy them sometimes. Occasionally. Rarely. But not now."

Gina's been reading over my shoulder. She snorts at this one. Whatever.

"Well… what do we do now, Nikola?"

The scratching stops. Now I know Tesla pretty well, I don't think I've ever heard him say "I don't know," or "it can't be done," so I'm positive he's cooking up something over there in 1943 with his supersized intellect. And sure enough:

"Master Chip. I will devise a repair for the lock. However, the process will require great care to avoid a temporal paradox – I will be fixing a 2017 mechanical problem here in 1943 – and thus will take considerable time, possibly creating some time slippage as well. In my stead, you will have to locate and engage another Nikola Tesla to help you."

"Wait. *Another* Nikola Tesla? There's only one you, dude."

"Chip. Chip. Again I appreciate the affection, but please – tell me how many Nikola Teslas there are."

"I know. I know. Infinite. Everything's infinite. But you know what I mean."

"Yes. I know what you mean. You will have to trust me. The Nikola Tesla you meet next will indeed be me, a slightly different version of me, but will help you nevertheless. Here are the coordinates for the INTERDIMENSIONAL NAVIGATION CONTROLLER: 824918.578 920e+482324.kr.mt."

"Uh, you keep a spare Nikola Tesla handy, with coordinates in your back pocket?"

"Certainly. Don't you?"

Jeez. First I find out Pete's got a posse of alternates, and now Tesla's got a spare of himself on call. I guess I'm last to the party. Maybe I should have a just-in-case Chip or two, ready to give me a hand at the right moment. Like when I need to move furniture. Or we could put together a bowling team, and challenge Pete's old nemesis, Tyler, that jagoff, freak the shit out of him, maybe even win one game for Pete. (Mental note: even if I don't do that, I have to get Gina onto Pete's old team, now that he's moved out and living here with Meg. She looks like she could bowl three hundred with a blindfold on. Who knows, maybe she could even shoot Tyler. Not to kill him or anything, just a little something to humble him for once, like a bullet in the foot. Whatever. Just fantasizing.)

Gina pokes me out of my reverie. "Collins. You're wandering again."

"Whoops. Hey, what's your bowling average?"

"What?"

"Never mind. Okay, listen, we've got a new Tesla to track down. So less talkee, more walkee folks!" I stuff the journal back into my pack, and step into the hallway. Gina follows me – ducking just in time. Damn, she learns fast. We both stop and turn to wait for Meg.

"I'm not coming."

"Huh?"

She's still sniffing a little. "I'm not coming. I'm afraid I'm, ah, a little too close to this. It could, ah, cloud my judgement. With the addition of Tesla, you'll have a three-person team. That should be enough. And my presence here could be helpful, in case another Pete shows up."

"You're leaving me alone with Collins?" Gina's miffed.

Meg laughs. "He's not that bad once you really get to know him. And if he gets out of line, you know what to do."

Gina lifts her gun, taps it to her temple. Grins. Oh for crying out loud. Really?

Meg laughs again. "I was going to say just give him the finger. Now promise me you won't go shooting one of my best friends."

Gina looks at me hard. Like she actually has to think about it. "As long as he doesn't deserve it." But she's half smiling when she says it, so she must be joking. Right?

Meg reaches through the doorway, motions for me to come to her... like she doesn't want to step into the hallway any more. She gives me a little hug, whispers. "My dear friend, listen. You get Tesla to help you figure out what this blue stuff is, and bring back Pete, you hear? I have a package waiting for him."

I whisper back. "A package? Just give it to me then. I'll put it in the backpack and get it to him no problemo."

She shakes her head a little, buries it in the crook in my neck, holds me a little tighter. She's shaking, I can't tell if she's laughing or crying. She lifts up her face and kisses me on the cheek. "You idiot."

From: Chip Collins
To: Julie Taylor
Date: November 19, 2017 11:43am
Subject: Re: I may have to change my pants.

Hi Julie,

Okay, it's back to just me and Gina. But at least we've got tools
and a plan, so I'm feeling better, strutting down the hallway in my
tux, going over how this is all going to work out in my head:

Exactly How This Is All Going To: Work Out In Six Easy Steps:

**1. We have the coordinates to find Tesla, who is sure to
know precisely what we need to do, therefore saving me
a shitload of work and stress.** Now he's not the Tesla I
know and love, but supposedly he's the same(ish) guy, so
I'm sure this step will be uneventful and breezy. (If your
reaction is "Chip - when was the last time anything you did
was uneventful and breezy?" I can't blame you. But trust
me on this one. And I know you just thought *"Trust me?
Really, Chip?* As soon as you say 'trust me,' every single
goddamned time, without exception, something bad
happens." But this time is different. Trust me.

**2. Tesla, Gina, and me will march right over to the Blue
Juice.** (That's what I just decided to call it – it needed an
epic name that was easy to remember.)

Gina interrupts me. "Blue Juice?"
"I like naming things."
"Because you're so good at it."
"Fuck you."

She balls up her fists. "Excuse me? What did you say?"

"Uh, 'foo-kyew.' It's Japanese for thank you."

"You know I know Japanese, right?"

"Whoops. Yeah. Of course. I was just testing you."

"Arigato."

"What?"

"Arigato. *That's* Japanese for thank you."

"You're welcome."

Her head almost explodes, but I continue before she can clock me:

3. We neutralize the Blue Juice and grab Pete. (Yes, this is a gross oversimplification. But when we get Tesla I'll have him flesh this step out and get back to you with the details.)

4. All the other Petes somehow miraculously go back to their dimensions. (Miracles. Or as Barry Manilow would call them, true blue spectacles. In the absence of any rational scientific explanation for the possibility, you just gotta believe. I'll come back and delete this step if Tesla's got something more scientificky. Or if, God forbid, it doesn't work.)

5. We all skip down the hallway back to Meg and you, singing "Climb Every Mountain" from *The Sound of Music*, until Gina ruins it with her terrible singing voice. (I have no idea if she can sing or not, but I like to imagine she can't. It would be nice to know there's something she *can't* do.)

6. You and me have a baby.

Whoops.

Yeah, Julie. What did you expect? You drop that bomb on me

literally the second I'm leaving for this mission, the *pregnancy* word, of course I'm going to roll it over in my head the whole time. I'm trying to stay focused on Pete, goddamn is he in some deep shit, but the words to *Goodnight Moon* keep popping into my head – *Goodnight comb, goodnight brush, goodnight nobody, goodnight mush* – wow, they're kind of trippy words, now that I'm actually writing them down. There they are, though, words begging to be read every night to wee little Chuck. And just as I finish the book and put him into his crib, his eyes are barely open, he's so tired from a full day of being cute and filling up diapers with toxic waste, anyway you walk in, and you say "So how's our little package?"

Package.

Wait.

Package?

Holy shit.

Meg's package.

Meg's pregnant, too.

From: Chip Collins
To: Julie Taylor
Date: November 19, 2017 11:43am
Subject: Re: I may have to change my pants.

Hi Julie,

TWO babies! Well, one baby and one maybe. Pete's going to either jump up and down, or shit his pants. I can't wait to tell him.

"So Gina. What about you? You ever think about having kids?"

"We're here."

The InController *breeps*. "You've arrived at your destination. The door is on your left."

God, Gina's got a funny way of not answering personal questions. Mental note: I must get even more annoying. That'll work.

She reaches for the lock of Tesla's dimension.

"No! Paradox!"

Her hand hesitates over the handle. "Paradox?"

"If we enter at the same time Tesla exits, it'll create a time paradox – the ITA can't resolve 1943 and 2017 at the same time. A paradox. Paradoxes are bad." Wow. I actually sounded like I knew what I was talking about there, huh? I must be learning stuff. "I'll let him know we're here."

So I write him a note in the journal:

"Hi. Chip Collins here. Original Nikola Tesla, or what I'm calling Original Nikola Tesla, from dimension #234,698,594,394,683, told me to contact you. We had a little lock problem – for the record, it wasn't my fault – and he can't make it. And there's something we need your help with. We're right outside your door, and we'd rather not create a paradox."

After a little while, scratchy-scratchy-scratchy:

"Master Chip! I have followed your adventures through
the journal with my fellow Alternate Nikola. He has told
me much about you as well. It would be my honor and
privilege to assist you. And the paradox? You're learning,
Master Chip. Give me a moment."

Wow. Two Nikola Teslas talking to each other – about me?
Cross that one off the bucket list! A minute later, the familiar
swoosh, and the door opens. But no one's there.

"Hello? Nikola?"

I can see into Tesla's north bedroom in the New Yorker Hotel,
but something's different. I know, I know, it's always something
different in here, but this is a different kind of different: it's dim,
there are only a couple of what looks like hurricane lamps lit, a
couple of high-back arm chairs face the window, and if I listen
carefully I can hear horse hooves clopping and some newspaper
kid yelling a headline from the paper: "Extra! Extra! New
Carriages Drive Without Horses - But They'll Never Drive
Themselves!" (I made that headline up in case it wasn't obvious.)
And the smell – a mixture of cologne, dust, whiskey, burning
lamp oil, and a hint of horse shit off in the distance. Nice. I'd call it
Eau de Gangs of New York.

"Yes, Chip. Please do NOT come in."

"Uh. *Not* come in? Kind of rude, don't you think?"

"No, no. Although there would not be a paradox in this case,
there is something else. Let me explain." And the familiar tall,
lanky figure rises from one of the arm chairs and approaches me.
Hmm. Not as stooped over as he usually is. Must be doing yoga. I
imagine Tesla in his Lululemon stretchy pants doing the Wounded
Peacock pose. You know, he could probably pull it off, he's such a
stud. Anyway, good for him.

And then he steps into the light, bends down into the little
doorway, and I get a good look.

Holy shit.

It's Young Nikola Tesla.

14. "WE?"

From: Chip Collins
To: Julie Taylor
Date: November 19, 2017 11:43am
Subject: "We?"

Hi Julie,

Before Tesla can explain why he's young (and being rude), Gina turns to me and slips back into her default mode: pissed. "Collins. Look. I don't pretend to know a lot about the ITA, but I know it's not a time machine." She points to Tesla. "He's fifty years old, tops. What the hell?"

"Well. Okay, first, I forgot to tell you our unofficial motto for the whole ITA: *'Shit's crazy. Don't ask.'* And second... uh... okay, since you are asking, my highly educated answer is... Nothing. I got nothing. No fucking clue." I turn to Tesla. "Nikola. Listen, you look great. Really. But do you mind telling us what's going on? The ITA is a dimension machine, not a time machine. Right?"

"You are correct. But it is quite a bit more complicated than that. You are, in fact, peering into a small fold in spacetime. It is called a closed timelike curve. The year inside here is" – he looks at his watch – "1917, and I am currently 61 years old."

Me and Gina stand there, looking into the doorway of 1917, gaping like the two kids who failed tenth-grade physics (which I did in fact fail, though I can't speak for Gina). I eventually blurt out, "How the hell did you fold spacetime?"

Tesla, of course, takes this as an invitation for a lecture:

The Official Quickstart Guide to Spacetime Manipulation
By Nikola Tesla

STEP 1: Create a massive gravitational force. As you know, from Albert Einstein's theory of relativity published in 1915, gravity is a geometric property of space and time, or spacetime. An extremely powerful gravitational field, such as that produced by a spinning black hole, warps the fabric of existence so that spacetime may bend back on itself. By devising a TESLA COIL of extremely large proportions, and utilizing the steel understructure of the New Yorker Hotel, I was able to produce the very first PORTABLE BLACK HOLE.

STEP 2: Create a Closed Timelike Curve. By modulating this artificial black hole, a customized Closed Timelike Curve, or CTC, is created – a loop that allows one to travel into past events. Time travel. Unfortunately, into the past and back only. Not the future.

STEP 3: Carefully enter the Closed Timelike Curve. When entering, remember to-

"Woah, woah. Hold on, Nikola. You created a *portable black hole*? In your *hotel room*?"

"Yes. But not I. We."

Tesla points to the other arm chair. A second figure rises into the shadows, taps out the tobacco in his pipe, and kind of shuffles towards us. The silhouette of his crazy, all-over-the-place hair is strangely familiar.

Oh holy shit. No way.

The figure steps into the light.

It's Albert Einstein.

From: Chip Collins
To: Julie Taylor
Date: November 19, 2017 11:43am
Subject: Re: "We?"

Hi Julie,

Yeah. I just met Albert Einstein.

"It's a pleasure to meet you, Herr Chip. I've read all about you."

"You've... read about... me?"

"Yes, of course. Nikola here has shared his journal with me. It's been most entertaining. I have to agree, however, that you swear far too much."

"I'm working on it."

Gina snorts.

I give her the finger.

Einstein turns and cranes his neck to look up at her. "And who is your attractive companion of such imposing stature?"

"She's Gina. Gina Phillips. Back home she's my boss."

Einstein laughs. "Well, well, Miss Phillips. You must have your hands full with Herr Chip!"

Gina looks like she's going to launch into a long monologue of her grievances against me, so I interrupt. "Okay, speaking of hands, Albert – may I call you Albert? – It would be my honor to shake the hand of the greatest physicist of all time." I stretch out my arm for a handshake.

Tesla and Einstein both scream "NO!!!" as my fingers breach the surface of their doorway.

Too late.

Whatever this closed timelike curve thing is, the invisible barrier between it and us just sliced off the tips of my fingers. Down to the first knuckle.

Yikes.

I pull back, sort of in shock, and it's like *Monty Python and the Holy Grail*, streams of blood spurting out from each of my severed fingertips.

And of course I throw up, and pass out, and my last thought is: wow, Einstein looks kind of funny with my blood and vomit all over him.

A face. Blurry.

Mom?

No. It's just Gina. Hovering over me. Probably laughing. No.

"Chip. You're okay. I'm right here."

She's holding my head in her lap. Wow. Compassionate Gina. I didn't know she existed. I chance a look down at my left hand. It's perfectly fine. "Whew."

"It's your other hand, idiot."

I lift my right hand to my face. The bloody bandage leaks a drop in my eye.

And I barf right into Gina's lap.

"Thanks, Collins."

Blackness.

A face. Blurry.

Mom?

Oh shit. Now I remember. The barf. Uh-oh. Gina's pointing a gun at my face.

No. She's still just looking down at me with my head in her lap. It's her finger. "How many fingers am I holding up?"

Yes. It's her middle finger. "I'm so sorry, Gina."

"Sorry and four quarters will pay for a washing machine to get the barf smell out of my pants. Now, you think you can get up without more of your insides exploding out?"

I slowly get to my feet. Strange. I feel fine. Like I can feel my fingertips under the bandage. Like they grew back or something.

Oh fuck.

They grew back.

I stare down at the bloody bandage, like somebody just gave me a Christmas package with a human head in it. The last time I grew something back, it was my foot. MY FURRY FOOT. I'm afraid to open the bandage. "Please let me not have furry fingers, please let me not have furry fingers, please let me not have furry fingers… (I say this eight hundred times while I slowly unwrap the bandage, you get the idea)…"

I finally unfurl the whole bandage, and wouldn't you know… my fingers are fine.

No fur.

Thank God. And you literally can't tell the first knuckle of each wasn't there a few minutes ago (or whoever long I was passed out). I stretch them in and out. Let the bloody bandage drop to the floor. Cool.

I can't resist. I wiggle my fingers and say "Ta-Da!"

Gina, Tesla, and Einstein are flabbergasted. (Is that enough of an old-timey word? How about "bowled over"? Or "thunderstruck?") And yeah, now, finally, I get to be the one lecturing:

Chip's Quickstart Guide to Spontaneous Organ Regeneration
By Chip "New Fingers" Collins

STEP 1. Befriend a three-foot, furry alien named Bobo. (Your alien may be named something else.) The important thing to note about this furry alien is that he can regenerate himself like a starfish, using asexual reproduction (it's not like that, get your mind out of the gutter). And because starfish have cells like stem cells that are immature (just trust me on this), they can grow into any limb or body part needed.

STEP 2. Cut off one of your limbs. If you'd prefer not to do it yourself, just step into the ITA. It's guaranteed to happen at some point shortly after you enter.

STEP 3. Ask Bobo nicely to chew his hand off – yes, it's super gross, maybe the grossest thing I've ever seen, but hang with me here – and then ask him to mold his regurgitated flesh to your bloody stump. (Yeah, that part's even grosser because you can feel his mashed up alien flesh touching your open wound. Fuck, that's DISGUSTING. I just threw up in my mouth a little.)

STEP 4. Pass out, vomit, or release some other bodily

fluids for a few minutes (at least that's what I tend to do), and wa-laa! Because Bobo's flesh bonded with your own, it triggers a signal to GROW BACK YOUR LIMB.

Important note: in the case of my foot, it grew back super furry like Bobo. It's embarrassing. Just letting you know. That might happen. Go out and buy a fresh razor just in case.

STEP 5. This one's new – I'm thinking (yes, Julie, I think a lot these days) that Bobo's DNA has fused with mine throughout my body, and maybe my human DNA has adapted to its presence, morphed or something, because this time I grew back four fingers *without* fur. Fucking A. NO FUR. I like this step. Well it's not really a step, but whatever.

"Hey Nikola. Thanks for the heads up, by the way. About coming through the doorway."

"I apologize. I did tell you not to pass through the doorway, however. You see, since you didn't exist in 1917, you cannot enter the loop."

"Why?"

"As you say, Chip, 'Feces is insane, do not inquire.' But since you did inquire, let me explain. When a–"

"No. Stop. My brain can't take anymore physics. I believe you. And the motto is *'Shit's crazy. Don't ask.'* Listen, can you pass an object from in there to us?"

"Certainly. Are you thinking of something that may assist you on your journey to extract Pete?"

"No. That ukulele hanging on the wall over there. I want to see if my fingers still work."

Tesla obliges, and passes his ukulele through the doorway.

And as it touches my fingers, through the invisible barrier of the closed timelike whatever, it instantly ages. Like from its pristine shape in 1917 to an old beat up antique in 2017. Crazy.

But it still works, and it's pretty much in tune, so I start strumming and singing:

"Here I am, stuck between dimensions with Gina,
I suppose it coulda been somebody meaner,
Yeah she's okay,
Sure kicks some A,
We're gonna get Pete and save the day,
Then skip home and have ourselves a couple of Pina (Coladas)
... One more time!
Here I am stuck betwee-"

Gina grabs the ukulele out of my hands, smashes it on the wall of the hallway. It splinters it into a million pieces.

"Hey!"

Uh oh. Now she's in my grill, even closer than usual. Red-faced. "Enough. I get it. *Roll-with-it.* You got it. You can go from getting your fingers sliced off one minute and puking on me to playing a song on a stupid ukulele the next. You win." She shakes her head. "That's not me, Chip. I don't know what I expected in here. Answers. But it's just questions. It's fucking crazy. I don't want to be here any more. I shouldn't be here."

"Yes you should. I... we... need you."

My sudden admission that it would suck even worse in here without her changes her face. Her hot glare is replaced with the look your mom gives you when she wants to kill you for spilling tomato sauce on the new rug, but she knows she can't send you back to wherever the stork brought you from. We're in this together. Stuck with each other.

"Then listen, Chip. Can we just move on? Get this thing done? And go home?"

"Uh. Sure." I pick up the pieces of the ukulele. "But just so you know, I'm trying to get this done just as fast as you. The goofy shit is just what keeps me sane in here."

She helps me pick up the last of the uke. "Yeah. I get it."

Hands me the neck with the strings dangling off. "I'll buy him a new one. And-"

A laugh interrupts her. It's Tesla. "Oh, don't worry, Miss Phillips. I've already gone back and gotten a replacement."

Yeah, that's right. Nikola Tesla, genius inventor, just went back in time ten minutes to pick up his unbroken ukulele, and is strumming it happily. And Albert Einstein is humming along, tapping his feet, wiping the last of my bodily fluids off his sweater vest. Yes. That is actually happening.

Gina shakes her head again. Sighs. She can't help but snort a little. "Well. You don't see that. Ever."

I feel bad for her though, she just kind of bared her soul, she wants the fuck out of this craziness, and I get it, I truly do, so I'm all down to business now. "Nikola. That's a really nice ditty you got going there, but Gina's right – we've got a job to do and time's a wasting. We were going to get Pete, that's how this whole thing started, and then Alternate Japanese-speaking Pete shows up covered in jelly and warns us to stay away. NOT to get him. Now it looks like you can't join us, you're in that loop thing, but can you help us figure out what the hell is going on, what that stuff is, and get him back?"

Tesla and Einstein look at each other and nod. And I swear to God, you can almost see the massive brain waves of these two geniuses sparking in the air. Tesla raises a finger and proclaims, "Master Chip, Albert and I will pass into the Closed Timelike Curve in search of clues, risking our own lives and dismantling the very fabric of existence for you. We will not return until we have traversed all of time and space and returned with an answer!"

Einstein leans over and whispers, "It should take about a minute."

They amble over and plop into their respective arm chairs (damn they look cozy). Tesla pushes a button built into his armrest (hey, I want one of those!) and their whole room starts spinning. Woah. Mindfuck.

And right on time, exactly sixty seconds later, the room stops spinning. Cool. Here come the answers.

But something's wrong.

Tesla comes lurching over to the doorway, barely able to breathe.

"Hey, Nikola. Where's Einstein?"

"Albert..."

"What, Nikola. What?"

"Albert Einstein is gone."

15. GREAT. NOW WE LOST ALBERT EINSTEIN

From: Chip Collins
To: Julie Taylor
Date: November 19, 2017 11:43am
Subject: Great. Now we lost Albert Einstein.

Hi Julie,

Yeah. It's bad.

So we get Tesla settled down a little, enough to talk. He's pale.

"Chip. When you saw Pete... the substance..."

"Yeah. He had some kind of jelly all over him."

Tesla turns even more pale. "Yes. What color?"

"Blue."

He turns even more pale. No. My bad. I think that's as pale as he gets. "Chip. There is an ancient substance, Albert and I were able to travel back thousands of years to see it ourselves, in a cavernous spring underneath what would now be, I believe, Madison Square Garden. A blue gelatinous fluid that the native Americans called "Igohidiv Oyohusa."

"Huh?"

"Forever Death."

"Cool name."

Gina smacks me on the arm. "That's terrible. Shut up."

Tesla ignores me and continues. "They believed that this substance, if you touched it, would suck your infinite soul into an eternity of darkness. A fate worse than death. So they built a pyramid to cover the spring." He puts his hands together. "And they prayed to the Earth Mother to rid the world of this abomination, this thing that did not originate from her womb."

"So… it's from another planet or something? The Blue Juice is some kind of alien goop?"

He sits down on the floor, right in front of us. He's spent. "Yes. We found the source… under the pyramid… to investigate and find a solution… Albert… accidentally touched it… one moment he was there… the next, gone."

"So, that's it? Now Pete *and* Einstein are trapped for eternity in the Blue Juice? We're just screwed? Come on, Nikola. What do we do? We gotta save Pete! We gotta get home!"

He shakes his head. "I am a man of science. What they told me, I'm afraid it wouldn't do any good."

"What? What did they say?"

"They said only one of their deities could slay the Igohidiv Oyohusa."

"A god?"

"Yes. ABBA."

"Wait. A Swedish pop group from the 1980s is the only thing that can slay the Blue Juice? Yeah. We're officially fucked."

"No, Chip. ABBA is an animal spirit. I don't know what kind of animal. This is all they gave me." He digs into his vest pocket and pulls out a scrap of animal skin with some hieroglyphics or something on it. Stares at it. "A primitive illustration of the spirit ABBA. I have no idea what it means, Chip. I'm afraid I'm at a loss when it comes to the spiritual realm with its incantations and religious iconography." He hangs his head. "Poor Albert… Poor Pete… would I could stand in their place…" and he closes his eyes. "For perhaps the first time, Chip, I simply… don't know what to do. They... us... all of us... are in grave danger if the Blue Juice is reaching out across dimensions."

I look down at Nikola. Man, I wish I could give him a hug without slicing off my arms. I glance at the pictogram or whatever it is he's holding. What the hell did the native Americans think he could do with this? Cover a ceremonial drum with it or something? Hang it on his wall in a frame that says "Me and Einstein went back ten thousand years but all I got was this lousy animal skin"? But you know, it is kind of cool looking. Gina steps over and takes a look too. She points to it. "Huh. Upside down it looks like math."

Tesla opens one eye. Lifts his head. "Excuse me?"

She twirls her index finger in a circle. "Upside down. That thing you're holding looks like math. Like an equation."

Tesla rotates the skin around so he's looking at it upside down. His eyes go wide. "Gina!" He peers up at her, and I swear the little Tesla coils start going in his eyes. "You're a genius, Gina!"

"Well, I don't like to brag, but..."

I punch her in the shoulder. "Hey, that's my line."

And while me and Gina argue over who's smarter, like the two kids who missed valedictorian by a hundredth of a point, Tesla's already back at his little table, furiously scribbling math and shit, and gesticulating (God, another word I love), and occasionally uttering "Yes!" or "If we put this here..." and finally *Eureka!* I've got it!" He rushes over to us – careful not to breach the doorway and cut himself in half – and shows us a mess of what looks to me like something my mom wouldn't even put on the fridge. "Look!"

Genius Gina, who'd love to say she knows what she's looking at, even has to admit – "Um, Nikola, what are we looking at?"

"Oh. Sorry. Yes. You were correct, Gina. The illustration was actually an equation, a way to formulate the exact place in their ancient celestial sphere – a direct analog to the ITA – that one could find ABBA! These are the exact coordinates for the InController!" He looks down, a little somber. "Perhaps I shouldn't be so excited. This is merely a first step in the right direction. To save our friends. We don't even know if this ABBA is real. But it is a step you two must take. I have faith in you." He slips the paper through the doorway and it yellows and ages as it touches Gina's palm. He turns and walks towards his chair.

"Wait. Nikola. Us two? What about you? You're not coming with us?"

"I shall return to the closed timelike curve, and search for Albert through time, and possibly a more complete solution. If I find anything, I will correspond with you through the journal. You are in good hands." He winks at Gina. Then he reaches back, takes the replacement ukulele from the wall, passes it to me, smiles. "A memento." He turns to Gina again. "And if his playing becomes too bothersome, feel free to smash this one into pieces as well. I have infinite more."

In the next moment, he's already in his chair, pressing his fancy time travel button.

The room starts spinning. And he's off.

Good luck, Nikola.

I shut the door, tap the coordinates to ABBA into the InController, and me and Gina take our next steps down the hallway. It could be a day, or a month, or a decade, but it doesn't matter, because time stops in here.

I reflect on Meg, and now on Tesla. "Gee. Nobody wants to come with us."

"Maybe it's because my pants smell like barf."

16. YOU'RE NOT GOING TO BELIEVE WHAT GINA'S SCARED OF.

From: Chip Collins
To: Julie Taylor
Date: November 19, 2017 11:43am
Subject: You're not going to believe what Gina's scared of.

Hi Julie,

We've been walking for a while, and I'll admit it, I've been
thinking about the kid thing again. Our little imaginary bambino.
Bundle of giggles. Factory of Obnoxious Smells. In fact, in one of
my daydreamy states (it happens a lot here in the ITA), I sort of
randomly came up with a story about it. Well, kind of – it's about
two stars who are in love.

"Hey, Gina."

"What."

"You want to hear a story? It's pretty cute."

"No."

"Come on. You don't do cute? You watch *Downtown Abbey*."

"That's not cute. It's–" she catches herself getting caught in an
actual conversation with me and shuts it down. "Whatever. Sure.
Go to town. I can't wait."

"Cool. Okay… a-HEM…

Baby Star: A Short Story by Chip Collins

Once upon a time there were two stars. And they were in love. They circled each other, endlessly, and found warmth in each other's glow.

One revolution, the first star pondered his love, the second star, and for the first time thought, "Is there something more? This love is a wonderful thing, but is it the end?"

The second star, sensing that something was wrong, reached out to her love with a solar flare. He felt the additional warmth of her flare and smiled. And he sent out flares of his own to her.

Soon there were many flares, too many to count, intertwining the two lovers in a warm embrace.

Yes, this was an even greater love.

But their shared heat began to do something else. It began to reach some critical mass, some cosmic point of no return. Something was about to happen.

"I'm afraid."

"Don't be afraid. We're together."

And in that moment, the two stars, sharing a mass now too large for either to contain, exploded in a massive supernova, sending glimmering plasma far into space.

It took a long time, but the plasma, and dust, and endless

small nuclear reactions remaining from the stars began to coalesce. To take shape.

And a new star was born.

"So, what do you think? You think it needs a ukulele soundtrack?"

I look over at Gina, expecting, at best, for her to be rolling her eyes, or pretending to gag, and at worst for her to pull out her gun and shoot me.

But her bottom lip is shaking a little. Her eyes are welling up.

"Hey, Gina. You okay?"

And of course, at that exact moment, the InController *breeps* and announces, "You have arrived at your destination. The door is on your right."

Gina turns away from me and faces the door. Sniffs. "We're here."

No way. Yet again, I've cornered Gina with a personal question and we've miraculously arrived at some destination, and she gets out of answering. "No. This is bullshit. We're not going in yet. I want to know."

"Cut the crap, Collins." She reaches for the door.

"No." I put my hand over the lock dials. "Look, I might not be your favorite episode of *Downtown Abbey*, but I know how to listen. I know how to have your back. I know how to be a friend. Tell me."

"You're not my friend, Collins." She brushes my hand aside. "You're a child."

"You know what? Thank you. Yes. I am a child, in a way. I am still filled with childlike wonder after all these years, and yes, I like to be tucked in whenever possible, and sure, if you make me a grilled cheese sandwich and tomato soup I'll do anything you want, and—"

"Anything I want? Like read my briefs?"

"This isn't about the damn briefs and you know it. What *is* it about? What's your problem?"

She's fuming. "Okay, you really want to know– *AAAAHHH!*" And she jumps back. Something just scared the piss out of her.

"What?! What?!"

"THERE!" She points to the floor, finger shaking. I don't see anything.

Oh wait. There it is. There's a cockroach skittering around on the floor. "You screamed about a cockroach?"

She can't even speak. Just nods and slowly pulls her gun.

"Wait. So you killed the million-toothed Purple People Eater back there with your bare hands, but this little – well, it's pretty big actually for a cockroach – this thing is freaking you out?"

She nods again, like a she just watched *The Shining* and now she has to go upstairs to her room in the Overlook Hotel, in the dark, alone. And the twin ghost girls are waiting for her.

I squash it. "Jeez. It's just a cockroach. It's not like–"

"AAAAHHHH!!!"

"Jesus Christ, what?!"

She points at another cockroach. Hmm. Looks like it might be time for another Official ITA Reset & Cleaning! But before I can step on this roach, Gina freaks out and shoots at it.

Yeah. She fires a gun at a cockroach. One inch from my foot.

She kills it (actually I can't believe her aim this time, pretty amazing), but the bullet goes ricocheting down the hallway.

"Gina! Dude! What the fuck? I told you! You can't keep shooting bullets down the hallway!"

"I'm… It's…"

"Yeah. I know. You'll file a report. Your stupid report's going to be three inches thick by the end of this. Look, promise me you won't do that again."

She nods, wary, eyes darting around, still afraid another cockroach is going to pop out and – I don't know, nibble on her toe or something?

So I finally get her to shake off all the crazies, calm down a little, and we enter the dimension where we're supposed to find ABBA (not the Swedish pop group). I don't know why, but I'm expecting a disco ball to drop from the sky and "Dancing Queen" to start playing, and this big giant god dude with white flowing hair floats down in a polyester suit with rhinestones on it and shit. Maybe he's even playing a giant synthesizer. But that doesn't happen. Darn. It's just another jungle. A dense, green, lush jungle.

"Uh oh. Gina, it's a jungle. Watch out for more Purple People Eaters."

"It's not the Purple People Eaters I'm worried about." Gina's frantically scanning the jungle floor, and sure enough, cockroaches are darting all over the place, hiding from her gun, and she's waving it at them like they're trying to rob a bank. I put my hand out. "Give me the gun. You're just going to run out of bullets."

She glares at me like I'm taking away her security blanket, you know, the one with the frayed edges and the silk trim that feels good when you rub it against your face, come on, Julie, I know you had one too – anyway, she gives it up finally, and we start poking around, looking for clues and crushing way more of these cockroaches than you'd expect in a jungle. Man, they need an exterminator here in dimension #685,420,295,324! What, did they leave out an old pizza or something?

It actually reminds me of that first night in our new apartment, remember? The old tenants hadn't been there for months, and they left full cereal boxes in the cabinets, and when we turned on the lights for the first time, it was like we interrupted the hottest cockroach party of the year, like one of them leaked the invitation on Facebook and Snapchat and every cockroach in the city showed up with their friends from Staten Island, and they scattered like they were hiding all their drugs, and we're there with rolled up magazines, thinking – foolishly – that we could take on this horde ourselves. I mean, I know it sucked, but it still makes me laugh to picture you swinging that issue of *Oprah!*

around like a medieval knight, spraying Raid all over the place and eventually into your own eyes. Ouch. But we had the FBI threaten an investigation (I'm not sure what the hell the FBI would have to do with New York City apartment pest infestations, but it was like the one perk the Bureau ever offered me so I pounced on it), and the landlord put us up in – of course – the New Yorker Hotel, and it wound up being one of the best weeks of my life, taking care of you and your puffy eyes. Remember they had that little cafe downst–

"Collins! You're doing it again!"

Oh shit. Back to the actual, real life story.

So anyway, Gina's nerves have had just about enough, when there's this sound.

Hhhhhmmmmmmmm.

It's sort of like a vacuum cleaner. Like a vacuum cleaner in a jungle. You know the sound, because you've been in a jungle with a vacuum cleaner, right? Haven't we all? Anyway, hhhhhmmmmmm. And all the cockroaches – shit, all the birds and monkeys, everything – disappears.

And something approaches us. Through the underbrush, some gigantic wave, not very fast but very fluid, is coming closer–

"OH SHIT! GINA! THE BLUE JUICE!"

We run. We run like hell back towards the doorway.

But mere steps into our escape, the wave consumes our ankles. Then our legs. Then our waists. We're both screaming, still running but slowing down, and at some point right before I perish I realize:

This isn't the Blue Juice.

I'm covered in fucking cockroaches.

From: Chip Collins
To: Julie Taylor
Date: November 19, 2017 11:43am
Subject: Re: You're not going to believe what Gina's scared of.

Hi Julie,

Have you ever been covered in cockroaches?

It kind of tickles.

I know, it's the last sensation I should be having when I'm being enveloped by a horde of cockroaches, but I'm just being honest. All their little legs all over you, all your sensitive spots, and I can't help it. I start giggling (trying like hell to keep my mouth closed). I can barely hear Gina over the din of all these bugs chattering away, she's a few feet from me screaming bloody murder – I mean, it's her only irrational fear in the world and now they're all over her – but I'm like a little kid, giggling.

Gina's right. I need to grow up.

Anyway, I also need to get some oxygen, my cute little nose holes – possibly my favorite body part, although they're holes, so do they count as parts? – my nose holes aren't cutting it, so I open my mouth and take in a deep breath.

And that's when it stops being fun.

My mouth is instantly full of cockroaches, scurrying back and forth, flicking their antennae around, checking out my teeth, wrestling with my tongue. It's like super full in there, so full I can't even breathe, or spit, or scream for the god ABBA to save us.

So I start to chew.

Crunch. Crunch. Crunch.

It's not because I like eating cockroaches. You know that. God, that one time we got sandwiches at that deli down the block and I bit into a dead cockroach in my chicken salad? You almost had to get the defibrillator off the wall and use it on me. Anyway, I start chewing these fuckers, just to clear my mouth, maybe spit them out so I can breathe. But every time I open my mouth more come in. God, this is worse than awful. But hey, now at least I know the final answer to that old joke:

What's grosser than gross?
Running while you're covered in cockroaches,
and every time you try to breathe they fill your mouth,
and chewing them doesn't really do any good because they never
stop.

So right before I start saying my near-death prayer – you know, the one I've said about a thousand times here in the ITA – there's this horn or something in the distance. "Waaa-HHHOOOOOO!" And the cockroaches instantly retreat. But not entirely. They skitter off our faces and necks, but they're still completely covering us otherwise. And they're silent now. And we're paralyzed by them. I look over at Gina, poor Gina, and I'm trying to find something to say. This is all I got: "Hey Gina, you know there might be a positive here. They say if you have a phobia, sometimes immersion therapy works, where they overload your senses with whatever you're afraid of. Did it work?"

She opens her eyes – and yes, she's shooting her flaming hot laser glare at me, as usual – but then she looks down at the sea of cockroaches holding her hostage, and a weird thing happens: a calmness comes over her. She doesn't smile exactly, I mean we're still literally covered in bugs, but the corner of her mouth curls up a little bit. "Actually, yes. I feel… *okay.* Huh. Weird."

"Great, cool. One problem solved. Now let's see if we can't mosey on over to the doorway and get the FUCK out of here and rethink how to find ABBA."

We start to slowly walk, crunchy step by crunchy step, to the door. But another "Waaa-HHHOOOOOO!" horn blast goes off, and I guess the cockroaches decide to take control. Their chatter starts up again, and they literally turn us around, while we're trying to walk the other way, and they start moving us toward the horn sound. I swear it's like having an exoskeleton – *Get it? Bugs? Exoskeleton?* – that has a mind of its own. My legs are moving, walking, but not where I want them to go. And every time I try to shake these things off me, even more take over the job.

Eventually, we're guided to what looks like an ancient outdoor arena, hundreds of little rows of stone in a semicircle, except it's covered in – you guessed it – cockroaches. We're on what kind of feels like the stage.

The chatter rises, like the crowd before a Broadway show, and then it gets quiet. I guess we're the show. Whoopee. My first show and you're not here to see it. Oh, and I'm covered in bugs, which is also not part of my ideal debut scenario. I was thinking more costumes, footlights, and orchestras, and less *covered-in-cockroaches*.

Anyway, if you can believe it, it get weirder.

We're facing the back of the stage, and right in the middle of it, about three feet in front of us, a shape starts forming out of piles of cockroaches. They keep piling and piling, until they form a column, maybe a foot round and five feet high. Exactly at Gina's eye level. The whole column of bugs moves over to within an inch or two of Gina's face. And one of the cockroaches gets up, stands on its hind legs, starts waving its arms and antennae. He looks exactly like all the rest of them, except for thick hair growing off the back of his shell, like he's wearing a coat or something. Gina's just staring at the thing, disgusted, looking over at me like "What the fuck?" and I'm like "You're asking me? This one looks like FBI jurisdiction, boss."

And then the column makes its way over to me – and yeah, it has to come down a bit to get to my eye level – and I'm looking straight at this cockroach dude wearing the coat.

~~So. Waddya think?~~

. . .

I look around. "Who said that?"

Gina looks around too. "Who said *what*? I didn't hear anything."

~~No. Over here, kid. Right in fronna you.~~

Now I've got pretty good eyes, but I can't tell if this little cockroach guy's got a mouth. And even if he did, I wouldn't be able to hear him. All I'd hear was a microscopic little squeak, squeak, squeak or something, right? "Hey. How the hell are you talking?"

~~Shit's crazy. Don't ask. Amiright?~~

Holy shit. He knows the motto.

~~Anyway, I'm not talkin'. I'm usin' telepathy.~~

"Uh, Gina. You hearing this?"

She shakes her head like I'm going insane. Which is perfectly understandable. Because I am going insane. I'm listening to a cockroach.

~~She can't hear me. I told you. It's telepathy.~~

. . .

I jiggle my brain around a little. This can't be happening. Then I realize that everything I've ever seen in the ITA can't be happening, so why should this be any different? "Okay, smart guy, if you're using telepathy, what am I thinking about right now?

No hesitation: ~~*Waffles. You and Julie eatin' waffles in bed as the sun peeks into your bedroom window.*~~

Holy fuck. He just nailed my go-to fantasy. "Uh-oh. Can you read... *everything* in there?"

~~*Relax, kid. I can only read what you push out there. Your dark secrets are safe. Unless you think of them right now, eh? Eh? Eh?*~~

I try like hell not to think about my dark secrets. *Don't think about your dark secrets Chip, Don't think about your dark secrets, Chip.*

~~*Relax, kid. I'm just funnin' witcha. You really gotta want me to know whatchya thinkin'. That's how it works. I can't just go pullin' shit outta you willy nilly.*~~

"Wait. How do you know English? And why do you sound like you come from Staten Island?"

~~*The language thing, whateva, it's just thoughts, language doesn't matta. Kapeesh? And the accent? I just like it, I don't know, you were pushing out the thought about your exterminator guy Phil. He's from Staten Island. I like it.~~*

Holy shit. This cockroach is talking to my brain. And he does accents. "Hey, can you do Michael Caine?"

And in a perfect Michael Caine voice, the cockroach replies: *~~Yes, Master Wayne. I believe I can offer you any accent you wish. But we're not here for accents, are we, Master Wayne?~~*

"I guess not. But I have one more question first – why can't Gina hear this?"

~~Her mind is closed right now. I usually have a good sense about things like this, but I guess she's not ready. You, on the other hand, are an open book, kid. Now… how can we helpya?~~

"We're here to see ABBA."

~~The Swedish pop group?~~

"No. Some Native American tribe said a god named ABBA lived here, and they think he knows how to beat the 'Forever Death' – the stuff we've been calling the Blue Juice. Do you know where I can find him? Can you guys take us to this god?"

The little cockroach dude laughs in my head.

I frown. "Yeah. That's what I thought. Pretty far fetched, right? We knew it was a long shot. Fuck."

• • •

~~No. I wasn't laughing because you're wrong.~~

"Huh?"

~~I've just never been called a god before. I'm usually called the Cockroach King.~~

"You...? You're...?"

~~Yeah. I'm ABBA.~~

17. ABBA, THE COCKROACH KING

From: Chip Collins
To: Julie Taylor
Date: November 19, 2017 11:43am
Subject: ABBA, The Cockroach King

Hi Julie,

"You're ABBA? A god? But dude, you're just a cockroach."
   ~~*And last year you were just a security guard.*~~
"Touché."
   ~~*I'm not a god though, really. Maybe someday. And maybe someday you'll be President.*~~
   Gina's had just about enough of listening to my one-sided conversation. "Collins! Come on. This is obviously a waste of time. We've got a pretty huge problem on our hands with the Blue Juice, and Pete, and now Einstein, and you're having an imaginary conversation with a BUG. You mind cutting it short so we can move on and make some actual progress?"
   The column of cockroaches immediately dissolves, creating a clear area around the one with the little hair coat, ABBA, who

then skitters over to Gina. Then the mass of cockroaches around Gina recedes a bit, revealing her right leg and foot.

~~Kid. Tell her to step on me.~~

"No. Dude. She didn't mean it. We'll figure out-"

~~Tell her to step on me, kid.~~

"No."

~~If you don't tell her to step on me, I'll push a thought into your mind about how our species reproduces, and you'll never wanna be intimate with another human being as long as you live. I promise.~~

"Gina. Step on him. He wants you to step on him. Now."

"What? Collins, is this one of your stupid games? Bugs don't have thoughts. You know what? I'm sick of-"

At that moment, ABBA starts pushing a visual into my brain, just a hint of the beginning of their courtship ritual. It involves about a million of these cockroaches, the sound of six zillion legs rubbing together, and something gooey, and lots of orifices, and "OH MY GOD GINA JUST STEP ON HIM!!!!"

I guess because I've actually given her a direct order for the first time ever, she instinctively complies and crushes poor ABBA with her free foot.

Crunch.

Ewww. There's little cockroach guts stuck to her boot.

What the hell?

Did the Cockroach King really just commit suicide?

While I'm trying to wrap my head around this, and think of an appropriate – and potentially hilarious – eulogy for this little cockroach, his guts snap back into shape – *pop!* – into pre-crunch ABBA. Both our jaws drop. And ABBA literally dusts himself off with his legs and antennae, like a boss, scampers up the pile of cockroaches on Gina, and takes a squat right on the tip of her nose. She's dumbstruck.

~~What can I say? It's good to be king. Now can you hear me?~~

Gina nods slowly. "Y- y- yes...?"

~~Good. Then let's make some 'actual progress.'~~

So I guess that little "squash me" routine must open your

mind a little or something, because Gina can hear him now just fine. Not that she likes it. Every time he speaks, she shakes her head to get him out of her brain.

I'm impressed. "Hey, ABBA, guess what? I can heal like you too. I just grew my fingertips back a little while ago. And check this out." I shake the cockroaches free from my left leg, and pull down my sock to reveal my foot fuzz. "This is a new foot. I grew it back. I swear."

ABBA scampers over to my foot, inspecting it. He seems especially interested in the fur that's growing in.

~~Hmm. How'd you get this ability, kid?~~

"Bobo gave it to me. Furry guy, about this high," I point to my hip, "with big, giant, black eyes."

ABBA's antennae freeze in place.

And the millions of cockroaches watching this whole thing fall silent.

The jungle seems to stop in time. Then, in unison, all the cockroaches withdraw from me and Gina, stand on their hind legs and begin to sway back and forth. It's like a flash mob, but I can't hear what song they're performing it to. All I hear is their murmured little chatter. Like they're chanting something, but, you know, I don't speak cockroach. "Hey, Gina. You're the linguist. You speak cockroach?"

She gives me the finger. "Yeah. This is what they're saying, Collins."

I turn to ABBA. "Okay, dude - what are they saying?"

He laughs. ~~They're chanting your name.~~

"Which is...?"

~~The Second Coming of The Furry One From Beyond the Great Door.~~

From: Chip Collins
To: Julie Taylor
Date: November 19, 2017 11:43am
Subject: Re: ABBA, The Cockroach King

Hi Julie,

I've been called a lot of things – idiot, douche, you name it – but this one's a first: *The Second Coming of The Furry One From Beyond the Great Door.*

"Kind of a long name, isn't it ABBA?"

~~*They say it fast. It rolls off the tongue if you say it fast. The-Second-Coming-of-The-Furry-One-From-Beyond-the-Great-Door.*~~

"Uh. Sure. But what the hell does it mean?"

ABBA turns to address the masses.

~~*Okay everybody. Our buddy here wants to hear the story.*~~

And a cajillion cockroaches lay down and snuggle up against each other, like ABBA's about to read them a bedtime story. Like if they had little blankets and teeny teddy bears, this would actually be pretty damn cute. You know, like what's cuter than a horde of cockroaches with little blankets and teddy bears? Anyway, here's the story:

The Insane Story of ABBA: A Telepathic Powerpoint Presentation, As Told By ABBA
In the Voice of Phil, My Exterminator from Staten Island

SLIDE VISUAL: ABBA as a young, streetwise cockroach
So. It's maybe forty thousand years ago. Me and my buddies are munchin' on a twig or some shit. My one buddy, I'll call him Moe, you know 'cause your exterminator's cousin is named Moe, anyway, so he's

telling me about a little get together they're having later that week, lots of food and females, but before I can say "sounds lit bro, what time should I be there?" this big foot comes outta nowhere and squashes me. Like complete and utter mush. Dead. Gone. The whole *white-light-at-the-end-of-the-tunnel* thing. It was freaky. And not freaky cool. Like freaky I was dead.

SLIDE VISUAL: The Furry One

I interrupt the story. "Holy shit! That's Bobo! That's Bobo! You guys know Bobo?"

~~Yeah, The-Second-Coming-of-The-Furry-One-From-Beyond-the-Great-Door. Can I continue?~~

"It's Chip. Just call me Chip."

~~Okay. Chip. Can I continue?~~

"You know what? I think I might like the longer name. Try that one again."

Gina snort laughs. She knows I'm just giving ABBA shit now, and since she likes him even less than she likes me right now, she approves. ABBA just shrugs it off and continues:

So while I'm having my near death experience, my friends tell me the creature that owns the big foot, this furry thing with big black eyes, stops and kneels down over my remains. And he chews off a little bit of one of his fingers, and mashes it up with whatever's left of me. And I slowly re-form, and come to. I look up, and the thing is off skipping on its merry way. My friends are like "holy shit!" and then we just go back to munchin' on the twig. It was a pretty tasty twig.

Meanwhile I'm stretching out my legs, and it's amazing – I feel as good as new.

No. *Better* than new.

SLIDE VISUAL: ABBA, now with furry coat on his back – presumably from Bobo's DNA mixing with his own – holding a little spear.
It turns out I don't get hurt any more. And in a coupla years, when all my old friends die off, I just keep on living. And living. And living. Generation after generation of us are born an' die, and I just stick around. This sucks for a long time, watching my friends die over and over and over, and I just keep on truckin.' Man, that part really blows chunks.

SLIDE VISUAL: ABBA riding a bird in flight
(Side note: this image is awesome. I want a poster of this for our bedroom wall.)
An' then, it takes foreva, but then I start the telepathy thing. Like I realize I can pick up thoughts, from any animal here in the jungle, including my cockroach buddies, which sometimes is a pain in the ass, because they're mostly having the same thoughts over and over again, either they're hungry or they're horny. But by an' large the telepathy thing's awesome, because I can use it to keep my peeps safer from the baddies, have other species help us, and organize the colonies to get better at gathering food and building shelters and shit.
Before long, they're calling me king, ABBA the Cockroach King, and all is well for thousands of years. Really, it's been a trip. I've been blessed with millions and millions of offspring, fuggedaboutit, the amount of sex you can have over that amount of time– but… that's another story…

SLIDE VISUAL: The beginning of their courtship ritua-
OH MY GOD MOVE ON TO THE NEXT SLIDE!

SLIDE VISUAL: An asteroid hurtling through the sky overhead.

SLIDE VISUAL: A neon blue lake in the middle of the jungle.

Okay, so at some point, maybe ten thousand years ago, this huge asteroid smashes into our planet, kills lots of stuff all over the place, and this blue gooey stuff appears in the impact crater – I guess the stuff you called the Blue Juice. Naturally, my main colony goes to check it out, and I'm like "DON'T TOUCH THE BLUE STUFF!" and of course one of my buddies isn't listening because he's an idiot and he touches the goo. And he disappears into it. So I'm like "fuck," and I dive in after him.

Of course you can only see a few inches in this shit, so I'm feeling around for my buddy, and I pick up this very strong thought. Just one thought, over and over again. Very strong. Over and over again. It was this freaky, single thought, repeated over and over and over and over and over and over-

"Christ, I get it! What was the thought?"

~~HUNGER.~~

"That's it?"

~~Yeah. Just 'HUNGER.' You done?~~

Anyway, all the Blue Juice knows is hunger. So I don't know what to do, so I push a thought into it: 'Hey buddy, you just ate.'" Nothing. So I push a little harder. 'Hey buddy, you just had a nice big meal. A whole bunch of meaty twigs. You're full.' Nothing again. And then I give it all I got, I swear my brain feels like it's about to explode. 'YOU'RE FULL, MOTHERFUCKER!" And wouldn't you know? The blue lightens up a little, just enough so I can see my buddy, and move around better, so I grab his ankle and paddle like hell to shore. Whew.

Of course, I'm happy I saved one of my own, but I gotta tell you – that Blue Juice shit took something outta me. Like *permanently*. Like I beat it, the white lake is over there a few miles if you wanna see, but I couldn't do it again. No way. So I'm like 'NOBODY TOUCHES THE GOO. EVER AGAIN. GOT IT?"

And it's been forbidden ever since.

SLIDE VISUAL: Far off mountain top, with a little Bobo sitting there motionless, like Buddha under the bodhi tree. Anyway, every hundred or so years since, I catch a glance of the Furry One, not doing anything, just being. But generally he's out of sight, and I never, even once, interact with him. Until…

SLIDE VISUAL: The Great Door

I can't help it. I blurt out, "The ITA! That's the INTERDIMENSIONAL TRANSFER APPARATUS!"

~~*Hey. Kid. Trying to tell a story here.*~~

I pretend to zipper up my lips. Then I say "sorry."

~~*Kid. How are you supposed to say 'sorry' if your lips are zippered?*~~

I unzip my lips and say "sorry" again, then zip them back up. He moves on.

So maybe seventy-five years ago, the Great Door appears. And the Furry One comes down from the mountain top the very next day, right into the center of our city. I hop on his finger, and look into those great big black eyes, and he says this:

BYE.

And I'm like "Bye? That's it? After all these years?"
He blinks coupla times, pats my head, and I'm waitin' for
some eloquent speech, somethin' real deep and
meaningful, something we can live by for the next
millennia, and he says,

YES. BYE.

And that's it. No explanation. He just hops away, and we
follow him, and he disappears out the Great Door. Poof.

SLIDE VISUAL: Me (Chip)

"Hey! That's me!"
~~We all know it's you, kid. For cryin' out loud, kid, you always this
annoying?~~
"Sorry."

Then seventy-five years later, today, you come strolling
through the Great Door with a furry foot. *The-Second-*
Coming-of-The-Furry-One-From-Beyond-the-Great-Door.

Now he's done, I guess. All the cockroaches are perfectly still,
asleep I think, I swear it even sounds like they're snoring. So I'm
standing there, awkward, like "ABBA, am I supposed to do
something now?"
~~Yeah. It's written in the Great Book. You have to marry my
daughter.~~
"What the fuck?"
~~Nah. I'm kiddin.' You're good, kid. It's all good. We're just happy
to see you. Now… I hear you have a Blue Juice problem. Your best friend
is stuck in it. And ironically, you need me to be your exterminator.
That's fuckin' hilarious. Well, I hate to do this, kid, but like I said, I'm

not what I used to be. There's no way I could take on another one of those things beyond the Great Door. No way.~~

"Fuck."

~~Hold on. I said <u>I</u> couldn' do it…. But <u>you</u> can.~~

"Me? Dude. I can't do the telepathy thing! I have trouble forming complete sentences in my head. And forget about math. Especially subtraction. Ask me what twelve minus seven is."

~~You can do it. You've got DNA from the Furry One. You're a shoe-in. I'll train you.~~

I shudder. "Training? Like exercise? Like brain pushups? Dude, I don't know if you could tell, but I'm exercise-phobic."

~~Sorry, kid. You wanna save your friend or not?~~

My friend. Pete.

"Yes. Of course. Okay, dammit. Just tell me it's going to be easy like an afternoon of thinking at each other over Earl Grey tea and triangle cucumber sandwiches. Easy like that. Right?"

ABBA belly laughs. (I don't know, does he even have a belly?)

~~No. You're gonna undertake The Three Terrible Trials.~~

The Three Terrible Trials. Me.

Great. I can't wait.

And out of the corner of my eye, I spy Gina, laughing like I've never seen her laugh before.

18. THE THREE TERRIBLE TRIALS

From: Chip Collins
To: Julie Taylor
Date: November 19, 2017 11:43am
Subject: The Three Terrible Trials

Hi Julie,

I know. I should look forward to working out. I'll live longer, it'll keep my body and mind in perfect balance, improve my well being, blah, blah, blah, bullshit whatever. But how long have you known me now? If I have to take the stairs because our elevator's on the fritz I consider that my exercise for the week. And when the pint of ice cream is too hard and I have to really work at scooping it out? *That's* my kind of workout, baby!

"Listen, ABBA, The Three Terrible Trials sounds really cool, with the alliteration and everything, but maybe we could go with something like, I don't know, the Path of Painless Pampering?"

~~No. Sorry, kid. No shortcuts. The Three Terrible Trials it is.~~

"Ugh. So how many students have you subjected to this torture over the eons? Hundreds? Thousands? Millions?"

~~None. You're the first. I just made the whole thing up.~~

Gina snort-laughs at me. "You're his beta tester, Collins."

ABBA hops up on Gina's finger. ~~*Oh, no. You'll both be attending class.*~~

I imitate her snort-laugh back at her.

She picks up a pebble and flicks it at me. It hits me in the eye.

Oh boy. Let the fun begin.

So ABBA guides us outside their little cockroach city – nice to get a little break from constantly crunching the poor dudes underfoot – and deeper into the jungle. It's amazing, to think that maybe Fifth Avenue is where we'd be standing in our dimension. Just because something different happened, like maybe some invertebrate never crawled out of the swamp like it was supposed to, there's no New York City, and no Fifth Avenue, and no guy on the corner selling meat on a stick.

Damn. I wish I had some meat on a stick right now.

Anyway, other than the fact that I'm wicked hungry for some New York comfort food, I have to admit: this place is beautiful. I mean, waterfalls and rainbows beautiful. Literally. We're actually walking behind a waterfall, to a secluded spot under some leaves that are bigger than me, with a double rainbow above us in the cloudless blue sky. If I had meat on a stick I could just stay here forever. Oh, and I'd need you. Of course, that just goes without saying. Me, you, some meat on a stick, and double rainbows in the jungle.

~~*I see you like it here.*~~

"Hey. I wasn't pushing that thought out."

~~*Wasn't pushing that thought out? You were practically writing a five-star Yelp review and screaming it at the top of your lungs.*~~

He skitters up onto the fallen tree trunk me and Gina are sitting on.

~~*So, kids, ya see, that's what I call 'liftin.' Listening to someone's thought patterns, and liftin' the most prominent ones they're pushin' out. That's the first trial. Liftin.' Now Chip: what am I thinking?*~~

"Double rainbows."

~~No. You're just guessin'. Try again.~~

I concentrate. Hard. I'm looking right at this little cockroach, really trying – I mean, I guess I'm trying, how the hell am I supposed to know if I'm doing this right? – And… nothing. "Nothing. You're thinking of nothing."

ABBA smoothes his coat with his antennae.

~~Okay. So that's your first lesson: you can't just wing this shit. It took me hundreds of years to figure it out. But you're in a rush, got a friend to save, so we gotta take some serious shortcuts. So kid, I'm gonna want you to imagine a silver thread, like a fine fiber optic line, goin' from my brain into yours. Next, imagine that thread pulsating with light, from me to you, me to you, in a constant stream.~~

He flicks a little pebble at my face.

~~Hey! Kid! Wake up!~~

I start. "Oh, sorry. It's just… your mind voice is so soothing, and the waterfall sound, and my eyes closed…"

~~You want a pillow?~~

"Actually, that would be really nice-"

~~I'm not giving you a fuckin' pillow! Now wake the fuck up!~~

"Sorry, sir. ABBA."

~~Okay, now again – you got the the thread image?~~

"Yes."

~~And what am I thinkin'?~~

"Boats. A big boat, like a cruise liner."

~~Nope. Kid. What the fuck is your problem? I don't even know what a cruise liner is. Come on.~~

So it goes on like this for an hour or so, I'm a total idiot, I can't guess shit, and Gina's shifting around, getting impatient, so I'm like "what?" and she's like "try harder," and I'm like "you try harder!" and she's like "this isn't about me, you idiot!" and suddenly I blurt out "ELEPHANTS!"

ABBA looks from Gina to me.

~~Hmmm. Emotional charge. Interesting. You were right, kid. I was thinkin' of elephants.~~

"Great. So I just have to be really pissed at Gina for this to work?" I sneer at Gina. "That shouldn't be a problem."

~~Well, let's use that as a startin' point. Keep that anger goin.' Gina, do me a favor, call Chip a douche.~~

I jump up. "Hey! I don't like this Terrible Trial anymore!"

Gina grins. "Just remember, we're doing this for Pete, you douche. Douchety-douche."

Man, my cheeks must be beet red, they're so fucking hot, and I'm so pissed, and I can't help it, I start spewing, "A thousand years ago, one of your sons made a little sailboat out of a shell and a leaf, and he took it right here, to this little lake by the waterfall, and he drowned. And for all the thousands of years you've lived, there was nothing you could do, nothing to save your boy, and even though you've had millions of kids who've lived and died, you'll never forget. You'd trade your immortality and healing for one more minute with your son right now…" and tears are running down my cheeks, I don't know why, and it won't stop, the thoughts just keep coming in a river, and I look over to Gina and her eyes are wet too, and ABBA finally hops over onto my knee.

~~Woah. Kid. I was actually thinking of double rainbows.~~

And I laugh, I don't know why, and so does Gina, and ABBA continues.

~~Listen, what you saw was a few layers down, I didn't think you could get that deep. It's okay, though, kid. Just release the thread.~~

So I release the thread in my mind, disconnecting from ABBA. It's a relief. I wipe my eyes.

He continues clambering up to my shoulder.

~~Sorry, kid. I hope that didn't freak you out. Maybe I'm pushin' you too hard.~~

"No… no, I'm okay. Let's keep going. Pete's waiting for us."

~~Okay, but a little expert tip: try to avoid the sex part of my brain.

Like I said, that's gonna cause some permanent damage if you see what's in there.~~

So we go on, each time using less and less anger and emotion to charge the telepathy, and pretty soon, maybe three hours later, I'm calmly lifting thoughts at will from ABBA (staying clear of the sex zone). While we're at it, I notice Gina's gone for a stroll, and it's getting dark.

We continue our practice, and Gina comes back and builds a little fire.

ABBA taps me on the ear.

~~Okay, kid. You're ready. For the Second Trial. So see? That first one wasn't so Terrible after all. And Gina's got the right idea. You're tired. Rest until tomorrow.~~

My stomach is growling like crazy. "ABBA, listen, I know you can probably go a week without eating, but I'm famished. You got anything?"

ABBA shakes his head. (At least I think he does anyway.) *~~Nah. Ask your friend.~~*

Gina's got her back turned to me, kneeling down across the fire. She's doing something over there, hiding something. I try to lightly "lift" her thoughts, but she's blocking me. Damn, she must've been paying attention to the Trial. Then she turns around, revealing a skinned animal, something like a rabbit, with a spit running through it. She hangs it over the fire, and grins at me.

"You looked hungry. So I got us some meat on a stick."

From: Chip Collins
To: Julie Taylor
Date: November 19, 2017 11:43am
Subject: Re: The Three Terrible Trials

Hi Julie,

Okay, the First Trial: *Liftin'*, as ABBA would say – check. I got an
A. I guess. He didn't hand out grades. But I'm giving myself an A.
If he gives me anything lower I'm complaining to the dean.

So… now yours truly can read minds! How cool is that? Yet
another gift from our little friend Bobo. I mean, look at all the cool
shit Bobo's done for me:

Cool Shit Bobo Has Done For Me:

1. Sacrificed himself to save me from beheading at the
hands of the Orange Dudes. *Whew!*

2. Took a massive electrical charge to the chest to create a
timespace continuum breach and help save Tesla from
WHO's interdimensional prison. (Wow, that's maybe the
most screwed up sentence I've ever written.) *Whew!*

3. Chewed off his own hands and mashed them together
with my ankle so I could grow back another foot. A furry
foot, which kind of sucks, but still a perfectly good,
working foot. *Whew!* (You know what? I'll stop saying
Whew! now.)

3. Blew himself to smithereens to create the Bobo Army,
millions of little Bobos that helped us win the Epic Battle
for the Multiverse. He fucking rocks.

4. Gave me the gift of growing other stuff back, so when I sliced my fingertips off back at Young Tesla's dimension, boom – good as new. *Whew!* (Sorry, couldn't help it.)

5. Now I can read thoughts! Holy shit! Bobo's the gift that keeps giving!

Man, what a good guy. Or alien. Or whatever he is. I miss him almost as much as I miss you, babe. I hope you're having fun with him back home.

TEXT MESSAGE
From: Julie Taylor
To: Chip Collins

Chip I am going to kill Bobo. I know you won't get this text, but I'm pissed and I don't know what else to do. Bobo's acting even weirder than usual. Restless, keeps tugging at my shirt sleeve like he wants to go out. When you get back you have to have a talk with him.

If this is what kids are like, I'm officially not prepared for this shit.

From: Chip Collins
To: Julie Taylor
Date: November 19, 2017 11:43am
Subject: Re: The Three Terrible Trials

Hi Julie,

I keep thinking about having kids. I can't help it. And I find myself thinking about my mom and dad for some reason, remembering those moments around the dinner table again, wrestling with with my dad over the prize pork chop, sitting with them trying to finish that impossible fucking jigsaw puzzle of the clouds – I mean, what kind of sadist makes a thousand-piece puzzle with nothing but blue and white pieces? – going ice skating at Wollman Rink and holding their hands to keep from falling on my ass. Jeez, I could go on forever.

You know what? I'm going to. Right now.

The Official List of Every Single Family Memory I've Ever Had
By Chip Collins

Memory One: I remember riding my Big Wheel through the house, maybe I was three? My dad was chasing me, a big scary monster, and I was giggling like mad trying to get away from him, and my mom was like Mothra, saving me and battling Godzilla to the death, right there in front of me. I had never laughed so hard in my short little three year life. It was heaven.

Memory Two: I remember throwing up on–

"Collins. Chip. For Christ's sake, don't you ever stop writing to Julie?"

"Dude. No. And I was compiling my *Official List of Every Single Family Memory I've Ever Had*. You mind?"

She laughs and throws a pebble into the lake next to the waterfall. "How deep would you say this lake is?"

"No idea. Now can I get back to my list?"

She grins. Man, she's way too happy this morning. "Nope. Come on, you're up."

"Up?"

"You're up. Time to push."

Oh yeah. We're starting the Second Trial today: *Push*. I assume ABBA means pushing thoughts into somebody, and not actually physically pushing things around, like a tackle dummy in football. Hey, did I ever tell you I tried out for football in junior high? I had this friend Jeremy who played, and he talked me into it, and the first thing Coach O'Brian tells me to do is push this tackle dummy down the field to see how far I could get. Well, I lunge into the thing with everything I've got, and of course it pushes back because it's made out of nine hundred pounds of steel springs and shit, and I bounce off easily five yards backwards, and O'Brian starts yelling and blowing his whistle, and I just get up and walk off the field, shedding all the pads as I walk away forever, waving my middle finger in the air. At least Jeremy and the whole team thought I was a god for being the first person to ever get away with flipping the bird at Coach O'Brian. So only half a fail, I guess.

Anyway, I just hope we're not pushing stuff like that.

ABBA flicks my earlobe.

~~Hey, kid. You wanna push this big rock? Think of it like a tackle dummy.~~

I look down. I was wondering why he had my ankle tied to this big-ass rock. "Crap. Are you kidding me?"

ABBA laughs.

~~No.~~

"How the hell is this going to help my telepathy? And the Blue Juice? And Pete?"

~~Trust me, kid.~~

Whatever. This push thing really is going to suck. But if pushing a rock tied to your ankle will help Pete, I'm in. I lean into the rock with all my might. Damn, this thing is even heavier than it looks. I could really use some Awesome Man strength right now, my eyeballs are popping out of my head with the effort, and finally… OOMPH! I nudge it like an inch. I go at it again, now I'm sweating, God this tux is NOT going to be returnable, and I'm huffing and puffing and blowing the goddam house in, and the three little piggies are NOT moving another millimeter. "COME ON, YOU GODDAM PIGGIES!"

~~Okay, stop kid. I can't watch you do that any more.~~

"BUT… IF IT'S GOING TO HELP SAVE PETE… URGGH…"

~~It's not gonna save Pete. It has nothing to do with telepathy. I just wanted to see if you could move it. I was curious. I'm satisfied.~~

Gina snorts.

And I can't help it, I guess I'm a little ticked – I squash ABBA with my free foot.

But he bounces back into shape, wipes himself with his antennae.

~~You know what they say, kid – sticks and stones don't do shit when you're immortal. Now, let's talk about push. See that bird up there?~~

I look up and there's a bird, like a sparrow but bright blue and yellow, darting from branch to branch, way up in the nearest tree.

~~Now watch the push.~~

The bird stops darting, looks around, then down at ABBA. He glides in little circles down to the ground, right at ABBA's feet. ABBA hops up on the bird's back.

~~Okay, remember this: I'm not tellin' the bird what to do. It's an agreement. You can never just tell somebody what to do in their own mind. It's always an agreement. So little bird guy here has agreed to take me on a ride.~~

And the bird launches back into the air, and I can imagine ABBA waving a little cowboy hat in the air, screaming "Yee-hah!" (or whatever the Staten Island equivalent is) and lassoing dragonflies, and dive-bombing his friends and shit.

Of course, me and Gina are standing there thinking this is a short little demo of "pushing," but ABBA's gone for at least twenty minutes. Do you have any idea how long twenty minutes is when you're waiting for a bird-piloting cockroach and you're tied to a rock? Finally, I'm like "Fuck this. Gina can you help me untie this? I know he doesn't want me wandering off, but I'm going back to bed." And at that exact moment the blue and yellow bird swoops down right onto my shoulder and ABBA hops off. (And yes, because it's a black tux, the bird decides to leave me a little white present, right there on my shoulder. I make a mental note to look up why bird crap is white when I get home.)

"Hey, ABBA. What the hell? You forget about us?"

~~Nah, kid. Like I said, it's an agreement. Little bird guy over there had some errands he had to run before he agreed to take me back.~~

"Yeah. Well he can check 'leave a crap on Chip's shoulder' off his to-do list." I wipe my shoulder with a leaf. "So, can I try this push thing finally, or what? Here, birdie-birdie!"

ABBA flicks my earlobe again.

~~Not a bird. You're gonna be doin' somethin' a little different.~~

He nods at Gina. She nods back, casually strolls over to the big rock my foot is tied to, and hefts it onto her shoulders. (Really? The rock I couldn't move an inch? Really.)

Then she throws the rock into the lake.

Of course.

The moral of the story: If you're ever near a body of water and you find yourself tied to a rock, you're going in. I should've guessed. As the rope around my ankle tightens and drags me down into the water, and I start to drown, my last thought is:

No wonder Gina's so goddamned happy this morning.

From: Chip Collins
To: Julie Taylor
Date: November 19, 2017 11:43am
Subject: Re: The Three Terrible Trials

Hi Julie,

"HELP!!!"

At least that's what I'm trying to scream, but it sounds like "GLHEGGLLLGGLLPPP!!!" because I'm drowning at the bottom of this fucking lake. I mean, it's a beautiful lake, crystal clear water, not too cold, refreshing actually, with the waterfall right there, bubbling the water, but it'd be much nicer enjoying it from the shore, dry and safe. With, you know, air in my lungs.

The water's so clear, in fact, I can practically see Gina standing there laughing about ten feet above me. Why would Gina and ABBA be trying to drown me?

~~We're not trying to drown you, kid.~~

It's ABBA. I spin my head around, losing more valuable bubbles of oxygen, and he's still there, perched on my shoulder.

~~Don't panic, kid.~~

~~DON'T PANIC?!~~

~~Don't panic. Listen, kid. This is what it's like in the Blue Juice. You gotta stay calm. Think.~~

~~THINK?! I usually like to be breathing when I think!~~

I claw at the rope, flailing, hoping I might have magical rope untying powers I didn't know about. I've got maybe thirty more seconds. How the hell am I supposed to 'push' my way out of this?

~~Kid. Stop thrashing around. You're NOT going to die. I want you to think about that eel over there. The big one with the sucker mouth.~~

I look over and yeah, there's a huge eel maybe five feet from us, ugly as sin, and I don't know what ABBA's thinking, but fuck that. I flail even harder, tugging at the rope like somehow it'll now be lighter, precious bubbles escaping my lungs with every tug.

~~Okay, MAYBE you're going to die.~~

~~You're funny, ABBA. Hilarious.~~

~~Listen. Gotta move fast now. I really need you to call that guy over here, ask him to give you some oxygen.~~

~~No. No fucking way. I am NOT making out with an eel. Look at that mouth!~~

~~Who said he'd be using his <u>mouth</u>?~~

~~Oh for fuck's sake, I don't even want to know what that means. I surrender.~~

~~Nah. I'm kidding, kid. It's his mouth. He'll give you air with his mouth. Don't give up, Chip.~~

I'm shaking my head, getting kind of dizzy, is it getting dark down here or is my brain shutting down? And suddenly the eel isn't looking so bad, like marginally kissable, compared to the alternative. So I look straight into the thing, forming a little silver thread in my mind going from me to him, me to him, and sure enough, it stops swimming and takes a look at me. Tentative.

So I ask it:

~~Would you mind helping me breathe?~~

And I swear, the look on this thing's face says "you're fucking kidding me, right? I mean, look at your *mouth!*" but it moseys over anyway, swells its body, puts its (OH MY GOD DISGUSTING) sucker mouth over mine, and releases such a foul-tasting burst of swamp gas into my lungs I think I'm going to puke. But I realize, somewhere deep, that it's not good manners to puke into someone's mouth, especially on a first date, so I hold back.

And the life-giving oxygen makes everything light again, and my head clears. Whew.

Yeah. Clears enough for me to realize I just went to first base with a fucking eel. Gross.

~~Okay, kid. First step done. He'll be your backup in case you need more.~~

~~No. I will not be needing more. Let's just get to the fucking second step.~~

~~Okay. Now look at the water around you. Looks perfect clear, right?~~

Bubbles start escaping from my mouth. ~~ABBA! NOT the time for a science lesson!~~

~~Sorry. Listen, the lake looks clear, but it's filled with microscopic algae. They don't have brains per se, but they're conscious. Conscious enough to push.~~

~~Push to do what?! Form a big bubble around me and lift me to shore?!~~

~~Wow, kid. That's exactly it.~~

~~I was kidding. I can't talk to a million algae, or algeas, is it algeas if it's plural? Anyway I can't do that!~~

~~No problem. We'll just stay down here and you can french kiss that eel for a while.~~

No. Okay. Time to talk to the animals. I send out a friendly greeting. ~~Uh, algae dudes, what do you think about helping out a buddy, see I'm kind of stuck here at the bottom of the lake, and I need oxygen to breathe, and-~~

And I swear to God I get this feeling they're like "just shut up, we don't need the ten-minute Chip explanation," and I sort of see them forming a group around me. If I remember anything from biology, which isn't much, I vaguely recall that algae eats carbon dioxide and releases oxygen, like plants. So they must be hyperventilating or something, because a bubble appears around my mouth, then my face, then my whole head.

Pure oxygen.

I CAN BREATHE!

I take some deep breaths, ahh, wow I'm feeling a little invincible actually, a little concentrated O2 buzz, and the algae dudes continue to enlarge the bubble until it's enclosing me and ABBA.

~~Now, kid. Cut the rope.~~

~~I can't cut the rope! I don't have—~~

In my tux jacket pocket. I feel it now. Motherfucker. One of the knives from the backpack.

~~*ABBA! You guys put this in my pocket and didn't fucking tell me?*~~

~~*Hey. Kid. You had to do it the hard way. You know that. And you did. You did it. I'm prouda you.*~~

So I cut the rope and we rise to the water's surface, and the bubble bursts, and I say a little "thank you" to the algae dudes and the eel (who, I'm not kidding, now seems to want one more smooch before I leave), and heave myself up onto the rocks, sit there dripping for a few minutes, catching my breath. Hey, my tux actually looks cleaner. Bonus. I skootch over a little closer to Gina.

"You enjoyed that a little too much."

She laughs. "Yes. I did."

I punch her playfully in the shoulder, and she full on clocks me in mine and I fall off the rock. "Ouch! Hey!"

"Don't punch me. Ever."

Jeez. Gina's got to be the most impossible person to figure out. One minute she's kind of nice, funny, even cooking me dinner, the next cold as ice. Whatever. I look down my other shoulder. ABBA's still there, I guess now permanently fused there. "You. What about you? You got another Terribly Torturous Trial for me? Or do I get to rest a little?"

~~*Oh, you'll be resting all right.*~~ And he cackles like a witch.

"Get away from me." I try to swat him off, but he's holding on like crazy.

~~*Not a chance, kid. You're stuck with me.*~~

I don't know why, I should be totally irritated, but I'm smiling. Two Trials down. One to go.

Bring that shit on.

TEXT MESSAGE
From: Julie Taylor
To: Chip Collins

911. Your stupid furry friend just bolted. He took one of your hoodies, figured out how to unlock the front door, and took off. Gotta go see if I can catch him. Although I think I know where he's headed.

TEXT MESSAGE
From: Julie Taylor
To: Chip Collins

Update: I was running after Bobo, and a fucking cab hit him. I thought he was dead. I was crying. The cabbie got out and instead of helping he just said "damn, that kid is hairy." And I lost it on him. I said "How dare you! He's my... he's my..." I don't know what I was going to say. So I just kneed him in the balls instead. Then Bobo got up and ran away. He was headed for the New Yorker Hotel.

TEXT MESSAGE
From: Julie Taylor
To: Chip Collins

You're in big trouble, mister. Your boss Fred is PISSED. He grabbed Bobo into your crazy hotel room thing, and told me to wait outside. I've been sitting here in the hallway for an hour now. Did I mention you're in big trouble?

TEXT MESSAGE
From: Julie Taylor
To: Chip Collins

I'm sorry. Sitting here thinking. About Bobo and how he looked like a little kid running down Sixth Avenue. I would have done anything to protect him. I must've looked like one of those hover moms chasing their brat through Central Park. Mom. Whatever. Please come home now.

From: Chip Collins
To: Julie Taylor
Date: November 19, 2017 11:43am
Subject: Re: The Three Terrible Trials

Hi Julie,

I hear a gunshot.

Is Gina shooting at cockroaches again?

Open my eyes.

Oh no… this definitely isn't the jungle.

I'm standing at the entrance to the Verrazano Bridge, on the Staten Island side looking across to Brooklyn. People are rushing around me, thousands of people, all right in the middle of the bridge, no cars or anything, and I realize: the gunshot was the start of the New York City Marathon. The scene is beautiful, actually – all these runners in their bright colors, hoofing it over a massive arch on a crystal clear November morning, little tugboats below spraying their water hoses into the air, the cheers of bystanders that seem to carry the runners along on the force of their collective positive will.

But I'm frozen. I can't seem to take the first step. I mean, I've never even run a 5k, so what the hell am I doing here anyway? I'm definitely pissing some of these runners off, too, adding seconds to their finishing times, making them navigate around the annoying anti-runner standing frozen in their way.

Suddenly one of the runners lightly grabs my arm. "Come on. I'll pace you."

"Thanks, dude," I say as I sort of stumble into a weak trot. God I'm pathetic. I really have to get out and start jogging one of these days. I turn while we're doing whatever this "pacing" thing is, to get a look at my new companion.

It's Pete!

"PETE!" I hug him, while we're both trying to run, so of

course our legs get tangled together and we fall and scrape our knees and elbows and shit, and the mass of runners squeezed onto the eight-lane bridge starts trampling us.

Pete fights his way back to a standing position, against this insane tide of humanity, and pulls me up. "Dude. First rule of running. Don't try to hug somebody. Ever. Now come on." He pushes me in front of him, and we get back into a little bit of a groove.

Funny. I've never run before, not in a race or anything, but I'm not getting tired. I must have some kind of hidden talent I wasn't aware of. "Hey, Pete, check me out! I'm a natural!"

"No you're not. You're an idiot. You're doing it all wrong. Your cadence is too slow for your leg length, and your hips are behind your feet, so your heel strikes are all fucked up." He pats my back and grins at me. "But whatever, this is your dream, so do what you want."

That's it. Of course.

I'm in a dream.

The Third Terrible Trial must have something to do with dreaming.

But why the hell am I dreaming about running?

I turn my head all the way around to get a good look at Pete, and shit, this feels so real. It's Pete all right, in incredible detail, right down to that little bump on his nose where he broke it playing rugby. I've never been in a dream that felt so real. "Hey Pete, dude. I'm worried about you."

"I'd be more worried about where I was looking if I were you."

And of course, as he says it, I spin my head around forward just in time to bump into the runner in front of me, and we both take another agonizing tumble. This time it's my turn to fight the crowd to get standing – get out of my way guys, it's my freaking dream, right? – and pull up the poor schmuck I just fell on. "Sorry, dude."

"No problem. But maybe listen to your good-looking friend over here and watch where you're going."

It's Pete! Another Pete! I instinctively go to hug him and he just puts his arms out, basically stiff-arms me like a football player. "Dude. How many times do I have to tell you about the hugging thing?"

I turn around in place, watching the sea of people run past me and the two Petes, and I don't know why, but I'm not surprised when it dawns on me: they're all Petes. All the runners.

Fifty thousand Petes.

"And that's just the ones you can see, dude." Pete's smiling, like he's proud of the world of Petes I've created in my dream. His smile turns to a frown. "Hey. Chip. Why are we here? You okay?"

"It's you. I'm worried about you. I'm coming to get you, but I need you to hold on."

He seems to remember something. And all the Petes, all fifty-thousand of them, all at once, stop. They turn around, looking. "Where's Meg?"

Something catches my eye. There's one runner still navigating his way through the crowd, all the frozen Petes, pushing a jogging stroller. His crazy white hair seems awfully familiar.

"Chip. Dude. Why is Albert Einstein in your dream? And why is he pushing a jogging stroller?"

"It's a long story. I'll tell you when we get back." As Einstein passes us, he nods and smiles. It's kind of funny. In my own dream, fifty thousand people stand around and watch Albert Einstein beat me in the New York City Marathon. In my own dream. Oh well. "But for now, Pete, dude, I want you to focus.... To remember."

Instantly the Verrazzano bridge is gone, and me and Pete are floating in the void of space. Every few feet, in every direction, is another Pete, to infinity. We're still in running gear, in space, but can breathe no problem. "My dream's fucked up, huh?"

"Did you have cheesecake right before bed?" he looks around, shudders. "Hey, remember when we were running from WHO, and his dimension was disappearing from around us? That's kind of what it feels like where I am now. But this time there's no rope."

Damn. No rope.

No hope.

I reach out my hand. "I'm your rope, dude. I'm coming. You know what I want you to remember instead? Remember that time we used that rope to rappel from the top of the library on to the Thomas Jefferson statue on campus."

"Why would it help to remember that? We got stuck. And then we got arrested."

"No, no. I mean yeah, that happened. True. But right after that."

He grins. "In the holding cell you got everybody to do the Hokey Pokey. Including the guard."

"And?"

"And we got off without any charges, and you talked the dean into only giving us probation."

"Yes. That's the shit, dude. That's me. I'll get us out of this. Just hold on a little longer."

All the Petes turn in space to face me. "You know what would help us hold on?"

"You name it. Anything. It's my dream, and I'm like Willy Wonka. You want an Everlasting Gobstopper?" I reach out my hand and offer him an Everlasting Gobstopper.

"No. I don't know why, but I've got a total hankering for your mom's lasagna."

In the next moment, it's just me and original Pete. Sitting at the little worn kitchen table in my mom's apartment in Green Point. It's dark except for the fake stained glass lamp hanging above us. The smells of garlic and onions and oregano beg us to breathe them in deep. It's warm, even though the snow is falling outside the window, and *Saturday Nights with Sinatra* is playing on the radio.

"Yeah, dude. That's more like it. This dream officially rocks."

We clink beer bottles. Mom splurged and got us a six-pack of New Belgiums. She's awesome. She puts down the lasagna pan – no fancy-schmancy serving dishes for her – and we ogle the culinary perfection before us. The cheese on top is brown and crisp, with little holes here and there for the sauce to bubble through, and I can tell already that the edges have that crunchy / chewy thing going on that me and Pete are both addicted to.

Pete smacks his lips. "Thanks, Mrs. Collins."

I pick up my fork. "Yeah. Thanks, mom."

"Eat up, boys. You'll need the strength."

Huh. Her voice sounds a little different. I look up.

"Gina?"

I bolt upright. "Hey, Gina! Stay the fuck out of my dreams!"

She wakes up with a start. Still sitting over there on the tree stump like she was before I went under. Groggy. "I didn't mean... I don't know how..."

"Dude. You don't know how weird that was. I look up to see my mom, and it's *YOU?!* How the hell did you get into my dream anyway?"

"I'm... sorry. I was just listening to ABBA's instructions, and I drifted off, I guess."

"His instructions to *me*, Gina. Not you."

"I said I was sorry, Collins. I didn't try to do that. Back off."

"Yeah. Well try harder not to next time." I jump off the little platform ABBA's got outside his teeny little cockroach mansion and glare at her with my best laser eyes (which aren't very hot and lasery, I'll admit).

ABBA strolls out of his front door waving his antennae.

~~Interesting.~~

I bend down and yell at him. "Interesting? Interesting? Now I have to process all the Oedipal implications of this?"

~~Relax, kid. First of all, you passed the third and final Terrible Trial. Congratulations. Dream Sharing can be a very powerful thing, and now it's in your toolbox. And second, don't read into the Gina thing. She didn't show up in your dream because you subconsciously wanted her there or some weird shit like that. She actively entered the dream on her own. I saw it. Hey, Gina...~~

"Yes?" She rubs her temples. She's still annoyed every time ABBA talks in her head.

~~*You ever been exposed to the Furry One?*~~

"No. He doesn't exist. As far as the FBI is concerned anyway."

~~*You ever know someone was gonna call you before it happened?*~~

"Sure. Everyone does."

~~*You ever know what someone was gonna say before they said it?*~~

She flicks a pebble at him. Misses. "You ever know you were almost as annoying as Collins?"

~~*You ever guess someone's phone number?*~~

"Of course no-" and she stops.

~~*I knew it.*~~

"What?"

ABBA starts jumping around, all excited. ~~*You've got it. The latent ability. Very strong. Every once in a rare while I run into a buddy, or a lizard, or a bird or whatever, that's got it. Maybe one in a hundred thousand I'd say. You're one of them. Hot shit!*~~

"No I'm not. If you live long enough, anyone will eventually guess someone's phone number."

~~*Really? Nine digits? Random guess? That's one in a billion or so. I'm not a math guy, but you'd have to make a guess like every second for fifty years to get it. No, you've definitely got it.*~~

Gina takes out her gun and points it at ABBA.

~~NO I DON'T.~~

We can both hear her. But her lips aren't moving.

She pushed the thought out to us.

Wow.

ABBA laughs.

~~*The Push? Dream sharing? Yeah. I knew it. She's good. Really good.*~~

Gina gets up. "Fine. Latent ability. Big deal. We can all talk about how great this is while Pete Turner gets digested by the Blue Juice."

ABBA skitters and hops right onto the end of the gun barrel.

~~*You know, it suddenly dawns on me why you're so hot and cold.*~~

"Don't psychoanalyze me, cockroach."

~~*I'm pretty sure you actually wanted to come. On this mission.*~~

"Get out of my head, ABBA."

~~*I'm not pullin' anything you aren't sending me. You wanted to come into the ITA. But you didn't want to come, too. Both. That's why you're so conflicted.*~~

"Why would I want to come into this insane ITA thing? Ever? With Collins, of all people?"

His antennae flick around.

~~*I don't know. But don't you think it's kind of strange that Fred got you on the clearance list the night before he was sending Chip in? The night before?*~~

"You think I had something to do with that? Are you crazy?"

~~*I absolutely think you had something to do with that. Fred seems like the kind of guy who might be manipulated with a subtle suggestion, a little 'push.'*~~

"You're nuts. Next thing you'll be telling me I wanted to come into the ITA to get answers to-" she stops herself again.

Me and ABBA look at each other.

ABBA skitters down the gun barrel onto her finger.

~~*Answers to what?*~~

She can't help herself. She squashes him between her fingers. Crunch.

And, of course, ABBA pops back into shape, brushing himself off.

~~*Remember, Gina. Sticks and stones. Listen, you wanna talk about it?*~~

"Screw off, ABBA. Both of you. Get out of my head. Out of my life." She marches off into the jungle. "This whole thing was a mistake. I'm leaving. You're on your own. I'm going home."

From: Chip Collins
To: Julie Taylor
Date: November 19, 2017 11:43am
Subject: Re: The Three Terrible Trials

Hi Julie,

I'm running as fast as I can, which is probably quarter-Gina-
speed, giant leaves slapping me in the face, vines tripping me up
every few feet, I'm wearing a full tuxedo in the most humid
jungle in the whole multiverse – because, I guess, you never know
when a wedding might break out – and I'm delirious, exhausted,
running after Gina, trying to stop her from leaving.

Wait.

Why am I trying to stop her?

I stop short. Bend over. Hurl.

I don't have to do this. I don't need Gina. I didn't even want
her in here to begin with. All I'm here to do is get to Pete. I've got
the journal and the InController, and now I can crank up my new
telepathic powers to take on the Blue Juice. Gina can go home.
Who cares?

I hurl again.

No, something's bugging me. In my gut. (Other than the
fourteen tiny bird eggs I had for breakfast that are now making an
encore appearance.) I know what you'd say if you were here,
Julie. You'd say "Chip, first of all, can you stop puking? It's gross.
And second of all, if something's bugging you, you have to get to
the bottom of it."

Okay, Julie, what's at the bottom?

I know.

She's looking for answers. Just like me. I don't know what
she's looking for, but she's not finding it. It's not fair. I get it.

I think I'm supposed to help her.

(Or I just don't like being alone. It could be that, too.)

I bend over and hurl one more time for good measure, and I notice: a foot. Uh-oh. It's Gina's. She's sitting on a log, glaring at me.

"Really? On my foot? You sure you don't want to barf on my pants again?"

"Sorry. But hold on. I came after you to tell you something you need to hear."

"Go away. Go bother somebody else."

"No. Now you listen here, young lady…"

"Young lady? Are you serious? What are you, my father?"

"God no. But you have to hear this. Don't you dare give up. Ever."

"Listen, don't you have an *Official List of Every Single Family Memory I've Ever Had* to write? Stop following me, Chip. I'll figure out my way back home, and wait at the home door until Fred fixes it and lets me in. You'll be better off, you're ready, from what I've seen in the Trials. You won't have to deal with my bullshit, and I won't have to deal with yours."

"Don't you dare give up, Gina. What are you, afraid?"

"That trick's not gonna work this time, Chip. I'm out. Now stop following me." She starts walking away.

I run up and grab her wrist. She glares at my hand like I'm about to lose it, so I let go. "Wait. I'm not done, Gina. I know you hate Chip soliloquies, but hear me out: I don't know what you're problem is, what you're looking for, but don't you dare give up. I know this place fucks with your head. I get it. But it can also give you answers. The first time I was in here I was totally lost. I know, no surprise there. But eventually I found what I was looking for. And it wasn't Tesla. It was Julie. The love I almost walked away from. The best thing in my life. And to think, in lots of these infinite dimensions," I point around, "some poor Chips never realize that, and they let her go. In those dimensions, it's over. She's lost."

Gina inhales sharply.

Oh.

I think I'm beginning to get it.

"Did you… lose someone?"

She nods, her eyes welling up, but still filled with anger, and she's gritting her teeth and shaking her head like if I say another word she's going to rip my tongue out. "Don't do this, Chip."

I put my hand on her shoulder. She recoils and bats it away.

"We're doing this, Gina. I want to listen. I want to help." And then I switch to telepathy. ~~*Would it be easier to tell me with your thoughts?*~~

I swear to God she almost punches me in the face, but she stops her fist from connecting, lowers it, and closes her eyes.

She exhales.

And she introduces me to T-Rex.

19. T-REX

From: Chip Collins
To: Julie Taylor
Date: November 19, 2017 11:43am
Subject: T-Rex

Hey Julie,

No, T-Rex isn't Gina's personal dinosaur. (Although that would be pretty awesome, right?)

It's her husband.

Gina floods my mind with images and thoughts. It's almost too much, my brain hurts, but it starts to paint a picture.

At first, it's what I expect: big, tough girl falls for big, tough guy. And Ty Phillips is *big*. Professional football player big. City block big. HUGE. I'm guessing six-nine, six-ten, and built like a brick wall. Like you think Pete is impressive? This guy makes an IMPRESSION. Literally, he leaves impressions in the pavement as he walks down Broadway. (Okay, not literally, but you get the idea.)

And of course, he's a welder. He's the guy up on the girder six thousand feet up, balancing a tank of gas on one shoulder and a steel beam on the other, like it's no big deal. You picture him chomping on a cigar and shouting orders like a badass.
Tough guy.

But no. That's not him. No cigar. No shouting. No tough guy act. It turns out this guy is a total surprise. Yes, by day he's a massive hulk of a guy, creating skyscrapers in New York City with his bare hands. But at night?

He's a standup comedian.

I'm not kidding. This behemoth doesn't have a mean bone in his body, he's a pussycat really, and he likes nothing better than a good laugh. Sure, he played football in high school, I mean, even just standing on the sidelines he had the other teams practically handing in forfeit letters written in their own poop, but the only part of it he really liked was getting his teammates to laugh so hard in the locker room they'd shoot chocolate milk out of their noses.

So some random Friday night at The Cellar Comedy Shop down on Macdougal Street, Ty is trying out his latest wares on the early crowd. The emcee shouts, "Okay, folks, straight from Skull Island, and trust me folks when I say you better laugh at anything he says, it's T-Rex!" And when Ty actually steps out on stage there's an audible gasp, and the poor half-drunk audience doesn't know whether to laugh or clap or run out of the place screaming. But they stay, tentatively shifting in their seats, and Ty launches into his new bit, about how aliens tried to abduct him, but they couldn't squeeze him out the window, and then when they finally did they couldn't fit him on their ship, so they had to do their tests on a park bench at three in the morning, and the aliens kept arguing about who was going to be stuck doing the anal probe on him, and finally they just gave up, and *that's* how he woke up naked in the middle of Central Park, officer.

That gets a big laugh, and the crowd and Ty ease up, and as he starts his second bit, about getting stuck in the middle seat in coach on an airplane with a jammed seatbelt extender and a full bladder, Gina walks in.

I know, you're thinking love at first sight, right? Six-foot-three beauty saunters into the room, with a back-lit glow and a fan blowing through her hair? WRONG. Gina's still in college at this point, still in her *let's-get-drunk-and-heckle-a-comedian* stage, so she stumbles in and immediately starts giving Ty shit. "Hey! Did you eat the other comedian? You know, the funny one?" and classics like "You're so big Mount Everest tried to climb *you*."

She's getting some chuckles, even Ty is laughing along, and then he lays this on her: "Listen. I know you're just afraid of me. But don't worry, girl, there's only one thing in this world you need to be afraid of."

"Oh yeah? What's that?"

"Ceiling fans."

The crowd erupts in "Oooh"s and "Snap!"s, and Ty and Gina start trading more *you're-too-tall* jokes, and pretty soon everyone's piss drunk and laughing their asses off, and Gina's now on stage, and suddenly they're kissing, right there, and the lights in her eyes are the brightest she's ever seen, and she finally found someone who would stand up to her, and tame her, and make her laugh, and hold her in his arms with the strength of a dozen men, but so gentle she felt like a little bird.

So yeah. They get married.

And it really is bliss. These two are made for each other. She loves being the Type-A and he just gives in and loves everything about her, even when she makes it into the FBI and starts working crazy hours, and jeopardizes his not-so-secret plan to have a family.

Oh, yeah. The family thing. She keeps promising him and promising him that someday she'll have kids, he's dying to hear even more laughter around the apartment, the laughter of babies, then toddlers, then tweens and eventually teenagers and maybe even grandkids. But she's not in a rush. She reached her goal, the FBI, and she's not about to throw a baby-size grenade into the middle of that.

And that's when it happens.

"When what happens? Gina, what?"

Gina takes another deep breath, closes her eyes, and sends me two more images.

An empty apartment.

A closed casket.

I open my eyes, it seems like an hour later, I'm bawling like a kid who just fell off his bike and scraped his knee, and Gina has her arms around me, patting my head. "Chip. Why am I not surprised that *I'm* the one comforting *you*?"

I sniff. "I'm sorry. It's just… so sad…" I look up. "How…?"

"It was an accident. At work. Down on Thirty-third and Eighth. He was doing foundation work, got trapped, and…" the tears are streaming down her cheeks, she's wiping them away as fast as she can, "… there was a sinkhole… so deep… they never even found the body… I was his little bird…" Her body's convulsing now, she's straining, but she's got to get it all out. "I'm so lost without him, Chip. I guess somewhere deep down I thought maybe, with all the possibilities, I don't know, maybe I could get some answers in here. But the longer I'm in this insane ITA, the more I realize: this is *your* place, Chip. The ITA gives you answers. Not me."

"Wait. Did you say Thirty-third and Eighth?"

She pushes me away. "Are you even listening to me at all?"

"Come on. Did you say Thirty-third and Eighth?"

"What's your problem? Thirty-third and Eighth. Yes. The new Madison Square Gar-"

She stops.

And we both know.

Young Tesla and Einstein went back in their closed timelike curve whatever, and found the Blue Juice exactly where Madison Square Garden would be thousands of years later.

T-rex. Madison Square Garden.

They never found his body.

"Gina... you think?"

She shakes herself lucid, wipes the last of her tears, straightens up, and makes two fists. "That Blue Juice is going down. Motherfucker. I'm getting some answers."

Wow. A hundred percent kick-ass Gina is back. I love it. I put my fist out for a bump, and this time she connects, even doing that little explosion thing at the end. "Thanks for listening, Chip. Maybe you're not such a child after all. But can you do me a favor?"

"Anything. Anything."

"Lose the bow tie finally. You look like an idiot."

20. LOOK WHO WE BUMPED INTO

From: Chip Collins
To: Julie Taylor
Date: November 19, 2017 11:43am
Subject: Look who we bumped into.

Hey Julie,

I don't know. I kind of liked the bow tie. I guess I still had a little
bit of the James Bond fantasy going on. But it was practically
strangling me the whole time, if I'm being totally honest. So I
untie it and let it hang around my neck. Hey, that almost looks
even cooler.

"Hey, Gina, you think this-"

"I know what you're thinking. That does NOT make you look
even one bit cooler." Gina's packing her backpack, making sure no
cockroaches are hidden in there tagging along for the trip,
plucking them out gently and shooing them away. She's laughing
when she flips the ends of my bow tie in my face though, so I'm
getting the distinct feeling that we're somewhere new, me and
Gina. Somewhere good.

"And stop smiling at me, Collins." He points into her pack. "I have plenty more bullets in here."

Oh well. Maybe scratch that last part.

I make my way over to ABBA's little mansion, and bend down and tap on a wall to get him and say goodbye, and I swear it's not me, this thing was built like shit, I knock an entire little wall down, and ABBA's standing on the other side, tapping his foot.

~~What the hell, kid? You got a problem?~~

"Sorry, ABBA. Shit, sorry dude. I just wanted to say goodbye. You should fire whoever built this crappy house, by the way."

~~I built it. It was me.~~

"Whoops." I kneel down and start picking up the little bricks and stacking them like a LEGO set. Hey, that would be cool, wouldn't it? New! LEGO Cockroach King Palace Set! Comes with four thousand pieces and a horde of live cockroaches! Okay, maybe not.

"So, you're not coming?"

ABBA hops onto my shoulder one last time. ~~Nah, kid. I'm good, but like I told you, I'm not *that* good anymore. I've given you what you need. You and Gina both. So go get your friend. I'll be here whenever.~~ He skitters up, right at the entrance to my ear. This is sweet, he's going to whisper somethi-

~~Fuck, kid. When was the last time you cleaned in here?~~

"Hey! My ears are fine. Get the hell out of there. Jeez, I thought you were going to tell me something nice."

ABBA whispers, for the first time, with his actual little bug voice, right up against my ear drum, "Listen, I can't see into the future, but I got a sense. This is bigger than your friend Pete. Be careful. The multiverse needs you, kid." And he skitters out of my ear and down into his half-destroyed home.

Well. I guess that's it. Goodbye, ABBA.

So we make our way back to the doorway. You'd miss it if you didn't know exactly where you were going, it's literally a gray door in the middle of the jungle. I don't know if I ever told you this, but in dimensions like this where there's no New Yorker Hotel, or New York, the door is just – a door. No wall around it, no back. In fact if you walk around back, it looks like there's nothing there at all, no door even. (WARNING: just because you can't see the door from the back, doesn't mean it's not there. I've run into the back full throttle and practically broken my nose like five times already.)

So I lean down to put in the zero-zero-zero-zero, and suddenly I hear some clicking. Not cockroach clicking, God, trust me, I'm like the world expert on that sound now, so no, it's something else. "What's that?"

Gina's looking around too, and then she looks at the door handle. "There."

I lean down closer to hear.

And I see the lock dials turn.

Oh shit.

Someone – or something – is coming in.

From: Chip Collins
To: Julie Taylor
Date: November 19, 2017 11:43am
Subject: Re: Look who we bumped into.

Hey Julie,

In the next blurry moments, after the "whoosh" of the door opening, Gina instinctively lunges at one of the moving figures in the doorway, the shorter one, and puts it into a choke hold. I ball up my fist and go to punch the taller one in the face.

And as my fist flies through the air, in super slow motion, I realize:

It's Nikola Tesla.

Original, eighty-six-year-old Nikola Tesla.

I am about three milliseconds away from knocking out a guy who could be my grandfather, who invented alternating current electricity, the INTERDIMENSIONAL TRANSFER APPARATUS, and five thousand other things, and who's looking at me with the kind eyes of a patriarch and true gentleman.

Fuck.

But then – also in frame-by-frame slo-mo – Tesla's hand comes up and grabs my fist.

Huh? is Tesla a fucking *ninja*, too?

He side-steps my punch, pushing my hand away from his face, allowing me to throw myself off balance and fall to the ground. Time returns to normal speed, and he calmly puts out his hand to help me up.

"Master Chip. It's a pleasure to see you too." He winks, and tousles my hair. (Man, I never get sick of that part.)

I give him a big hug. "Nikola! But how did you…? With the punch…?"

"I've had many teachers in my long life. Did you know that Theodore Roosevelt knew judo? We sparred many times. He had a dojo in the White House basement. And speaking of judo, your friend here must be Gina."

Whoops. I forgot about Gina. I look over, and she's definitely doing some karate shit on.. wait... is that...?

BOBO!

Poor Bobo's just trying to hump some leg, and she's going all Bruce Lee on him. She chops him across the neck and he goes down.

Schlunk.

Wow - she's actually breathing heavy. I don't think I've ever seen Gina winded. Good job, Bobo. You probably just thought she was dance-partying with you and busted out some of your extra special disco moves. Nice. Anyway, she looks over at us, suddenly realizing these two are friends, not foes.

"Oh. I think I... killed it."

I laugh. "You sound like Pete the first time. Nah, you can't kill him. Even a plumber's wrench to the head doesn't do anything. That's Bobo. Just give him a minute."

And sure enough, a minute later Bobo opens his eyes and pops up.

And starts licking her hand.

"Ewww! Get off!" She shakes him away, but he doubles back and gets in a little leg hump sneak attack. (God, on the cuteness scale that one was an eleven.)

"Awww. He likes you."

"Wonderful."

Tesla steps into the space between us, petting Bobo's head. "Good day, Miss Gina. I am Nikola Tesla, inventor of the INTERDIMENSIONAL TRANSFER APPARATUS. To answer the questions I'm sure you both must have, yes, I did in fact repair the lock on the ITA doorway to our home dimension. It was quite the project, resulting in a minor time slippage. When I finally finished and entered the ITA, I corresponded with Fred – after taking the appropriate moments to chastise him and the entire Federal Bureau of Investigation for tampering with my invention – and he sent Bobo here to join me, and find you. Oh, and he handed me this as well. It's for you."

Awww look. Fred wrote me a love note. I can't wait to read it.

CHIP,
WE SPEND EIGHTY-MILLION DOLLARS SECURING AND SANITIZING EVERY MILLIMETER OF THIS HOTEL ROOM INTERDIMENSIONAL PORTAL, I'M WEARING A FREAKING CLEAN SUIT FOR GOD'S SAKE, AND YOU'VE GOT AN UNSCREENED, UNCATALOGUED, OFFICIALLY NON-EXISTENT EXTRATERRESTRIAL RUNNING AROUND MANHATTAN IN A HOODIE? WHAT THE HELL ARE YOU THINKING?
NOW GET PETE AND GET THE HELL BACK HERE. YOU'RE IN BIG TROUBLE, MISTER.
– FRED (YOUR BOSS. FOR THE MOMENT ANYWAY.)
P.S. TELL GINA I SAID "HI."

"Hey Gina. Fred says 'hi.'"

"He sent a note with Tesla just to tell me hello."

"No. Whatever. I'm in trouble. What else is new? Oh, but the FBI in our dimension now finally has to believe me about Bobo, so there's a silver lining. In any case, I'll deal with Fred later. Now, let's get Pete."

Bobo starts jumping up and down, saying *"BEEZNEEZ."* I guess he's anxious to get Pete too. I lean down and look him straight in his big, black eyes, and push a thought to him.

~~Hey, buddy. Your friend ABBA taught me telepathy. Pretty cool, huh?~~

Blink. Blink.

"Oh, for crying out loud, Bobo. Really? Nothing?"

Blink. Blink.

Now I'm just irritated. "Okay. How about this... how many fingers am I holding up?" I am, of course, giving him the finger.

He gives it back to me, his weird, three-fingered sign of Universal Peace, and leans his head against my hip. I pet him. "Oh well. Someday I'm going to figure you out, dude."

Okay. The good news is we've finally got our team. And as we leave the jungle, rev up the InController with the location of the anomaly, the Blue Juice, and start strutting down the ITA hallway, I swear to God we look like one of those scenes in the movies where the heroes walk in unison toward the camera, and it freeze-frames on each of us:

CHIP COLLINS
Tuxedo-wearing Master of Interdimensional Travel
(if he doesn't mind saying so himself)

NIKOLA TESLA
Genius Inventor, Spreader of Light
(who practices judo at age eighty-six)

GINA PHILLIPS, FBI
PhD in Badassery, with an extra Masters Degree in Laser Eyes
(seriously, watch out for that shit, it burns)

BOBO
Self-replicating, leg-humping, telepathic, immortal alien
(who digs dancing and only talks in annoying rhymes)

I can almost hear the soundtrack now, like we're in some kind of action-crime flick from the seventies, horn section and a guitar with a wah pedal, like "wacka-wacka-wacka." All we need is an explosion going off behind us. Man, this feels goo-

"*STOPDROP.*"

We all look down at Bobo, while we follow the path set by the InController. "What's up, dude? You just interrupted my soundtrack."

"*STOPDROP.*"

"Look, Bobo. We're not stopping. We have to make it to Pete. You have to pee or something?"

"STOPDROP."

"Bobo. No. If you say that one more time I'm gonn-"

And the floor drops out from under us.

We're falling.

"STOPDROP."

"Yeah. I get it Bobo. You can shut the fuck up now."

From: Chip Collins
To: Julie Taylor
Date: November 19, 2017 11:43am
Subject: Re: Look who we bumped into.

Hey Julie,

The air's rushing past my face. We're all screaming. (Except Bobo. As usual, he's having the time of his life.)

We're in free fall, inside some massive chute, like a big laundry chute, with four metallic sides, straight down. Our bodies are flailing around like crash test dummies, with no will of their own. We can see each other, there's some kind of light source, like the hallway of the ITA, so it's not quite my worst nightmare – but it's pretty fucking close. I grab Tesla's jacket and scream over the din, "Hey Nikola. Didn't cross your mind to tell us you designed the ITA with trap doors?"

"I didn't design this!"

"Then who did?"

He shrugs and raises his eyebrows, like "how the *1920s-swear-word* should I know," and in that moment the Truth Of The Multiverse finally sinks in:

The Truth Of The Multiverse:
Shit really is crazy, and if you ever think you've got a
handle on it – think again. Even Nikola Tesla doesn't
know what the hell is going on.

"Nikola! How could someone else build this? This is *your thing!*"

"Remember, Chip! The INTERDIMENSIONAL TRANSFER APPARATUS is real, but it is also *not* real. It is not "built" per se. It is a framework for perception. It is an infinite, ever-growing connection to each event outcome. Its existence and design may be manipulated by forces other-"

"Okay! Okay! I get it! It's always a teachable moment ! Just tell me when we're going to stop falling!"

And at that exact moment, our butts hit the bottom of the chute as it changes angles, becoming more of a slide.

He grins. "Now."

I'll give it to Nikola, injecting a moment of levity, trying to calm me down. But we haven't stopped, we've just slowed down a little, and we're now sliding on an angle on our asses, down one of the sides of this chute. It's kind of hot in here too, so of course this bowel-emptying thought barrels through my brain: *we're going straight to Hell. The actual Hell.*

Bobo has his hands in the air, and I'm like "Bobo! This isn't a ride! It's a slide to Hell!"

"SLIDERIDE! SLIDERIDE!"

Oh, that's fucking great. Yeah, that rhyme won't be too annoying for the next hundred years we're sliding down this thing on our way to meet Satan.

When we finally get to the end – I don't know, a thousand years? – It's like that time when we went down that slide together, remember that babe? Pretending we were kids even though we were way too big, and we tumbled over each other at the end into the sand, and some stranger's kids piled on right after us, like four of them, giggling and kicking me in the nuts, and you were giggling, too, and wow, I suddenly remember exactly what you said at that moment, pointing to the girl with the little light-up sneakers: "How cute are these feet? I want a pair." And I was like "you mean the sneakers?" and you were like "No, the feet. Can we get a pair?" And I thought you were having a brain spasm, but I just realized what you meant. And you know what? I think I want a pair, too. It's just… feet need shoes, and shoes cost money, and now I have to have a job *and* be a dad? I don't–

· · ·

Wait, where the hell was I? Oh yeah, so we're all piled up at the end of the slide, and Bobo immediately jumps up and tries to climb back up the chute and do it again. *"SLIDERIDE! SLIDERIDE!"*

I want to strangle him, but I know it wouldn't do any good, and hey, at least we're not in the everlasting fires of Hades, right? "Okay, Bobo. Come on, man. Focus. Focus." Tesla and Gina have to reach up into the chute to keep him from climbing back up.

I'm so distracted by the three of them, I hardly notice the tap of a finger on my shoulder.

Tap. Tap.

I turn around.

And scream.

Eight feet tall. Blood red skin. Leathery wings. A forked tail. Horns.

Yup. It's Satan. Standing right in front of me.

Shit, he even has the goatee. I almost want to laugh, he matches my goofy picture of what the Devil should look like a little too perfectly. I spin around and try to scramble back up the chute past Bobo. "GINA! SAVE US! You're the boss! You're the boss! FBI Jurisdiction! Shoot the fucking thing!" I must look like an idiot, because I'm not getting anywhere, I'm like running in place, shuffling at the floor of the chute, these stupid tuxedo shoes have zero traction, and the three of them are just standing there, staring at me like I'm an exhibit at the zoo.

"Why are you standing there staring at me?! Look! It's fucking SATAN!!" They are literally standing next to the Prince of Darkness, not giving one fuck. "WHAT THE HELL – EXCUSE THE PUN – GUYS?!"

"Collins. It's a police officer. Calm down. What, did you take mushrooms before we left ABBA?"

Tesla taps his chin. His lightbulb goes on. "Chip. Gina. I believe it is neither Lucifer, or a police officer."

"Nor. I think it would be neither Lucifer NOR a police officer."

"Or."

"Nor, dude."

"You are incorrect." He moves over to Satan. "But grammar

issues aside, I would postulate that our friend here is neither of those two things, nor an angel, which is what *my* visual perception tells me he is. And Bobo, let me ask you…" Bobo reaches up and grabs Tesla's hand. "…What do you see, Bobo?"

Blink. Blink.

"Nikola. You really thought Bobo was going to answer you?"

"No. I just like to see him blink like that sometimes." He turns to Satan, puts a hand on his shoulder. "Am I right, my friend? That your visual display matches what another expects to see?"

Satan Cop Angel looks down at all of us, and smiles.

I back up further into the chute, falling on my ass. "Hey! Not true! I didn't expect to see Satan!"

"Master Chip. What were you thinking the whole way down here?"

"That we were heading straight down to Hel– oh."

Tesla walks around our new companion, looking closely at his skin. "It must be some kind of specialized defense mechanism. Manipulating perception like that. Perhaps that is how he adapted the ITA as well, changing our perception of how the structure of the hallways works. Some effect on its observers. Simply astonishing. My friend, do you think you could show us what you really look like?"

Satan Cop Angel smiles again, nods slowly, and starts to morph. Wow. It's like he's made of light and mirrors. Pretty fucking psychedelic, actually. Who needs mushrooms when you're hanging out with this guy?

So we're all kind of anticipating what this dude's going to look like. My bets are on a bulbous green slimy thing, like the ghost from *Ghostbusters*. But no, he's looking pretty humanish. Very human. Hmm.

And right before I pass out (yes, again), I look into his eyes, and his smile is a smile I've seen a million times.

It can't be.

"Dad?"

From: Chip Collins
To: Julie Taylor
Date: November 19, 2017 11:43am
Subject: Re: Look who we bumped into.

Hey Julie,

I haven't opened my eyes yet. I want to stay here for a little while.

I just saw my Dad.

I'm not going to go into hero worship, you know it wasn't like that with my dad. We didn't exactly skip along through life together, going to Yankee Games and sharing Cracker Jacks and having pop-fly catches in the back yard until the sun goes down. He pretty much did his thing, and I pretty much did mine. He was probably pissed at me more than he wasn't, or frustrated at something that wasn't matching up with what he was expecting from life, I don't know. He was an enigma.

But there was always something about his smile.

He could be sitting in his corner on the couch, doing the *New York Times* crossword puzzle, and suddenly he'd put down his pen, all serious. "Get over here, kiddo." And I'd jump on his lap, and he'd ask me a five-letter word for the club a golfer uses in the sand. And I'm like ten years old, so pretty much every time he asked for a five-letter word, no matter what the clue was, I'd say "penis!" and he'd pretend to get all pissed off and say, "Get out of here, you rotten kid!" and push me away, and as I'd run out of the room, I'd look back, and sure enough he would flash me that smile.

God, that smile.
I miss that smile.
I miss you, Dad.

"Come on, Chip. Open your eyes. It's okay."

No. I don't want to leave here. Not yet.
"Come on, Chip. You're just faking it now."
I open my eyes.

It's Gina. Holding my head in her lap. Again. "God. You have to stop passing out like that, Chip. It's becoming a habit."

"I'm sorry. It's kind of my thing. Hey, you should have kids. You're good at this."

"Who needs a kid when I have you?"

She pulls me up until I'm sitting. "Before you ask, Chip, yes. We all saw it. I saw T-Rex. Tesla saw Einstein. It was pretty powerful. She was trying to show us she's one of the good guys. She doesn't have total control over what we wind up seeing as the observers."

"She? Satan's a *she*?" I turn around to get a look. Wow. She's beautiful. Very glimmery, like a skinny, super tall WNBA player covered in tiny mirrors, with her own light source. I can't tell if she's got arms or legs, it's all pretty fluid.

"So. You've been talking to her?"

Glitter Girl smiles and hands me Tesla's journal.

"Wait. The journal?"

Tesla pats my hand. "It's another copy. Her copy. Her species found it in one of the dimensions. They've been following us. They want to help. Here, read this." He points to the open page.

> *HUMANS: THERE IS DANGER. TO US ALL. HUMAN*
> *PETE TURNER TRIED TO BAR THE DOOR. TO KEEP THE*
> *STUFF OUT. BUT THE STUFF TOUCHED HIM. TOOK*
> *HIM. ALL OF HIM. THE DOORWAY IS NOT SAFE. NOT*
> *SAFE TO TOUCH. IT IS SPREADING. WE BUILT THIS*
> *BACK DOOR FOR YOU. IT IS SAFE.*

I look around. "Wow. You built all this, just for us?"

She gently takes back the journal, and writes on the next page with what looks like a finger.

NO. NOT JUST FOR YOU.
FOR ALL OF US. WE NEED YOU.

"Nice. No pressure."
She writes:

NO PRESSURE.
JUST EXISTENCE ITSELF HANGS IN BALANCE.
DON'T SCREW THIS UP.

And she smiles.
Well, at least she's got a sense of humor.
"Okay. Cool. Whatever. Where's the door?"
Glitter Girl waves her hand, and a doorway appears, opening to bright sunlight that make us squint. When I adjust to the light, I gasp.

21. THE BLUE JUICE

From: Chip Collins
To: Julie Taylor
Date: November 19, 2017 11:43am
Subject: The Blue Juice

Hey Julie,

I don't know what I expected, I've seen a lot of crazy shit in the ITA, but I've only seen something like this once before: in WHO's dimension.

It looks like New York City must have been hit by a bomb. A big one. Some buildings left, but it's mostly rubble. And not a single living thing anywhere – no people, no rats, not even a leaf. The only sound is the whistle of the wind kicking dust up into our faces.

No, wait. There's another sound.

We step into the dimension, and Glitter Girl waves again, sealing the back door behind us. I lean down to listen to the other sound. It's like plastic stretching, or somebody trying to squeeze into a scuba suit that's two sizes too small. Hmm. Hard to place.

Oh shit.

It's the Blue Juice. It's everywhere.

All around us, what looks like little blue roots are slowly growing, attaching to everything, stretching, stretching.

I look North, to where the Glitter Girl told us the ITA doorway would be, and sure enough, I see the doorway, hanging in space, I guess the New Yorker Hotel didn't survive whatever happened here, and it's covered in blue roots, dangling, connected all the way down here where Madison Square Garden used to be. The thing that took Pete.

"GUYS! DON'T TOUCH THE BLUE JUICE!"

Gina's gingerly walking around the roots about thirty feet away. "No shit."

I look up at the buildings. "Christ. It looks like World War Three in here."

She freezes, sudden realization in her eyes. "Chip! Quick. Check the radiation levels. It's the red pouch. In your pack."

"The red pouch? I thought that was granola."

"No, you idiot. It's a one-shot radiation detector. Come on, man. Think."

I pull out the red metallic pouch and rip off the top strip. Well, she was right. There's no granola in here. It's just a piece of paper. "It's just a piece of paper, Gina. What am I, supposed to scribble a cartoon version of the deadly radiation level I think we're being exposed to? There's not even a pencil in here."

"Shut up. Just shut up and hold it up in the air and wave it around for a few seconds."

So I'm waving this sheet of paper like I'm surrendering to the Blue Juice, and numbers start to appear. "Cool. Invisible ink."

"No. Not cool. What does it say?"

"One Zero Five."

"Fuck."

"Fuck? Fuck what?"

"We have one hour to get Pete. Or we're all dead."

"ONE HOUR?!"

"The radiation level is too high for prolonged exposure. No time to explain. Hurry. Get the yellow pouches."

"What, we're taking urine samples now?"

"You've never read a single instruction from the FBI, have you?"

"I wouldn't say tha-"

"Don't even answer. Just take the tubes from the yellow pouches and get the hell over here."

"Tubes? Uh-oh. I don't like the sound of this."

And yeah. It's actually worse than I expected. The tubes contain this bright yellow radiation protection cream that we have to rush like hell to slather all over us. We look like a bunch of bananas. Literally. This stuff must be like SPF fifty bazillion.

"Gina. Please tell me we don't have to put it... you know... down there..."

"Depends. You want to have kids?"

"Got it."

So I shove this stuff down my pants, and Gina tells me that if I so much as glance at her while she's applying the stuff to herself she will kill me on the spot with no regrets at all.

"Um, hey, Gina. Sorry to interrupt. Can you do my back?"

She glares, but we don't even have time for her to murder me with her bare hands, so she just goes ahead and rubs it in. And yes, I have to do her back, and it's all the most awkward scene you've ever imagined, and we both have to help Tesla, and he's squirming like he's never been touched by another human being before, and by the time we get done with him, we turn to Bobo, all that fur, and we're both like "Fuck it." I mean, we're absolutely positive Bobo could withstand a direct nuclear blast and be totally fine, so why bother?

Suddenly I'm struck with a terrible thought: "The radiation… what about Pete? He's been down there for over a week!"

Banana Tesla pats my arm. "Master Chip, based on my initial observations, the radiation, from what appears to have been a nuclear blast decades ago, has done two things: first, it has given the Blue Juice, as you call it, a way to escape its subterranean confinement and grow. Second, as it utilizes radiation for fuel, the Blue Juice may convert it to some inert form during absorption."

"Uh, on that second one… English?"

"The Blue Juice may be, ironically, shielding Pete from the radiation as it digests him."

"Great. Remind me to say thanks after we send it back to last Tuesday. Hey, one more question…"

"Yes, Master Chip?"

"If – WHEN – we get Pete, how the hell do we get an infinite number of him out of here?"

"Hmmm."

"Please don't say hmmm."

"Well, it would be purely speculation, but I would assume that whatever force plucked the Petes from their normal dimensions would reverse if the Blue Juice was to be neutralized."

"So they'd be de-plucked."

"If that was a word, yes. They would appear instantly back in their appropriate dimensions."

"Good to know. Because otherwise, I have no idea what the hell we do with infinite Petes trying to make for the door." I accidentally step on one of the tiny blue roots, and my foot gets stuck. "Yikes!" I try to free it, and my shoe pops off. "Dammit. There's no way they're going to take back this tux now, with only one shoe. Fuck you, Blue Juice." I reach down to pull the shoe away. It disappears.

"Dammit."

"Chip, stop fooling around. We've only got an hour to find Pete and get the hell out of here. Start looking for a way down into the sinkhole that's not full of the blue stuff."

I look down at my shoeless foot. "I'm not fooling around. That was my fucking shoe. *Wait*. Gina. Why don't I just let the blue stuff take me? Like the shoe? Suck me in? Then I'll go right to where Pete is."

"Sure. Sounds like a rock solid plan."

"No, listen. It took Pete from near here, so if I get plucked here, it should take me to the same place."

"Should?"

"Should. Right?"

"Chip, you have no idea how the Blue Juice works. It could bring you to another dimension. It could bring you to wherever it originally came from, in the middle of space. It could be smart enough to keep you as far away from Pete as possible. We can't take that chance. Right, Nikola?"

Tesla nods.

"Whatever. If you guys are so smart then, what do we do?"

"Just… shut up and start looking for a way down to the main pool."

We're looking across an entire two city blocks of rubble. "Gina. There are a million ways down. But they're all dripping with goo."

"There's got to be a way. Keep looking."

I point around. "Impossible. We'd need Pete himself here to tell us where he-" I stop. Tap her on the shoulder. Tap. Tap. Tap.

"You're annoying! What?"

"*A dream.* If I get to him in a dream, I can find out where he is!"

"You're going to fall asleep? Right now?"

"No. Knock me out."

"Collins. As much as I'd like to knock you out, I can't. It's agains-"

"KNOCK ME OUT GODDAMMIT!!!" And I punch her square in the gut. She actually staggers back, trying to catch her breath, and looks down at her stomach like "did that just happen? Is there a single possibility anywhere in the multiverse where Chip Collins actually strikes me?" Then she whips her eyes back up to me – and smiles.

Permission has been granted.

And before I can say "good night," I feel Gina's knuckles on my chin and I'm seeing black.

From: Chip Collins
To: Julie Taylor
Date: November 19, 2017 11:43am
Subject: Re: The Blue Juice

Hi Julie,

We're in a nursery, an infinitely long and wide nursery, with infinite babies screaming their infinite heads off, nurses are running around trying to shush them, and me and Pete are looking through the glass, down at the two nearest us. One of them has Pete's eyes. She's cute. The other one has shit on his leg – that one must be mine.

Pete turns to me, points at all the babies. "Dude. Something you want to tell me about?"

"Julie's pregnant. Maybe."

Pete laughs. "Awesome! Wait, you? A *dad*?"

"Yeah. Is that so hard to imagine?"

"Yes. I mean, no. Just roll your kid up in bubble wrap and you'll be fine."

"Ha ha. I can't wait to see what kind of dad you're going to be."

He whips around to me. "What?"

"Nothing. Forget it. But you might want to talk to Meg when you get home."

"Why? We're perfectly happy where we're at. No kids. Childless by choice. Hey, speaking of Meg. Dude, when am I going home?"

I take a closer look at him. His whole body is shivering. And he's white as a ghost. "Man, hey Pete, we're working on it. But I need your help. I need you to show me where you are. Not in the dream. Where your body is right now, in actual reality."

And we're immediately floating in the semi-dark, in a

suspension of blue jelly. "Here's where I'm at. I don't move, or think, or anything. I just dream."

Dammit. This doesn't help. I can't tell anything, up down, blue, blue, blue, no context at all. "Okay, dude. Next step. Take me to the edge of the pool. Closest to where you are."

"I don't know..."

"Pete. Please. Try."

Now we're standing at the edge of a neon blue underground lake. The only light source is a little glow from the Blue Juice itself. Pete points down. "I'm there."

I can sort of make out a human shape in the goo. And then another. And then another. It keeps going. It's all the Petes. As far as I can see.

"Okay. I need a landmark. Something to mark this spot." I look around, and wouldn't you know – an old Budweiser can. Right here. A full mile into an alien sinkhole in the Earth after World War Three, you can still find an old beer can without even trying.

"Now. Up."

"Up?"

"I have to find out which way to get down to you." It's pitch black as soon as we get a few yards away from the Blue Juice, so I take out my wand and whisper "Lumos."

Pete's like "Really? A wand?"

"Hey. It's my dream. I feel like being Harry Potter."

"It's all good. You're a little more Ron Weasley though. Just saying."

We climb up and up and up. God, this cavern goes up forever. Pete's above me, spraying pebbles into my face as we get closer to the surface. I can't see shit.

Clink.

"Wait. What the fuck was that?"

"A rock. I don't know. It's your dream, dude. You tell me."

No. That wasn't a rock. That was a clink. Like metallic. I wipe the pebbles out of my eyes and look around. "Show yourself, scary metallic dream thing!"

Silence.

Then another clink. "There." I point my wand up and to the right.

It's a pipe. Not scary at all. Just a stupid pipe-

Wait. There's something to it. "Listen."

Clink. Clink. Clink-clink-clink.
Clink. Clink. Clink-clink-clink.
Clink. Clink. Clink-clink-clink.

"Pete. It's a beat!"

"Well, not exactly the most rockin,' but yeah, I guess it's a beat. So?"

"So that's it! That's how we can find you! Follow the pipe!" I rush up to Pete and bear hug him. He doesn't even have the strength to push me away like he always does. I look him straight in the eyes. "Pete. Hold on just a little bit more. I'm leaving the dream, but I'll be back for real before you know it. I'm coming to get you." I take his hands. "I'm bringing you home. And then I'm never letting anyone hurt you again. I'll always be there. I'll always watch over you."

Suddenly we're back in the nursery, with the infinite screaming babies.

"Pete? Why are we here? I didn't do this."

"I did." He reaches through the glass, gently picks up the dream baby with the shit on his leg, wipes it off with the end of his shirt, and hands him to me. Then, as Pete begins to disappear, he whispers.

"Forget what I said about the bubble wrap. The kid'll be lucky to have a dad like you."

From: Chip Collins
To: Julie Taylor
Date: November 19, 2017 11:43am
Subject: Re: The Blue Juice

Hi Julie,

"…the pipe!… the pipe!…"

I open my eyes, and suddenly feel the most excruciating pain in my jaw. Ouch! Gina's hovering above me. I rub my chin. "Wow. You really got me."

She grins. "Yes. And I'd be lying if I said it wasn't satisfying as hell." She takes my arm and lifts me to my feet. Woah. Dizzy. "Chip, you were rambling something about a pipe…"

"The pipe! Yes! That's how we find Pete! There was a clanking in my dream! I think if we can find the clanking pipe, we can follow it all the way down to Pete. Where's Nikola?" I look around, almost falling over, and spy Banana Tesla off in the distance, sifting through some rubble looking for a path. Nothing I guess. "How about Bobo?"

"He's over there." She points to a mound of rubble down closer to where Thirty-Seventh street used to be, maybe a couple of hundred yards away. Bobo's just sitting there. Man, Pete's being digested, we're busting our asses trying to figure this out before we all get radiation poisoning and die, and he's sitting up there meditating? So I run over and up the hill, ready to bitch him out, he's being such a-

Hold on.

What's that noise?

I look down at Bobo. He's hitting a rock against a pipe.

Clink. Clink. Clink-clink-clink.
Clink. Clink. Clink-clink-clink.

From: Chip Collins
To: Julie Taylor
Date: November 19, 2017 11:43am
Subject: Re: The Blue Juice

Hi Julie,

"Bobo! You found the pipe! This is the way down to Pete!"

He jumps up, gives me a little leg hump for luck, or just because he can't get enough of that shit, and starts trotting down into the hole, following the pipe. *"MEETPETE! MEETPETE! MEETPETE!"*

"Woah, hold on, buddy. Let's get Gina and Tesl-"

Gina's almost on us, but poor Tesla. He's not looking so good. We've only been exposed to the radiation for about fifteen minutes and he already looks like he's a goner. I mean, he's freaking eighty-six, right? Can't blame him. I call to Gina, "Go back and take Nikola back to the back door! And meet us on the way down!"

She gives me the one-finger salute and turns to get Tesla the hell out of here. I'll see you later, Nikola. Hopefully.

So me and Bobo begin the endless descent into the bowels of New York City. I hand an extra flashlight to him, and of course he starts using it like a disco ball, twirling it around and doing the hustle while we climb down and down, using it to clink his beat on the pipe, *clink-clink-clinkclinkclink,* and I have to laugh, because I'm trying to be all serious, this is some serious shit after all, and Bobo still finds a way to get in touch with his inner kid. So I'm like "what the hell?" and I follow him into his subterranean disco, clinking on the pipe, feeling a little more hopeful, a little lighter. Bobo's right: why take everything so seriously?

That's exactly when my foot, the one with the shoe still on it, crunches something.

I look down.
It's a human skull.

MENTAL NOTE
To: God
From: Chip
Subject: I just stepped on a human skull.

Dear God,

Listen, I know the only time I talk to you is right before I think I'm going to die, which is a lot lately, but I think the first time was that hangover in college, remember that? Like my body was literally giving up, it was so tired of puking up everything and nothing, and I was bent over the toilet, begging you to let me live, looking at the little chrome flush lever, getting ready to pull it again, and I saw myself in the reflection, all distorted like a funhouse mirror, and one of my eyes was huge and one was tiny, and I laughed at how ridiculous and wretched I looked, and suddenly I felt a little better. And after a minute something somewhere said, maybe it was me, maybe it was you, it said, "You're not going to die today, Chip."

So other than the *please-don't-let-me-die* prayer, yeah, we're not exactly calling each other every day, but I really could use your help with Pete. I don't care if you take me instead, really, I mean you know the last thing I ever want is to experience any kind of pain at all, and definitely not death, so you know how serious I am if I say I'd rather have you take me than Pete if you have to.

Please.

He's alone. He's afraid. He's dying.

He can't die. He's got so much more life to live.

Actually, we've both got so much more life to live, together, so scratch that last part about taking me instead of him – this prayer is for both of us. I want him to meet my kid. And I want to meet his. And I want our kids to grow up like cousins. Going clamming along the shore on an endless summer day. Playing Super Smash Brothers until their thumbs hurt and they're aching from laughing. Jumping into the pool together to see how much water they can empty out onto the lawn.

And maybe even some day going to college together, and making their Philosophy teacher lose it so bad he quits on the spot, and playing frisbee in the dorm hallway until they hit the RA in the throat, and throwing their graduation caps so far into the air they take off like kites. And then finding the loves of their lives, and getting married, having kids of their own, and starting the whole crazy cycle all over. Into infinity.

Is that too much to ask? I mean, that's rhetorical, of course it is. You don't owe me anything.

But I'm asking anyway. Please. Let me find Pete and bring him home.

Even if I could just get a sign that all hope's not lost, that I'm headed in the right direction. Anything. A little sign.

I know you're not that kind of guy, but-

"Ouch! Motherfucker!"

Something just ripped through my sock and stabbed me in the foot.

An old beer can.

Budweiser.

From: Chip Collins
To: Julie Taylor
Date: November 19, 2017 11:43am
Subject: Re: The Blue Juice

Hi Julie,

So we made it.

Right around the corner from the beer can.

We're at the edge of the pool of Blue Juice.

All the Petes are in there, floating in it, still like corpses. My heart sinks, I want to cry. But now's not the time. You can cry later, Chip.

"Okay, listen Bobo. I've got to get myself centered, make sure I'm mentally ready, remember everything ABBA taught me. I don't want to just jump in there without being prepared. I'm going to meditate for a few minutes, so just do your thing, the perfectly still thing, and when you see–" and Gina comes flying around the corner, trying to catch up to us, and crashes into me, sending me head first into the Blue Juice. I distantly hear her whisper: "Whoops."

So much for being prepared.

Before I can scream "thanks for the helpful push, Gina!" I'm gripped by the Blue Juice, and sink maybe six feet down.

It's just like the dream.

I'm suspended in this blue jelly stuff, able to move a little, but I'm definitely not going to be doing laps in this shit. Not that I would ever be doing laps anyway, but you know what I mean.

The Petes are all around me.

They're in some kind of coma state.

Poor Pete. I mean, you actually look kind of peaceful, but you've been stuck in this jelly for a week, that can't be good. You're alive, I can see your chest rising and falling-

Wait – how the hell are the Petes breathing? I look at him up close, I can barely see more than a couple of inches and I notice one of those blue root things going up his nose, and out up to the surface of the pool. Ewww.

The Blue Juice is keeping him alive while it digests him over god knows how many years. Motherfucker.

HUNGER.

Oh. There it is. I'm picking up the thought from this stuff. Just like ABBA said. Every second or two.

HUNGER. HUNGER. HUNGER.

Holy cow that's creepy. It really is all this thing can think. Suddenly I get a cramp in my gut, and I realize I'm starving for oxygen. Uh oh. I can't move enough to swim to the surface. I look around, starting to panic, though I don't know why, because how the hell could I see microscopic organisms, especially in this shit? But I try to remember what ABBA taught me, calm down Chip, create a silver thread from you to them, you to them.

It's not working. The only thing coming at me are some of those blue root thingies. Going for my nose. I'm swatting at them, trying to keep them away from my nostrils. Not the nostrils! Ever since I was a kid and I got a bracelet bead stuck up my nose (don't ask), I've been super-sensitive about my nostrils. (I know, I know, I'm sensitive about everything. But even more so about my cute little nose holes!)

They're multiplying, fucking relentless. Come on, you fucks! Give me a break!

But then I notice a little bubbling. With some organization to it, too. Holy cow, there actually are some mutant algae or something that can live in the Blue Juice, responding to me! I call them over, and slowly but surely they envelope my head in a bubble of pure oxygen. *Whew!* And their little bubble helmet is keeping the blue root thingies at bay too. Bonus.

Okay, now on to the hard part.

I form a silver thread in my mind from me to the Blue Juice. Me to the Blue Juice.

And I'm assaulted again by the word: *HUNGER. HUNGER. HUNGER.*

I know there's no negotiating with it, nothing but my best effort will do, no pussy-footing around, so I get right to the point: with everything I've got, I scream with my mind, "YOU'RE FULL, MOTHERFUCKER!!!"

Nothing.

I scream it again: "YOU'RE FULL, MOTHERFUCKER!!!"

The blue maybe just got a little lighter. But I can't budge Pete.

Dammit! What the hell? ABBA said that would work!

Wait. The Blue Juice has been feeding on radiation for God knows how long, growing, spreading. It's much stronger than the pool of it ABBA had to deal with way back when.

It's useless. I'm screwed.

Wait - was that a splash? I look over my head, out of the corner of my eye.

It's Bobo.

He scootches right up next to me, sharing my little bubble helmet, and puts his eyes right up next to mine. "Hi Bobo. I assume this means you have a plan."

YES.

"So what's the plan?"

THINK.

God. Would it kill Bobo to communicate in full sentences? Once?

"All right, dude. I'm going to have to guess you want me to push out that thought again. Then you'll do… something?"

He nods.

"Okay, here goes…" and as the next thought leaves my brain it happens.

I lose my mind.

From: Chip Collins
To: Julie Taylor
Date: November 19, 2017 11:43am
Subject: Re: The Blue Juice

Hi Julie,

Wow, babe. I just went somewhere, and I'm not even sure I can describe it.

But I have a giant-ass big mouth, so I'll try.

As the next thought leaves my brain to the Blue Juice, it connects with a thought coming out of Bobo, and then everything goes white. It's like lightning in my mind, I can feel it expanding a million miles an hour, and I realize this is how Bobo's brain must work all the time, and then I realize I'm in Bobo's brain and he's in mine.

Holy shit.

In a fraction of a millisecond I see how little of our brains we use, and how much of everything out there we miss. And how powerful thought can be. How on a quantum level our thoughts are literally creating our reality, and how awesome and beautiful and cooperative the multiverse really is. Our minds are limitless.

And then I see the Bobos.

Infinite Bobos, glowing, stretching out to the horizon, doing a little slow motion dance in perfect unison. I suddenly feel more joy than I've ever felt in my whole life, it's my love for you, and for our unborn baby, and for Pete, and for everyone I've ever loved, even for Gina, and of course for all the Bobos.

From somewhere far off, I can feel tears streaming down my face, because I've finally seen it.

I've seen infinity. All at once.

Mind.

Blown.

And then I see my thought, and I understand. Bobo has some

strange, infinite power that extends out beyond time, but it's not enough. He needs a co-creator. My act of sharing, giving my thoughts to him and him giving them to me, creates the power. *There is no creation without co-creation.* We need Bobo. And Bobo needs us. We need each other.

And then our creation, the thought, the thought of being full and satisfied, plunges deep into the heart of the Blue Juice, and together, we feel it begin to change.

Then it lets go.

Suddenly we can move again. Together we grab the nearest Pete, pull the nasty blue root out of his nose (it's like nine inches long btw, gross), and swim to the edge.

Gina's there to pull us out.

I kneel next to Pete and wipe the Blue Juice off him. It's actually turning white, and drying, and flaking off pretty easily. He's breathing, but not responsive. What do I do? "Pete! Pete! Wake up!" Nothing. "Pete! Come on, dude! Wake up!" Nothing.

Gina steps in. "Here. Let me-"

"No. I've got this." And I slap Pete hard across his cheek.

His eyes shoot open and he bolts upright.

He looks at me, wild-eyed.

And he punches me in the face.

I dab the blood from my nose. "Yeah. It's definitely Pete. He'll be fine."

Pete goes to smile, but instead turns on knees, bends over, and hurls. Oh God. I've never seen so much of anything come out of somebody so fast. It's like that joke:

What's grosser than gross?
Pete throwing up a week's worth of Blue Juice.

Then he turns again, and collapses on his back. And I realize: I'm fucking exhausted, too. Like not tired from exertion, more like somebody plucked a battery out of me. Or like I'm supposed to run on Duracells, and somebody put in those shitty no-brand batteries from the corner convenience store. Or like some other bad battery metaphor. You get the point. I'm beyond exhausted.

I lift Pete's head onto a rock. "Dude. Am I glad to see you. We're here now. We're going to get you all out."

He smiles weakly, I can't wait to hear his voice, and he finally lets out a whisper.

"Gracias, amigo."

Of course. It's Spanish Pete.

I mean, what were the chances I'd pick out Original Pete on the first try? Luckily, my Spanish isn't as bad as my Japanese, so I reply, "De nada, amigo." And I give him a little hug. He whispers back, "Deja de abrazarme. Ahora." I'm pretty sure that means he's happy, so I hug him a little tighter.

Gina laughs. "He's saying 'Stop hugging me. Now.'"

So I pull back, and he says. "¿Por qué eres amarillo? Pareces un plátano."

"He's asking why you're yellow. Says you look like a-"

"Banana. Yeah. I still know my fruit in Spanish. Well, Pete, I'd love to get into the way-too-long explanation, but I've got to start grabbing the other Petes, in case Tesla's theory wasn't righ-."

But Tesla does prove himself right, once more, as the Pete I'm holding disappears right from my arms. *Poof!* We turn to the pool of blue-now-white, and the Petes start going *Poof! Poof! Poof!* back to their own dimensions.

HOLY SHIT! WE DID IT!

I stand, and I don't know why, I'm just so overcome…
I hug Gina.
I've never done that. Uh-oh.

As soon as I realize my error, I back up and cringe and wait to feel her knuckles on my chin again. "Sorry."

But she doesn't clock me. She pulls me back into such a tight hug I'm gasping for breath, and whispers in my ear, "You did it, Chip Collins. I'm proud of you."

"Wait. Did I hear right? Do I still have that blue shit plugging up my ears? Can you repeat that?"

Now she pushes me away. "You heard me."

So we sit there until we stop hearing the *Poof!*s, and I'm like "is that it? Do we just go home and Pete'll be there waiting for us?" and I hear splashing coming from the pool. And Julie, we all practically shit ourselves thinking it's the Blue Juice coming back to life, we're getting into *save-the-multiverse* mode, even though I'm exhausted and I can barely stand. But it's not the Blue Juice…

It's Pete! Original Pete!

He swims up to the edge, dragging something. "Hey dude. Did you forget something?"

"Pete! No. I don't know. I mean, I always have that nagging feeling like I'm forgetting something, but I thought that was just part of being a guy. Like it comes with the package."

"No, you idiot. I mean did you forget *this?*"

And he lifts Albert Einstein from the pool.

From: Chip Collins
To: Julie Taylor
Date: November 19, 2017 11:43am
Subject: Re: The Blue Juice

Hi Julie,

Whoops.

I actually let out a laugh.

I was so focused on getting Pete out, I totally forgot about Einstein. The most famous mathematician and physicist in history. Arguably the last person you'd ever forget. And I forgot.

"Come on dude. Stop staring and help me get him out."

"Oh. Right." So we drag Pete and Einstein out of the Blue Juice. They're wiped out, collapsed on the ground. I go over, kneel down, and lift Pete into my arms. "You're safe, buddy. We're here."

He looks up. "I don't remember anything. Just dreams. You were in a couple of them."

"I'll explain the dream thing later. We gotta get going."

He smiles weakly and looks at my tuxedo, holding on to the jacket lapel. "Well, at least you dressed for the occasion. I assume the one-shoe thing is a fashion decision. And the yellow makeup."

"Yeah. It's the latest craze with the hipsters. It's called One-Shoe-Banana-Formal."

Einstein, now up and wiping the drying jelly off his hair, coughs up the last little spittle of blue. "Herr Chip. Thank you."

And I realize. He's been in here since… "Albert. I never thought about… How are you even…? It's been how many years…?"

He blows some blue stuff out of his nose. "I believe there is an explanation…"

"No. No. We don't have time. Gotta go. Explanations later. Stop." *Ah shit.* Too late. Einstein's already waving his arms and blathering about something called consciousness energy. I try to stop him with warnings of the radiation poisoning that's going to kill us in fifteen minutes, but he doesn't care. All these genius types are the same: a teaching moment stops for nothing.

How It Works: The Blue Juice: Another Theory by Albert Einstein

"When considering the 'Blue Juice,' as Herr Chip calls it – I, of course, would call it something different, something more scientifically appropriate, perhaps Extraterrestrial Plasma Consciousness – in any case, first we must understand energy.

"Energy is the property that must be transferred to an object to make change, whether it be movement, or heat, or growth. Living organisms need energy to move and grow. And so does the Blue Juice. I believe it uses radiation, such as a nuclear explosion, and Human Consciousness Biophotons for this purpose.

"You see, the biophotons emitted by living organisms, a form of bioluminescence, are very subtle. But the human brain, in the process of storing, recalling, and executing large amounts of information – our consciousness – creates an incredibly complex mathematical pattern, and a resulting vibration, that energizes these biophotons. I'm not sure it's ever been measured, but clearly it can act as a powerful fuel. More powerful than nuclear radiation."

"Hold on. So this stuff was feeding off your brain power?"

"I believe so. That is why all the Petes and myself were in a coma-like state, not even consciously aware of our predicament. The Blue Juice was *not* digesting us, our physical forms. It was harvesting our consciousness. In fact, it seems our physical forms were preserved. And since Human Consciousness Biophotons are a byproduct of our normal thought processes, there doesn't appear to be any damage to our minds either. Pete, would you agree?"

"Uh. Sorry. Was I supposed to be listening?"

Einstein continues. "So, the native American tribe Nikola and I encountered was correct: that if we weren't saved by you, we would literally be experiencing the Forever Death. And that is why, to answer what I believe to be your original question Chip, I stand before you, in 2017, exactly as I was in 1917. One hundred years later. Remarkable."

"But… you came from another dimension. Not this one."

"Yes. Interesting. Clearly the Blue Juice, once it had assimilated Pete Turner here, gained some trans-dimensional ability. Remember, Pete was the first person snatched that had been to other dimensions. The Blue Juice in this dimension must have channeled Pete's unique connection to take its prey from any dimension, all of the Petes, here to this massive subterranean pool. Since I was grabbed *after* Pete, I came here instead of staying in my own dimension."

Gina steps in. "What about someone who was grabbed *before* Pete? Before it could reach across dimensions?"

"They would not have travelled here, then, so I assume they would remain in their own dimension, currently experiencing The Forever Death. Unless…"

I put up my hands in surrender. "I give up. This is fucking confusing. Can we go now?"

Gina punches my arm. "Chip, stop. Albert… you said 'unless'?"

"Unless its new ability and connection has created another kind of dimensional portal, to all the other pools of Blue Juice. In that case, its human captives may be in their original dimension, but *connected* to this central pool right here."

"So I could reach someone in *another* pool from *this* pool?"

"It's a rather tenuous theory I admit, based mostly on conjecture, but if it is correct-"

"Albert. I could?"

"I suppose. Yes."

"T-Rex is in another pool. Somewhere. I'm going after him."

Uh-oh. Gina's running for the edge of the pool. I go to grab her. "Don't!"

But she's already in midair, diving into the bluish white.

I crouch to dive in after her, I'm exhausted and useless, but what can I do? Gotta go after her. Then she pushes a thought into my head:

~~You won't stop me, Chip. And you're spent. You can't help me. So go home to your wife. And your baby. Go be a dad.~~

~~But Gina...~~

~~And for God's sake, please raise your kid to be less annoying than you.~~

Boom. Gone.

We're all just standing there, in shock.

I guess that's it.

She's going to find T-Rex.

Holy cow. That's some serious love shit right there.

But she's swimming through dimensions, into some pool of active Blue Juice somewhere, with untested telepathic powers, to find her lost husband, who could be anywhere, without even a Bobo to help her. It's suicide. Though I guess for her it would be better to go down trying at least. Respect, Gina.

Bobo tugs my shirt sleeve. I look down.

"MEGEE. MEGEE."

"Huh?"

"MEGEE. MEGEE."

"Oh. You and Gina? Yeah, makes sense. You gotta go."

He nods. And dives in after her.

Maybe it's not a suicide mission. Well, it probably still is, but maybe she'll have a better chance with Bobo.

Crap. I forgot to ask him to chew off a hand or something, so I could grow a copy of him. Ugh.

Later, Bobo.

I guess my kid will never have a furry alien to play with.

I turn to Pete. "They're gone."

He tries to lighten the moment, pointing to Einstein's mop of hair. "Hey, Albert. Ever hear of a comb?"

Einstein chuckles. "Herr Pete. I will comb my hair for the remainder of my days if the two of you can recite the mass equivalency equation that proves special relativity."

We both reply, "E equals MC squared. Everybody knows that."

The shock on Einstein's face is priceless. I guess he didn't realize that if there was one equation everyone in the world knew, even two idiots from the future, it would be that one. I dig around in my backpack, in awe of Fred's prescience, and pull out the comb and hand it to him. "Here you go, Albert."

Einstein's equally shocked at the sudden appearance of a comb, but takes it in stride and runs it through his hair. "How do I look?"

"I wish I had a mirror."

"That good, eh?"

Pete grabs Gina's backpack and starts climbing. "Hey. While you guys catch up and get radiation poisoning and die, I'm heading out."

Einstein smiles at me. "Herr Pete is right. You can tell me how good I look on the way. Let's go home."

22. SO NOW WE GET TO GO HOME, RIGHT?

From: Chip Collins
To: Julie Taylor
Date: November 19, 2017 11:43am
Subject: So now we get to go home, right?

Hey Julie,

So we make it to the back door with five minutes to spare, I'm
even more exhausted now, and Glitter Girl waves us in. And Julie,
I don't know if I can describe the reunion – Original Nikola Tesla,
from 1943, looks at his dear friend Albert Einstein, from back in
1917, I don't know how they don't have a million questions for
each other, they just grin and embrace.

Nikola whispers to his friend. "You've been traveling in a
closed timelike curve, I see."

"Yes, Nikola. It's fascinating. You should try it."

"Apparently I already have." He walks off a bit with Einstein,
but I can still hear him. "Now Albert. About your experience
down there in the Blue Juice…" and they start murmuring
scientific shit and I stop paying attention.

Pete looks up into the huge slide. "Dude. We supposed to climb up this thing? There's nothing to hold on to."

Glitter Girl takes this as her cue, and waves again, and incredibly, the slide begins to rotate, *Inception*-style, right before our eyes, until it leads *down* instead of *up*.

I look at her, and try to push a thought at her to say thanks. Nothing. Huh.

But she gets the idea anyway and pats me on the head.

And all together, the four of us skootch on our asses over to the lip of the slide. "Ready folks?"

Pete stops me. "Hey. Remember that time on the slide at the water park?"

"Yeah. That was a pisser."

"No. The part where you puked on me."

"Oh. Yeah."

"Yeah. Well, please don't do that."

"I've done it like five times on this trip. I think I'm all puked out. I'm sure of it. There's nothing left."

"You're sure."

"I'm sure."

So he pushes me off, and jumps in behind me, and Einstein and Tesla jump in too, and soon we're all careening down this massive slide to God-knows-where. I'm feeling pretty good, actually: I've got my best friend next to me, we've got Einstein and Tesla with us, we're all safe and sound, we're going home, the wind's blowing through my hair, and I don't have even the slightest feeling like I'm going to hurl. I smile over at Pete. "See? I'm perfectly fin-"

And Einstein barfs all over him.

Hey Julie,

"Dude! Gross!"

Einstein's got his oops face on, while we're hurtling down this chute, little pieces of his vomit spraying off Pete onto me and Tesla. We're all pretty disgusted.

"Gentlemen! I should have mentioned! My stomach is not the biggest fan of falling!"

"Wouldn't have guessed, Albert!"

A million years later, we tumble out of the slide, which of course is now the ceiling of the hallway, so we fall the eight feet or so to the floor, and Tesla's elbow nails me in the small of my back, sending bolts of white hot pain through my body.

Pete's on his feet in a second. Man, he looks as good as new, and I'm... I don't know. Like Old Man Chip. Christ, even Tesla and Einstein have to help me up.

Tesla pokes and prods me, stretches out my eyelids, takes a good look in my ears.

"What's up, doc?"

"Master Chip, your interaction with the Blue Juice must have impeded your body's ability to restore your normal energy level. What exactly happened down there?"

"You wouldn't like the explanation. Very unscientificky. But basically, me and Bobo mind-melded with the Blue Juice and convinced it that it wasn't hungry anymore. Neutralized it. It was pretty psychedelic."

"And the Blue Juice… neutralized everywhere? Across all dimensions?"

"I don't think so. I don't know. How the hell would I know?"

"This is not good."

"Not good? Nikola, we just saved Pete and knocked out the Blue Juice. It's over. We won."

"It's over in *one* dimension. But the multiverse has infinite dimensions."

"Infinite schminfinite. It's over."

Tesla gets stern, more stern than I think I've ever seen him. "Master Chip, I celebrate our victory as well, and I am beyond happy to have Pete safe and sound. But our current situation is not like WHO. WHO was one man, from one dimension. This Extraterrestrial Plasma Consciousness, this Blue Juice… it is *everywhere*. This is far from over."

I'm about to give in, I mean having Tesla admonish me is like my dad guilting me into mowing the lawn on a summer Saturday, like you want to say "no way fuck you," but you know he's right and it's gotta get done anyway, so I'm about to give in and –

Rumble rumble.

"What the hell was that?"

"What?"

"That rumble."

"Maybe Nikola farted. Or your stomach. Whatever. You're always hearing shit, dude. Let's go."

Rumble rumble.

"No. Hold on. It was like people running." I put my ear to one of the doors. Nothing. I walk to the next door and put my ear to it. Footsteps, rushing. "See? I told you I wasn't imagining-" and the door swings open, right into my ear, and throws me back on my ass, and eight guys with guns and sunglasses fall over each other onto me. All eight of them. On top of me.

"…dudes… do… you… mind…"

The eight guys eventually – right before I suffocate – break up the dogpile. One of them, I couldn't tell you which one, they all look identical, like the agents from *The Matrix*, one of them walks right up to my face, tips his sunglasses down his nose to get a good look. "Woah. It's really you."

"Really who?"

He salutes. "Really you, Mister President."

PART TWO: PRESIDENT CHIP

23. I DON'T WANT TO BE PRESIDENT.

From: Chip Collins
To: Julie Taylor
Date: November 19, 2017 11:43am
Subject: I don't want to be President.

Hey Julie,

The guy in charge walks through the ITA door behind the sunglasses/guns dudes, chewing gum, straightening his nerd glasses, holding *The Lost Journal of Nikola Tesla.* "Men. Silence. This is not the President."

Pete snickers under his breath. "Thank God."

The guy continues. "...But he will be for the next ninety-six hours."

I turn on Pete. "Thank God, huh? I'll have you know I would make a great Presiden- wait." I turn back to the gum-chewing guy. "What the fuck did you just say?"

"Mister Presiden- I mean, Mister Collins, sir. I can brief you on the flight. Now if you'll come with me." He hands me a handkerchief. "Um, and you have something on your face."

I start wiping the yellow shit off. "Okay, first: no, I'm not coming. And second: who the hell are you?"

"Arthur Ashe, sir. I'm the-"

"Wait. Like the tennis player?"

"What's tennis?"

"You know, tennis. The game." He looks at me blankly. "With rackets. And balls. And a net." More staring. "Right. I should know better by now. Forget it. Continue."

"I'm the President's Chief of Staff, and head of the National Security Council. There's been a development. We need you." He offers me a piece of gum.

I wave it away. "Look, Artie – is it okay if I call you Artie? – I know 'development' is code for absolute-fucking-out-of-control-shitstorm, but I have to tell you, I just came from a 'development.' I'm shot. Sorry. I have a strict one-development-a-day limit. Enjoy yours, dude." And I switch the InController back on and turn to head home. Goodbye, Arthur Ashe. Good luck with your development.

Tesla reaches out his hand. "Master Chip."

"No. I know where you're going to take this, Nikola. You're going to say something about how us Masters of Interdimensional Travel have a responsibility to all dimensions, how we're the guardians of all the beings in the multiverse, sworn to give ourselves to the ideals of peace and justice until there's nothing left to give. And then you're going to admonish me again for wanting to bolt, and tell me how I should look forward to serving as President of the United States for ninety-six hours, for the greater good of dimension number whatever-the-swearword-it-is."

He takes the handkerchief from my hand, and gently rubs the tip of my nose. "No. I was just going to say you missed a spot. Now you're good. No more yellow."

But he's smiling that smile, the smile that knows I just stepped in my own shit, and that, like it or not, I am here to help. That's my job. It's been my job since the moment I first stepped into the

ITA. "But Nikola, I wanted to go home. I have a wife, and maybe a baby, waiting for me. And I hate to sound ungrateful, but I don't want to be President of the United States."

He pats me on the head. "You will get home. I promise. But for the next ninety-six hours, it appears we have an opportunity to help someone in great need. And during our stay there, I can work on a solution to the Blue Juice problem, assuming that Mr. Ashe here supplies me with a small laboratory–"

Artie steps between me and Tesla. "Woah, woah. As much as I'd like the extra assistance, we have extremely strict rules about the ITA. Only a handful people in our entire dimension even know of its existence. Not even the President. To minimize risk of exposure, we're authorized to take Mr. Collins only. It's either just him, or no one. And for the record, I have no idea what this Blue Juice is, it's not a problem here, so we won't need any extra help on that either. I'm sorry."

"Fuck. Artie, you have to make this as hard as possible, don't you?"

"I'm sorry."

Tesla takes my hand, pats it. "Master Chip. Perhaps this is best. I will return Albert to Alternate Nikola's dimension, and while there we will attend to the matter of the Blue Juice. You can help our new friends, and join us later." He points to the copy of the journal Artie's holding. "I will keep in touch."

I look around to Pete, and Tesla, and my newest companion Einstein. And they nod in unison, and I understand. I'll catch up with them later. But for the next ninety-six hours, I've got a side gig to take care of.

And Julie, I'm sorry I've got to keep you waiting again. But you literally won't even notice I was gone, I'll be back before you know it. So forgive me, I've got to go help some people out, see if I can make a difference with their 'development.'

"Hey, Artie, just so I know what I'm getting myself into, what's this 'development' anyway?"

He hesitates, like he doesn't know how to form the words.

"Artie?"

"Sir. You've been assassinated. We're trying to avoid World War Two."

From: Chip Collins
To: Julie Taylor
Date: November 19, 2017 11:43am
Subject: Re: I don't want to be President.

"World War Two? You mean World War *Three*, right Artie?"

"No, sir. Two comes after one."

"I know two comes after one, smart ass." And it hits me. "Oh. Let me guess. You didn't have a World War Two."

"That's what we're trying to avoid, sir."

"No Hitler? No nazis? That shit didn't happen?"

"I have no idea what you're talking about, sir."

Wow. I try to wrap my head around that one for a second. Think about it, Julie. I guess in this dimension Hitler finished art school and maybe sold a painting or two, and wasn't such an angry fuckup. And maybe the reparations from World War One didn't happen, so there was no festering resentment in Germany. Who knows?

"And assassinated? What the fuck? Who would want to assassinate President Collins? I mean, us Chips are gentle as lambs, and yeah, we get into stupid shit here and there, but we mostly keep the blast radius small and stay out of major trouble. We're just regular guys."

"You, sir – or I should say your alternate, sir – is anything but a regular guy."

So while we're taking the chopper to who-knows-where, Artie fills me in on why I'm here, snapping his gum here and there for emphasis. It's kind of a long story, Julie (and by kind of long I mean it's literally the never ending story), so I've condensed it for you, into my latest easy-to-read mini novel…

The Rise of Togo: Prelude to World War Two (Based on a True Story)
An FBiPad Novel by President Chip Collins
(Yes, I'm going to start using "President" in my name from now on. Get used to it.)

Once upon a time in this dimension, four-ish billion years ago, as the Earth cooled, a massive diamond deposit formed in the planet's mantle, right under – you guessed it – the spot where the tiny African country of Togo would later plant its flag.

Two billion years later (wow, time flies in this story!), due to ever-so-slightly different humidity levels in this dimension, the world's dinosaur migration patterns led many more of these creatures through the very same land, where, when the giant asteroid struck sixty-five million years ago, they keeled over and died.

And became oil.

And so, in the year 1919, when poor Togo yam farmer Abi Kossi found himself at the bottom of a large hole in the ground, digging his new well, four diamonds landed on his shovel, in a small pool of black oil. "Shiny stones? Black liquid? What good are these for growing yams?" he growled, as he climbed out of the hole and started digging his well in another location a quarter mile away, forgetting forever the riches the ground had offered him.

The end.

No, I'm kidding. Abi wasn't an idiot. As soon as he saw the diamonds and oil, he shouted "HOLY SHIT!" and jumped up and down, and declared himself King of Togo on the spot.

And sure enough, as his diamond mine, oil fields, and fortunes grew, along with his influence, he did become king. He declared independence from German and French rule, kicked them all out in a bloody revolution, and sat his ass down on a throne – literally made of diamonds.

Soon little Togo was doing some empire-building of its own,

and by 1980 the House of Kossi ruled over the entire continent of Africa (which King Abi's grandson Kodjo renamed Togo – and the map people went nuts, like "Dude! Every three years we have to re-do all our maps because of you! Can't you just do it all at once?").

When King Kodjo died in 2015, (btw, can you guess what his coffin was made out of?) his sixteen-year-old son Kookee (yes, I swear that's his name, and as you'll see it's a perfect fit) took the throne, and the very first thing he shouted from the balcony of the imperial palace was, "This continent is not big enough for my – *I mean, our* – ambitions! I – *we* – must expand Togo to the corners of the globe! Even though it's obvious that globes don't have corners!" Yeah. The kid was bat shit crazy. Oh, and did I mention the bat shit crazy kid had nukes?

So the rest of the world collectively gulped and said "oh fuck," and rushed to create alliances, and shit started getting very heated, lots of fingers on lots of buttons, military buildup, civil unrest, celebrities freaking out on social media, you name it.

And that's when President Collins stepped in.

He calmed the nerves of the Chinese, then the Russians, worked tirelessly to push through international laws that could contain Togo and other rogue nations, and vowed to forge a lasting worldwide peace.

Then, on the eve of his historic diplomatic mission to Togo, where he would speak one-on-one with King Kookee (dude, I couldn't make that name up if I tried), A motorcycle rammed through a police barrier towards President Collins' motorcade in D.C. and threw an IED under his truck.

Boom.

The End.

"So, sir. I hope you can see the gravity of our situation. If the President dies, it will be the spark that ignites World War Two."

"Hold on. What do you mean, if the President dies? I thought you said he was assassinated? Like already dead."

"For all intents and purposes. But against all odds, he is holding on to the thread of life. For the moment."

"I want to see him. Now."

"I anticipated that, sir. That's where we're headed."

The chopper slows, and begins to descend.

"Uh, why are we stopping now? We're in the middle of nowhere." We're literally in the actual desert somewhere, not a landmark in any direction for a thousand miles. So unless we're just stopping on the way to take a quick leak, I don't see- *hold on.* Something's moving down there.

Woah.

The floor of the desert opens up, forming a gigantic ramp. The pilot aims right for it, and the Earth swallows us whole. Then darkness. You know what I'm thinking, right? This time we're definitely on our way down to Hell. The President is Satan. I'm sure of it.

Artie clicks a little light on above us.

"Welcome to Area 51, Mister President."

From: Chip Collins
To: Julie Taylor
Date: November 19, 2017 11:43am
Subject: Re: I don't want to be President.

Hey Julie,

The helicopter lands in this massive space, it looks like a hangar I guess, God knows how many miles beneath the surface. There are planes and choppers and rockets everywhere, none of which I could identify (not that I could ever identify an aircraft, but still). There's a ton of activity, folks rushing here and there, guys in lab coats looking at us suspiciously, loads of military. Anyway, they hand me a suit (which fits more perfectly than any other clothes I've ever had in my life, I'm embarrassed to say), and we go through a little swearing-in ceremony, and I sign a bunch of stuff that I assume means they're allowed to kill me if I divulge anything I'm looking at.

On the way to the elevators, I look around and shake my head at Artie. "Jesus, dude. What's with the Area 51 drama? Couldn't you have just taken him to a hospital?"

"Sir. Area 51 is the most secure location on Earth. And there are… things here that may help."

"Aliens! I knew it!"

Artie laughs. "No, sir. Advanced medical technologies that I'm not at liberty to discuss. There are no aliens. Not that I'm aware of."

"Hold on. You've followed the journal. What about Bobo? He's an alien."

"Well, officially, sir, Bobo is a construction of your imagination."

"What the fuck? God, you government types really don't want to believe in Bobo. I don't get it. I wish he was here. Then you'd believe me."

"I certainly would, sir. If he were here." He looks around, at the obvious lack of a Bobo.

"Wise ass."

He points to the door on our left. "We've arrived. You'll have five minutes with the President to brief. Then, I'm sorry, we've got to get him into an induced coma. It's the only thing that may save his life."

I walk in, alone, and regret that I didn't prepare myself for what I'm seeing – I almost throw up. It's an alternate me, I can tell, but with both legs missing below the knee. Just one eye peeking out from a headful of bandages. It looks like he's made out of bruises. Tubes everywhere. God, he looks worse than when Chuck got run over by that car.

I tentatively walk over. He's awake. "Hey, bro. You look like you could use a beer."

He smiles weakly. Groans.

"I would try telepathy, it'd probably be easier for you, but I think I lost it. I got nothing. The Blue Juice did me in. Knee-capped me like Tonya Harding."

He musters up his voice into a hoarse whisper. "Maybe it's the drugs, but I have no idea what you're talking about."

"Oh. Yeah. Sorry. Well, in any case I'm here to help, Mister President. So, you're the President of the United States. How cool is that?"

"So, you're the Master of Interdimensional Travel, if you don't mind saying so yourself. How cool is that?" And we both laugh. He coughs. A little blood comes up. "You know, I wasn't aware of any of this until this morning. Tesla's great invention. The multiverse. You." He coughs again. "And by the way, you're not a bad looking guy." He forces back another cough or laugh. I think the next one might kill him.

I lean in close. "Hey, I'm sorry about what happened to you."

"From what I've heard just now, you've stuck your neck out a few times, too. Comes with the territory, am I right?" And he takes my hand. "Now I'm sure Arthur has you up to speed. But I want to tell you something that I think will help when you meet King Kookee."

"Let me guess. You're going to tell me not to spit soda through my nose when he introduces himself."

He can't help it, he lets out a little chuckle.

And starts heaving. And then shit goes berserk. Alarms blaring, people rushing in, trying to push me out of the way, the monitors are going crazy. Fuck. It's happening, right before my eyes. He's dying.

A nurse yells at me. "Get out of here! We've got to get him into the coma. NOW!"

But the President clutches my hand tighter. He won't let me go. And he pulls me in, as close as he can, and we lock eyes. And he lifts our hands up, and taps my temple with his index finger, and whispers, *"Remember…"*

"Remember? Remember what?"

"…Kookee…"

"Kookee? Remember Kookee what?"

"…he's just a boy."

Hey Julie,

I'm a mess.

I'm watching myself die.

But Artie pulls me out, cool as a cuke, while the monitors go flatline and about twenty doctors and nurses shout instructions at each other. It's mayhem.

He grips my shoulder. "All right, sir. First, we have to make an appearance in public in D.C. Then we'll take the chopper to-"

I grab his jacket collar. Tears are rolling down my cheeks. "Hey! Who the fuck do you think you are? Did you just see what happened back there?! He just died!"

He slaps me hard across the face. "Calm down, sir!"

Did Artie just fucking slap me? I slap him back. And yeah, it turns into a Russian slap fight, until we're rolling on the ground like a couple of hockey players, slapping and grunting, and the Secret Service dudes have to play referee and pull us apart.

"Dick!"

"Sir! This isn't about him! Or you! Or me! It's about–" he looks around, like he's looking for something, then grabs his wallet and pulls a picture out and throws it at me. "-THEM!"

I bend down and pick up the photo. It's Artie and his wife, and their four kids.

And I get it immediately. He's right. The President is a guy, a human being, and I am too. But we're really just here to protect *everyone else*. To guide them. To push the boulder forward for the next generation. I take a deep breath. "Is he...?"

"No. They'll revive him, and place him into a coma, and in some short span of time, he'll be back on his... he'll be back."

God, I can feel Artie's faith like heat coming off him. I reach out my hand. "Artie. I hope you're right. Now let's hit the road."

We brush ourselves off and march down the hallway, a gaggle of Secret Service dudes following in our wake.

"Clarence? Dear? Please, is that you, Clarence?"

Artie winces. "Oh shit."

I stop marching. "Did someone just call my name?"

"Um, no. I belched. Let's keep moving."

"Dude. That wasn't you belching. Someone called my name. It sounded like my mom."

"Sir. Our ride is waiting. Please don't-"

But I'm already walking back down the hallway. I definitely heard a woman call my name, and dammit I'm checking it out. Here, there's door ajar on the right. Artie rushes between my hand and the doorknob. "Sir. Please. It's... the First Lady."

"The First Lady?! I'm *married?*"

"And you're madly in love. It's true. But you can't see her."

"You didn't tell me?! Is it Julie? Get your hand away, Artie." I try to push past him but now he's spread eagle, clutching the doorway like a crab over a pot of boiling water. "No. Please, sir."

"I'm going in, Artie. Just tell me if there's anything I should be aware of."

He surrenders with a sigh. "Just make it quick, sir. We'll drug her up afterwards so she doesn't remember anything. She's physically stable. It's a miracle she only has two sprained ankles, some bad burns, and a concussion. I don't think it's a version of your Julie, however, sir. No red hair, and much taller. And her name is..."

I rush into the room as I sort of half-hear that last part, about it not being Julie, and about how she's taller, and her name, and the words don't register until it's too late.

I look down at my wife, laying like an angel in her bed, the woman I'm supposed to be madly in love with, and she smiles broadly and reaches out her long arms.

And then Alternate Gina Phillips speaks.
"Clarence! Come to me, my darling!"

From: Chip Collins
To: Julie Taylor
Date: November 19, 2017 11:43am
Subject: Re: I don't want to be President.

Hi Julie,

Yeah. It's the fucking weirdest moment ever. And I've seen a lot of weird shit in here. Not even in all the infinite possibilities would I have bet on this one. The toughest FBI agent I've ever met, tough as titanium nails, whose only love for me is the love of despising me, is laying there like a fragile girl, hurt, reaching her arms out for me to comfort her.

"Clarence! Darling! What happened? I have no memory. Why are we here? Come give your snuggle bear some love."

Run away. Run away.

That's all I can think. I've never wanted to run away from something more than I want to run away from Alternate Gina Phillips at this moment.

"Clarence…?" And she starts crying.

Oh shit. Don't cry. Come on. Not the tears, Gina. Dammit.

I tread, as slowly as possible, over to her bed and lean down to give her a little hug. You know, I feel bad, It's Gina after all, who has already saved my life more than once, and has been an actual friend at moments here and there. And she's hurt. She deserves a little hug. Just a little one. Then I'm the *hell* out of here.

But she grabs me with so much force it knocks the wind out of me, and her bear hug finishes the job, squeezing any remaining air out of my lungs, and I'm about to pass out, and then it happens.

I'm sorry, Julie.

I wish I never had to say these words:

Gina Phillips kisses me.

Passionately.

I back off immediately – of course – and she's got this weird look on her face. It's dead silence for a full minute, and then her face hardens. "You're not Clarence."

"Of course I am. I'm just-"

"You're not Clarence. Who are you?" Her grip tightens.

"Uh, honey. You're hurting my arms. Snuggle puppy."

"It's snuggle *bear*. You're not Clarence. Guards!" She starts screaming, and crushing my rib cage, and I can't breathe but I manage to shout, "Help! The First Lady is killing me!"

"Guards! There's a fucking impostor! In my *bed!*"

And three Secret Service dudes and a nurse rush in (I swear to God I think I hear one of them snickering), and pin her down, and the nurse whips out a giant horse tranquilizer and finally calms her the fuck down.

And then she goes bye-bye.

Whew.

I skulk out of the room, and Artie's waiting there for me.

"Sir. I trust that went as planned."

"Shut up, Artie."

From: Chip Collins
To: Julie Taylor
Date: November 19, 2017 11:43am
Subject: Re: I don't want to be President.

Hey Julie,

So I just wanted to apologize again. I never meant to kiss Gina, alternate or not. I think you know that. I think you know what I want.

I want to be with you.

These last few months living together have been magical. I know that's not the macho-est word in the world, way too Disney, but I don't care, it describes our life right now perfectly: *magical*.

How else can you describe those funny moments where we look at each other, and without words, have entire conversations? How else can you describe the moment I pick up peaches from Gristedes and you say, "weird, I was just thinking about how much I'd like a peach." How else can you describe the moment you pick up the sugar shaker at the diner and offer it to me at the same exact moment I pick up the creamer and offer it to you?

And how else can you describe that life growing inside you right now?

It's magic.

Right now, somewhere out there in the multiverse, a life is starting. A little ball of life, growing, getting ready to arrive on the big stage, with a scream and a splurt of amniotic fluid. (That last part was gross, sorry.)

You know, when I think about that moment, and I've been thinking about it a lot, I hope it's okay if I tell you I have about a million different feelings. I'm in awe of the magic of it, and excited as hell, but I'm also scared to death. Is it okay to say I'm scared? That I have no idea what I'm doing, and I'm afraid I'll break our kid the minute I hold him for the first time? Afraid that every time he cries I won't know what to do? That maybe Pete's right and I should wrap him up in bubble wrap, to protect him from me?

And is it okay to admit that I'm even angry a little, at my Dad, for leaving too soon, before I could find out how I'm supposed to do all this? How I'm supposed to guide our kid through junior high, when all the other kids are being total assholes? How to talk to him about asking a girl out for the first time? How to teach him to fix the screen door? How to show him what really matters?

I know what you'd say. You'd say to relax, that he'll learn everything he needs to, it just sort of happens, and that as long as we're together, and we love him, everything will work out just fine. That's all good. But I still don't know if I'm ready.

"Sir. I hope it's all right if I ask you a question."

I look up from my letter. "Huh? Sure, Artie."

"You write constantly, I notice. Why?"

"It keeps me sane. And it keeps me connected. You remember how you said the President and First Lady were madly in love?"

"Yes."

"I have someone like that, too. Julie. The letters keep me connected to her. I'm madly in love with her. If I didn't write to her I'd be lost."

"She must be very special, sir."

"Yeah. Tesla calls her the 'bee's knees.'"

He raises an eyebrow. Grins. "May I show you something, sir?"

"Sure. Of course."

He pulls out his phone. It's an email from his wife:

To: Arthur Ashe
From: Kitty Ashe
Date: November 12, 2017, 8:04pm
Subject: Hi

Hi Art,

I know you're busy. With terrible stuff beyond my imagining. But I just wanted to share a random moment: Kate came home from school today with a poem they had to write in class. Here's hers:

> *My Daddy likes cheese.*
> *He always says please.*
> *He helps me climb trees.*
> *He's the bee's knees.*

Me and Artie smile at each other for a while.

Yeah, that's the shit right there.

"Hey, Mister Bee's Knees."

"Yes, Mister President?"

"Let's go stop World War Two."

24. DUDE - PICK UP

The Journal of Nikola Tesla, 1941-
Journal Entry
From: Pete
To: Chip

Listen, I know you're trying to avert World War Whatever, but you better hurry up and get back to me. There's a problem. If I'm actually writing, you know there's a problem. Tesla's freaking out. It's bad.

Here's what happened:

We got to Young Tesla's dimension, where you sliced your fingertips off, to drop off Einstein, and it turned out Young Tesla had a little mishap with the closed timelike whatever-it-is, because we opened the door and the hotel room was full of Teslas. You would have loved it, it was total chaos, about twenty Teslas, all different ages, trying to figure out what the fuck went wrong with their stupid machine. So just for kicks I shouted "Hey

Nikola!" And they all turned around at once, and I took a picture on my phone. I'll show you when I see you. I made it my home screen. It's priceless.

Back to the point: original Tesla had them shut the whole curve thing down, it took maybe a day and a half, apparently it wasn't meant to ever stop, then he brought me inside and briefed them all on what happened with us, and the problem with the Blue Juice, and they put their heads together, all twenty of them plus Einstein, and this is the gem they came up with:

"We must peer into the future."

So I said, "What the hell does that mean?" And they said, "Pete, the Blue Juice, using normal radiation and its newfound transdimensional ability, will eventually expand to fill the multiverse. To choke off life itself. We haven't reached the 'tipping point' yet, but we must locate that tipping point in space and time in order to prevent it. That place and moment is in the future."

Einstein got pissed and said "Impossible."

One of the Teslas, I don't even know which one, said, "Albert. Is there no way to peer into the future? Even for a moment?"

"None. It is impossible."

"Wasn't it you, Albert, who said that the difficult can be done now, and the impossible just takes a little longer?"

"No. I think an American President said that. Taft, if I'm not mistaken."

"No. Perhaps Madison?"

"Polk." "Roosevelt." "Lincoln." "Hoover." Dude – every single one of these Telsas had a different opinion. I had to shut them all up. "A-HEM! Guys. Is it possible or not?"

Einstein and the twenty Teslas stared hard at each other for an eternity.

"We would have to manipulate entropy. It's never been done. But…"

And then they all went over to his little lab table, the whole team of them, and harrumphed for three hours, and then one of them shouted, "Eureka!"

. . .

I literally have no idea what the fuck they did, so I had Original Tesla try to explain it in normal person terms. That didn't work either, so I just had him write it down:

Dear Chip,

First, I hope your mission is proceeding apace. I trust, based on our previous experiences, that it is going smoothly, without a single hiccup. (I jest, of course: your paths tend to be quite bumpy!)

Secondly, Master Pete has asked me to explain what we are doing. I am not sure it will be of interest to you, as terms like "entropy" and "quantum states" usually cause you to fall asleep during my explanations. But in any case, here is what we are attempting:

Because of entropy, a system moves in the direction of the highest possible state of disorder, and never will reverse – thus the single direction of time. By understanding the direction and amplitude of every particle in said system, it is theoretically possible to predict – with amazing precision – the future outcome of events.

However, this prediction ability would require a device that harnessed the power of infinite parallel dimensions, and the ability to bend spacetime. Fortunately, we have such a device! By linking the INTERDIMENSIONAL TRANSFER APPARATUS with the PORTABLE BLACK HOLE, we can, I believe, create the opposite of a closed timelike curve: an OPEN TIME INFINITE QUANTUM STATE PREDICTION SIMULATOR. (I apologize, we could not all agree on a shorter name. And also, please make sure any references use all capital letters.)

We should now be able, for the first time in human history, to see into the future! Or at least an extremely accurate simulation of the probable future. I shall hand the journal back to Pete now, as we are about to start up the PORTABLE BLACK HOLE.

Did you get that? Neither did I.

But they went ahead and did their thing. And they put me and Original Tesla back out in the hallway, to protect us from getting trapped in there with them forever, and started up the machine. And as soon as they did – it happened.

They saw the future.
And it wasn't good.
All dimensions.
All blue.

It gets worse, too, and this is why I need you to hurry the hell up.
This doesn't go down in some random dimension.
This isn't years out.
It happens in the dimension you're in *right now*, dude.
And it happens in *forty-eight hours*.

We're coming to get you. You better be in the hotel room when we get there.

25. HOW TO STOP WORLD WAR TWO

From: Chip Collins
To: Julie Taylor
Date: November 19, 2017 11:43am
Subject: How to Stop World War Two

Hi Julie,

The first leg of the Fake President Tour was easy. Stand at the front door of the White House and wave my hands. Don't say a word. Limp and walk with a cane. Let them take pictures. Prove to people around the world that I'm alive and well. (By the way, my hair is a little shorter now babe, I guess the President doesn't go in for the *I-don't-give-a-shit* look.) I smile and wave my hands some more. Easy. Only forty-eight more hours to go.

The second leg? Not so much.

Artie's been prepping me nonstop since the moment we met, two days ago, because there's no way around it, I have to talk to people, reporters and leaders and shit, so I have to know what the hell I'm talking about if I'm going to pull off the Alternate President thing. I've got it pretty much down, though, I think:

Top Ten Things I Learned About Dimension #921,034,455,231,594 In No Particular Order

1. Africa is now Togo, ruled by King Kookee. Yes, Kookee. It's not a joke.

2. Tennis doesn't exist. Don't ask me how this didn't happen, I mean everything else seems pretty much the same, and they have hockey and football, heck they even have a famous athlete named Serena Williams, but she's a figure skater. I forgot to ask Artie if they have badminton. Or ping pong. Like do they have a problem with net games in general?

3. Their favorite beer is something called Moshpit. I tried it. It tastes just like Bud. (Which is to say, like cat piss.) I asked Artie if they had like a microbrew version of Moshpit, something with a little more depth maybe, and he looked at me like I had three heads. Everyone just drinks plain old Moshpit I guess. I might have to sign an executive order to change that shit. This country needs good beers. I told Artie we should make one and call it White House, how cool would that be, and he regurgitated about thirty-five rules that would break, so I just said forget it so he would shut the hell up.

4. The First Lady, Gina, even though she's an alternate of Gina Phillips, doesn't seem like the tough-as-nails agent type at all. Supposedly, she's super sweet, just like you. And fiercely loyal, and the American people dig her a lot, like a modern Jackie O. I don't see how that could be, I mean it's Gina, you know, the one who smiled wide as she knocked me unconscious? The one who shoots her gun at cockroaches? But, as Tesla once told me, the personalities of our alternates can be as different as the circumstances we find ourselves in. I'm not convinced she's as sweet as she seems, though – she did almost crush my ribcage,

and call me a fucking impostor, and it literally took a horse tranquilizer to take her down.

5. You can become President at thirty years old here. So immature man-children like me can be leader of the free world.

6. The major international players are: the USA (of course, we rock), The European Union (except for Portugal. Portugal here is called "Fortugal." With an F. And in this dimension they're like Switzerland, impartial and apolitical. And yes, they have a cheese, too. Fort cheese. I'm not kidding.), China, Russia, India, Australia, and honestly I forget the other two or three. And of course, Togo.

7. Everyone in the world is obsessed with a TV show called *Origami*. It's the most bizarre mix of game show, singing competition, Survivor, and a semi-scripted drama. Julie, they interrupted a top-secret classified briefing to put it on. So I reached over to turn it off because it sucked so bad, and Artie actually put his hand on the remote to stop me, and the Secret Service guys went for their holsters. I swear to God. And you thought we were obsessed with stupid shit in our dimension.

8. If President Collins (not me, the first one) ever gets back on his feet, meaning prosthetic legs, he'll be limping. So they got me a fancy cane and told me if I walk normally at any time in the next forty-eight hours, they'll break my legs for me to make it more realistic.
9. President Collins (not me, the first one) liked to quote previous presidents, like all the time, so they had to give me a crash course in U.S. President Quotes. They set it up like *Jeopardy*, which made it fun, but still, out of something like five thousand quotes, I think I remembered four: the JFK "don't ask what your country can do for you" the Lincoln "all men are created equal," the FDR "we have nothing to fear but fear itself," and... oh shit, I can't even remember four. I am so screwed.

…. And the biggee…

10. There is no strawberry flavored ice cream. And thus, no strawberry milkshakes. It's official: this dimension has some serious issues.

Anyway, we arrive on the tarmac at Andrews in D.C., and I kind of gasp, because there it is: Air Force One. Julie, you have no idea how impressive this plane looks up close. Like if it was your Delta flight to Minneapolis, it might not faze you at all. But this giant bird is for ONE GUY. It's crazy. So we walk to the little podium with a carpet leading up to the plane, and at least a hundred reporters are nudging each other to see who can get their microphone up my nose the farthest. My hands are shaking.

Artie leans in and whispers. "All right, sir. Deep breath. Take just five questions. Keep your answers short. You'll be fine. I'm right here."

I nod and step up to the mic. Point to the least annoying-looking journalist.

And the very first question is this:

"Mister President, there are concerns that with the First Lady injured, you may not be able to focus on the important task at hand. Will your wife be too much of a distraction?"

"What the fuck kind of question is that?"

Artie rushes over, between me and the mic. "Ah, what the President means is that-"

I push him back. "No, Artie. I got this." And I turn back to the reporter. "Hey. You ever love someone?"

The reporter dude is in shock. "Um, I, ah…"

"Here's the truth: love doesn't distract you from the important stuff. Love *is* the important stuff. And that love pushes you to work hard, to focus even more on making a life that's worth it, focus on being your best self, focus on creating a better world. So yes, I love my wife, perhaps to a fault. But I'm going to do what I have to, to avert this calamity, to make this planet a safer place, so I can make it back home to her. To hold her in my arms..."

There's a sniffle from the reporter. Another is wiping a tear from her cheek.

"... and to hold our baby for the first time."

Artie spits out his gum. The fucking reporter pool goes nuts. "Sir! You're having a baby?!" "Sir! The First Lady is pregnant?" "Sir!" "Sir!"

"Um, as FDR said, 'We have nothing to fear but fear itself!'"

Artie rushes in and grabs me and says, as calmly as possible into the mic, "No more questions."

Limping as fast as I can away down the carpet to the plane's stairs, I turn to Artie. "Dude. I'm sorry. That question just pissed me off, and I lost my center. It just made me think of Julie, and I never told you, she thinks she's preg-"

"Sir. Don't worry. Let's keep moving forward. We'll just have to spin this a little."

"*Spin this a little?* Artie, I just lied to the whole world. I told them the First Lady is pregnant. How are you going to spin that?"

He pops another piece of gum into his mouth. Squints at me. "Actually, Sir..."

"No. Stop. Don't tell me."

"...no one knows this, only the medical staff at Area 51. The First Lady is expecting."

Oh for crying out loud. Another baby? This is getting ridiculous. The multiverse is clearly trying to tell me something. Something to do with babies. Lots of babies. Babies all over the freaking place. How many more babies are there going to be?

"Oh, and sir? Since we're on the subject – it's triplets."

From: Chip Collins
To: Julie Taylor
Date: November 19, 2017 11:43am
Subject: Re: How to Stop World War Two

Hi Julie,

"Welcome to Beijing, Mister President."

It's the Chinese president, Xan Xing. He bows, and hands me a fluted champagne glass to match the one in his other hand. "First, a toast. To your miraculous recovery. And your impending fatherhood."

I can't tell if he's being a dick, or if he means it. I look over to Artie, who nods. So I clink glasses, and kick back onto my tongue what I expect to be some seriously fine bubbly.

It's Moshpit.

So of course I spit it out, full force, onto President Xan Xing, who's utterly horrified that his *enemy-turned-temporary-ally-by-necessity* just showered him with the foulest alcoholic beverage known to man. Artie's just standing there shaking his head, probably trying to find the nearest exit.

"Yikes. Sorry." I take out my pocket square to help mop some of the swill off him, but twelve samurai guards jump in and stare me down, like I'm going to kill their president with a hankie.

"Woah. Guys. I said I was sorry. It's just, sir... Moshpit?"

Xing grins, waves off his minions. "It's your national beverage, Mister President. I was simply trying to make you feel at home."

"More like you were trying to kill me."

He laughs nervously, like he can't figure out whether I'm the one being a dick now, subtly accusing him of maybe being behind the recent attempt on my life, or if I'm just joking. Then he gets a strange look on his face. Uh-oh. Artie warned me Clarence didn't have exactly my sense of humor. Can Xan Xing tell? They've only met twice before. Shit. I've got to stick with the script. Don't let him think I'm not me. Don't be like Chip, Chip. Be like Clarence, Chip. Think of a president quote or something quick.

I bow to him. "Perhaps a nice little glass of Baijiu instead?" I motion to one of our aides, who presents Xing with our ceremonial gift of a bottle of fine Chinese hooch.

He raises his eyebrows and smiles. But before he can dismiss his servant dude and we forget about the whole episode, I snatch the bottle, crack it open, pour out the shitty Moshpit onto the floor, and fill our glasses with the good stuff. I raise mine high.

"President Xing. As Thomas Jefferson once said, 'Out with the bad. In with the good.'"

He chuckles, relaxing a little, and slaps me on the back and we both take a deep drink.

"And now, President Collins, my new friend, it is time to join the other leaders in the Great Hall." And his entourage follows him down the long hallway, avoiding the little puddles of Moshpit.

Artie's shaking his head. "Sir. Number one, Thomas Jefferson never said that. But number two, the Chinese president just called you 'my new friend.' Not a small thing. Well done, sir."

"Cool. Maybe I should spit Moshpit on everyone in the Great Hall. You know, take a good thing and overdo it."

"Excellent idea. But perhaps another time, sir."

"And remind me. Why are we here again?"

"The five world leaders requested your presence to finalize the plan. But really, to grill you for five hours. To make sure their eggs, now all in one basket, that basket being you, haven't been broken – broken being your brain after the explosion."

"Gotcha. Any last advice?" The samurai guards at the doors begin to close them between us, sealing me in, alone, with the other five most important people on the planet. I hold them open for one last moment to hear Artie's response.

"Yes. Be yourself."

"Wait. Really?"

"No." But he winks at me, and I think that means that it's okay if I inject a little Chip into the proceedings, judiciously. Just a little. A smidge. Don't overdo it, Chip. Really. I'm serious.

FIVE HOURS LATER:

The doors swing open, and leading the way out, swinging her shoes in her hand, swaying a little from side to side, barefoot, giggling, is the EU Prime Minister, Eileen Hart. Behind her, Xan Xing walks arm in arm with Russian president Alex Sokolov. They're singing a sea shanty or something, which sounds awful, it's a mashup of Chinese and Russian and they have absolutely no sense of key or timing (and they're piss drunk which doesn't help). And bringing up the rear is me and the Indian Prime Minister Deepak Sodhi, and the Australian Prime Minister, who hiccups and shout whispers, "...and then the horse says 'I've fallen and I can't giddyup!'" and she practically falls on the ground laughing at her own joke.

Meanwhile, everyone's aides are jumping in like disapproving moms, trying to hush up their bosses and make sense of what the hell just happened. Artie takes me by the arm. "Sir. I was kidding when I said be yourself."

I laugh. "Artie. I love you."

"Oh Christ. What happened in there, sir?"

I put my index finger to my lips. "Shhhh... super secret world leader stuff." And the other five leaders join in. "Shhhhh..." and we all start laughing again. "Artie. Listen, buddy, I got nervous, and there was a bar in there – *surprise!* – God, the most well-stocked bar on the planet I think, so it just kind of happened. Sorry. You wanna see it...?" I try to stumble lead Artie back into the Great Hall, but he's not having it. He's pissed.

"Sir! You've made a mockery of this meeti-"

The Russian president interrupts him, putting his giant meaty paws on both our shoulders. "Mister Ashe. A mockery? I have never felt more hopeful, thanks to your President Collins here. We may be on the verge, not just of avoiding a world war, but of ushering in and era of peace and-" and he burps. "Excuse me. What was I just saying?" And he starts cackling like a Russian witch (is that even a thing?), and wanders off to find the rest of his brain.

Prime Minister Hart stumbles in to complete the thought. "What he was trying to say, dears, I think, is that we've got a chance here. A better chance than we thought."

Artie grudgingly gives me a smile, he knows we nailed it, but I guess he feels like he still has to act pissed. He waves a hand in front of his face. "Sir. You smell."

I grin wide. "As Abraham Lincoln once said, 'You're welcome.'"

The Journal of Nikola Tesla, 1941-
Journal Entry
From: Pete
To: Chip

Dude. Where are you? What's with the radio silence?

I realize you're saving the world or whatever, but I know you
– you take everything to the absolute limit, and your Chipness
spreads like a virus to everyone around you. Pretty soon you'll be
drinking buddies with the Chinese president or some crazy shit
like that. And you'll forget about the other little problem we've
got. You know, the blue stuff that's going to absorb the whole
multiverse. Yeah, that little issue.

So cut the crap, get the job done, and write back to me in the
journal ASAP. We'll be at the hotel room soon.

– Pete

Hi Julie,

The thing that strikes me first is the drapes.

They're easily thirty feet long, from the ceiling to the floor. Stitched with images of kings and conquest, lined with gold, and covered with, of course: diamonds. I'm pretty sure King Kookee didn't order these from FabricWorld.com. I wonder if there's a TogoCustomCurtains.com. If we save up for a couple of hundred years maybe we can get one for our apartment.

Anyway, I'm sitting in this impossibly big room, the palace dining room in the capitol of Togo, you know one of those ornate rooms that has such a long table you'd have to have the butler run down to the other end to fetch you the salt because the person at the other end wouldn't even hear you yell for them to pass it. It's so long, you'd have to–

Oh. It's him. He's here.

Kookee.

Don't laugh, Chip. It's just a name.

He's been keeping me waiting for two and a half hours. Just to rattle me. Not a surprise, actually. Artie called it. Artie warned me about lots of things. He told me we'd be alone, but that you're never alone here. He told me that I was about to understand the true definition of intimidation. Yeah, well I can be intimidating too. Super intimidating.

I know, I know Julie, I can't even intimidate the guy at Baskin Robbins to give me an extra scoop of ice cream. Whatever. I'm trying.

Anyway, I'm sitting at one end of the table, at the head, and I fully expect him to stroll way over to the other end and sit down where I can barely see him, and we'll have to talk with walkie talkies or smoke signals or butlers running back and forth.

But he comes right over to my chair. "Move. That's my seat."

Okay. He's young, but he's definitely learned how to be a total dick just like a grownup. "Your highness, if I might say, your English is perfect, I'm really–"

"No 'your highness'."

"King Kookee, I'm–"

"No 'Kookee.' Just King. You may call me King."

"Uh, okay. Let's start over. King."

He brushes past me to sit in his chair. "You sit there." Points to his left. I walk around behind him and take my seat. "Listen, King, why don't we start with–"

"No. I'll start."

His right palm presses on the corner of the table, and instantly a little panel in the table in front of him slides back, and a small square box rises up. The lid pops off.

It's a button. A red button.

Yes. *That* Red Button.

With a spot for a key at the base. So he reaches under his collar, removing a long necklace with a key on the end, takes the key and inserts it in the keyhole and turns it.

The Red Button lights up.

I gulp.

He smiles. "Yes, Mister President. This button does exactly what you think it does."

"Orders Dominoes? Cool." I touch my palm all around the table. "Is there another button around here for extra mushrooms?"

His finger taps the top of the button lightly. I practically shit myself. "You're hilarious, Mister President. I can hardly contain myself. No, it launches nuclear missiles. At New York City."

Jesus, Chip. Strike one. Pete would smack you. Maybe don't be hokey-jokey guy for once, will you? "Sorry, your highne- KING. Uh, why don't we start over?"

"That would be twice now. Are you sure you've prepared for this visit? You certainly don't act like any leader I've ever met. And I don't mean that in a *that's-so-refreshing* way."

Damn. He's got me off balance. And my blood pressure's starting to shoot through the roof. This fucking kid is asking for it. But I swallow hard. "I apologize, King. It's just not every day I get to meet someone with such… influence."

He dismisses my comment with a wave. "Very well. As you know, as you all know, Togo is now the richest country – no, continent – in the world, and it is time that we spread our wings, and claimed our rightful lands."

"King, I understand that you believe the Middle East to be-"

He laughs. "Only the Middle East? I'm afraid your intelligence is a little dated, Mister President." He stands and strolls over to the big antique globe in the corner and spins it. He doesn't even need to say the words.

It's my turn to laugh. "King. The world is a big place. With a lot of people. Who already have a place to call home."

"They will still have a home. Togo will be their home."

I rise, head over to the globe, and point to the various nations. "No. They already have a home that is rightfully theirs. Your rights do not supersede theirs. These are their homes. Not yours. It can never happen. I'm sorry."

"Mister President, why are you here? To talk some adult sense into a young, inexperienced, impulsive monarch?"

"Well, I wouldn't say it like that. I would say-"

"You will fail. I represent the destiny of Togo. My entire life has been for the furthering of Togo. There is nothing that can stop this great nation's destiny. Nothing."

"King. I'm here to talk about balance. And about peace. And about the future of us all. Do your people even want this conquest? Does anyone other than you really want th-"

"Nothing will stop us! Do you hear me? *Nothing!*"

Julie, I don't know why, but I suddenly just get really calm, take a deep breath, and go completely off script. "Nothing will stop you? Are you sure?" and I walk back over to the table and lean over to press the Red Button.

King Kookee lunges across the table, under my arm, grabbing my finger a moment before it hits its target. "NO!! ARE YOU CRAZY?!"

I jump on him, we're both on the table now, rolling around, an inch from the button, and I get back on top finally, and take his finger, and hold it a millimeter above the button. He's pressing back, desperately trying to keep it away, keep it from launching whatever the hell is aimed at New York.

"Come on, kid. Do it." I touch his finger to the glowing red plastic.

"You…!!" He glares at me, a mix of fear, and disgust, and the definite knowledge that he's met someone truly insane.

I lean in. Our eyes are an inch apart. "You think I'm crazy, kid? Nah. I just know something you don't. You want to know what it is?"

"No!" He's trying to keep his finger from pressing The Button. His hand is trembling.

"Well I'm going to tell you anyway. You probably think you're the center of the universe, right? What if I told you that not only was there no center, but that there were so many universes there couldn't possibly *be* a center? What if I told you that, at this very moment, there were versions of us, infinite versions, not fighting like rats over an old piece of pizza, but sitting like men, at this exact table, talking out their differences and reaching compromise? What if I told you that if you blow this world to smithereens, there are infinite other versions that don't, and that make it work, so what's the point? And what if I told you that I've already seen entire universes collapse, and that being King of the World doesn't mean squat, it's like being king of a speck of dust…"

"Please… stop…"

"I'm not done. What if I told you that the only thing that

matters, then, the only thing, is love? Yeah, I know I'm a mush, but I don't give a fuck – it's true. Somewhere out there, right now, a mom is holding her infant, wondering if they'll have enough rice to make it through the week, and doing whatever it takes to keep them alive, and that's all that matters. Somewhere out there, someone's graduating from college, and their parents are cheering through their tears, because that kid's the first one in the entire family to make it, and that's all that matters. Somewhere out there, two best friends are putting on a talent show in their basement, and no one will ever see it, but that moment will become their most cherished memory until the day they die. And that's what matters. And somewhere out there, a father is wondering if he's done enough for his son, because money and power mean absolutely fucking nothing without love."

He pushes hard against me. "My father…"

I take a good, hard look at his pained face.

The President was right:

He's just a boy.

I let go of his finger, and roll off him, looking up at the ceiling thirty feet above, breathing heavy. "I'm sorry. That wasn't fair."

For a long time, we both just stare up, at the mural on the ceiling, of angels and devils, locked in battle above us.

He speaks first. "What… have you seen?"

I almost laugh. If he only knew. "Enough."

"I… have only known one thing. Togo."

"It's okay, King. You've helped unify an entire continent. You've fed a lot of people. You've tried to follow your father, and your grandfather, and your great grandfather. And you haven't started any wars yet."

"…your assassination… it wasn't us. But I knew." He looks over at me. "And I knew what could happen. The war."

"Yes. But it didn't happen. It's not too late. I'm here." I turn my face to him and smile. "And now you're not alone. I'm here."

His eyes well up, and I guess that's the first time in a long time, because he quick sniffs it back and jumps off the table and puffs out his chest. "Ahem. Mister President. That box. What is in it?"

I hop off the table too, reach down, and hand it to him. "A gift. Open it."

He tentatively lifts the lid. Doesn't know what to make of it.

"It's a ukulele. A dear old friend gave it to me."

"I... don't play."

"That's why I brought it. So I could teach you a song."

I take the ukulele for a moment, and show him a couple of chords, and sing:

When the late afternoon sun
Bends down it means we've won
We've made it through another trying day.
So come along and take my hand
As the twilight coats the land
The sun will rise again, just hours away.

I pass the ukulele back to him, and he fingers the fretboard awkwardly, plucking the strings, laughing a little. "Did your dear old friend teach you that?"

"No. My dad. He taught me that before he died. I was eleven."

He looks up at me, and half smiles, and stays silent for a while.

Then he plucks the strings, for a long time, and starts to make music.

Finally he looks over at me, and nods, and says, "I'm glad we had this meeting. I look forward to more."

And we both know.

It's an ending.
And it's also a beginning.

Somehow, miraculously, some of the wisdom of the multiverse seeped into this boy's brain, enough to make him stop and think, really think about it all, maybe for the first time. And this world will live to see another day without war. I'm so damned happy and relaxed, and yeah, I'll admit it, proud of myself, that I laugh, let out a big breath, lean back against the table…

And press The Red Button.

From: Chip Collins
To: Julie Taylor
Date: November 19, 2017 11:43am
Subject: Re: How to Stop World War Two

Hi Julie,

I know, I know. Only I could start a world war with my ass. But it wasn't my fault! The stupid button shouldn't be right where I wanted to sit!

So me and King Kookee are running around each other screaming like spider monkeys for someone to come in and click "undo," we're trying to pry The Red Button back up, like that would do anything at this point, and sirens are blaring, and we're fucked. The nukes are in the air. Game over.

And that's when five armed guards march in, and the lead one, dangling a key on a chain, announces, "King. I'm afraid you took the wrong key this morning. The key you used is only for drills. Here is the correct one – in case you'd like to do that last part over." And Julie, I swear the guard looks specifically at me and gives me the slightest little wink. Like, of course, they weren't going to let two idiots blow up the world. They must have switched out Kookee's key. Smart dudes.

And instead of bitching out his lead lackey, King Kookee surprises everyone in the room and reaches out and shakes his hand. "Uncle Koy. Thank you."

Uncle Koy seems genuinely touched, it's probably the first time he's heard a thank you from his nephew instead of getting slapped, and he pulls Kookee in for a proper Togo hug. It's awkward as hell, but awful sweet, too. So I use this tender moment as cover to get the hell out of here.

"Peace out, dudes."

And *that's* how you stop World War Two.

PART THREE: BATTLE THE BLUE

26. THE BLUE JUICE, PART TWO

From: Chip Collins
To: Julie Taylor
Date: November 19, 2017 11:43am
Subject: The Blue Juice, Part Two

Hi Julie,

Don't get me wrong. Dimension #921,034,455,231,594 still has a lot of work to do, a lot of long, dangerous rivalries to smooth out, and a U.S. President to keep alive and get back on his feet. But I think they can make it. I'm optimistic. (Or I'm just an idiot. It's a toss-up.)

So as I sit in the early morning light of the Oval Office, watching *Good Morning, New York!* with Artie, the last thing I expect is an emergency call on the Red Phone.

"Oh, shit. Artie. Do you know what this is about?"

"It's probably nothing, sir."

It's probably nothing. God, I would love to believe Artie right now. But I've got an uneasy feeling, because it's on my top-ten list of phrases uttered immediately before something colossally shitty happens:

Chip's Official Top-Ten List of Phrases Uttered Immediately Before Something Colossally Shitty Happens

1. "It's probably nothing."
2. "What's the worst that could happen?"
3. "Hey. Check this out."
4. "You might feel a little pinch."
5. "Oh. It's you."
6. "Seat belts? Why?"
7. "It doesn't look so bad. Just put some cream on it."
8. "What does this button do?"
9. "Wait – did you hear that?"
10. "What's that coming this wa- HOLY SHIT RUN!!"

Against my own will, I pick up the phone. "Chip– ah, President Collins here. "

"Mister President. It is King Kookee."

"Kookee! How's it hangin'?"

"Not good. Not good at all. We have a large problem."

My stomach turns. Shit. "Okay. Give it to me straight."

"Remember the missiles aimed at New York? They weren't nuclear missiles. They were new, um, technology."

"Technology?"

"Technology I am not at liberty to discuss."

Fuck. I don't even have to ask. *I know.* "It's the blue stuff, isn't it?"

His shock is palpable. "How…? No one knows…"

"I told you. I've seen a lot."

"Mister President. One of these missiles has been stolen. By Al Mofo. Terrorists. I believe they have loaded the weapon into a submarine, and are headed your way. Soon."

I turn to Artie. "Dude. You told me there was no Blue Juice problem in this dimension." But it's a rhetorical question, there's nothing he can say. We're fucked.

The chef walks in pushing a cart with my breakfast. Artie tries to shoo him out. "Sir, I'll call in the cabinet, and we can all–"

"No. Go. Get out. Just let me have my waffles in peace. I need to think."

From: Chip Collins
To: Julie Taylor
Date: November 19, 2017 11:43am
Subject: Re: The Blue Juice, Part Two

Hi Julie,

While me and Artie are shoving back and forth about getting into their stupid bunker, to save Dear Leader Chip from the terrorists' Blue Juice missile attack, (and ruining my breakfast, btw) I decide to give the telepathy thing another go. It's been a few days, so I must be back to normal super-human Chip, right?

I form the image of a silver thread from my brain to Artie's, and imagine it pulsing from me to him, me to him, just like ABBA taught me. Push. Push a thought into Artie's brain.

Nothing. Fuck me.

I reverse the flow, maybe I can at least pick up his thoughts. Him to me, him to me. Lift a thought. Any thought. What's he thinking?

Nothing. Fuck me again.

Damn. That Blue Juice really did me in. I'm used up.

There's a Blue Juice missile coming this way. And there's nothing I can do.

Wait.

There's something I can do. Of course there's something I can do.

"Artie. Get a hold of Pete. Pete Turner. And hand me that journal."

"Sir. Chip, sir. The regulations state–"

I grab the journal from his hand, slam it down on to the desk, and open it to a blank page.

"It's time to call Nikola Tesla."

But as soon as I open up the journal, to the last page, it starts scratchy-scratchy-scratchy and filling up with text.

Uh-oh. It's Pete.

Something about seeing the future. The Tipping Point.

Oh my God. It's bad.

I turn to Artie.

"Get a chopper. We're going to the New Yorker Hotel."

It's crazy, being on this side of the ITA, sitting in the New Yorker Hotel, waiting for someone to come to my dimension. No sooner had I scribbled "I'm here" and closed the journal – and there's a knock on the door. Like it could have taken Tesla and Pete five years to get to us, but since time stops in the ITA, it's instantaneous. Weird.

I don't know if I mentioned this last time, but the government, actually some super covert group who I assume is with the government, has commandeered the hotel room permanently. It looks like Churchill's War Rooms, barely any lights, maps all over the walls, red phones and shit.

Pete steps in first and peers around in the dimness, then to me. "Nice haircut."

Tesla steps in behind Pete, walks over and smooths out my jacket. "And that suit! Master Chip, your tuxedo was… interesting… but this! You look like a thousand dollars!"

I'm about to say "fuck you" but it hits me that Tesla's still stuck in the 1940s. "Thanks, dude. Hey, Nikola, what could you buy with a thousand dollars back in 1943?"

"A brand new Cadillac La Salle."

I turn to Pete and puff out my chest. "Hear that? I look like a *thousand dollars*, dude."

"Yeah. That's a third of one month's rent in 2017. Don't get too impressed with yourself."

I get down to business. "Okay, guys, the Blue Juice…"

Tesla claps his hands together "I have a solution!"

"Wow that was fast."

"I apologize. Pete didn't include this in his journal entry to you. Assuming you would succeed in your mission of stopping World War Two…"

"I did. Like a boss."

"Of course. Assuming that outcome, I began working on this." Tesla reaches into his pocket, pulls out a thin metal cylinder with a red button on the top, and begins.

Nikola Tesla's Quick Start Guide to Ridding The Entire Multiverse of The Blue Juice

"Step 1: Understand the Blue Juice.

After thorough analysis of a contained sample of the Blue Juice, I have confirmed: it is an Extraterrestrial Plasma Consciousness – a sentient being with a decentralized nervous system, suspended in a matrix, parts solid, liquid, and gas. As Albert theorized, it does in fact feed on energy from radiation, whether it be something as immense as a nuclear explosion, or as tame as the emissions from a television set. It also feeds on the energy emitted by biophotons excited by consciousness in other sentient beings – by capturing and placing them in a permanent stasis that the Native Americans called 'Forever Death.'

Pete's staring out the window down towards Madison Square Garden. "Been there. It sucks."

"Step 2: Understand how the Blue Juice Traversed Universes.

As you know, the infinite universes that make up the multiverse are discreet. Once a new universe is spawned, in every moment, based on every event outcome, it travels on its own path, untouched by all other universes. HOWEVER, …*are you listening, Pete and Chip?*"

Whoops. We were having a little sword battle with a letter opener and a stapler. "Sorry, Nikola. But this is BOOOORRRIINGG. Can you hurry it up? We kind of have some shit to take care of."

He tugs the lapels of his suit dramatically and moves on.

"Very well. Step 2, continued… HOWEVER, while universes, or dimensions, normally do not touch each other, the emergence of the INTERDIMENSIONAL TRANSFER APPARATUS has led to beings, including you and I and Pete, that have been to other dimensions. And we have created a new form of quantum entanglement, where our atomic structure, the particles that make up our bodily forms, have become correlated, or synchronous, with our alternates elsewhere, and that entanglement has propagated throughout the-"

"DUDE. Stop. I'm sorry. I know you live for this shit – stuff – but come on. Bring it to a close. Whatever you say I'm going to believe you anyway. Next."

"Chip!"

"Nikola." I point out the window. "It's not about me. It's about them. They need us. Now."

"All right then. Quickly: I believe that by absorbing Pete, The Blue Juice also achieved quantum entanglement, but in its case it was able to use it to capture more Petes, and more, across dimensions, and become the very first truly multidimensional creature. Living in all dimensions at once."

"Which is bad."

"Which is *very* bad. It will not stop. Never stop. Its hunger will never be satiated. We have seen the outcome. Complete multiverse absorption." He shudders. "That is why we must initiate-"

"Let me guess: quantum disentanglement."

His eyebrows arch. "That is correct, Chip! You *have* been listening!"

I point to the metal tube he's holding. "No. You wrote it right there. On a piece of tape."

Tesla just *tsks* and moves on:

"Step 3: Disentangle and neutralize the Blue Juice.

"Albert and I have devised a small machine, housed in this

tube, that creates spontaneous parametric downconversion, with mutually perpendicular polarizati-"

"Enough. Enough. Sorry. Just tell me where we stick it."

"Directly into the Blue Juice. Chip, I believe if you submerge yourself in it, activate this QUANTUM DISENTANGLER, and simultaneously- *oh, dear.*"

"Simultaneously *oh dear?* That doesn't sound very scientific."

"No. Oh dear. Chip. Have your powers of telepathy returned?"

"Nope."

Tesla plops down on the couch, defeated. "We can disentangle the Blue Juice, but we must also neutralize it, through telepathy, to prevent it from re-entangling. I assumed your telepathic abilities would return by now. Without them, all is lost."

Damn.

No. No fucking way am I letting this thing beat us. The gears start grinding in my head. Hmm. "Telepathy. Wait. Think. Think. Yes, I'm definitely out. ABBA's definitely out, he wouldn't be able to do it. Bobo's gone, he's with Gina – HOLD ON!"

"What is it, Chip?"

"*Gina!* She had the latent power – ABBA called her an anomaly, one in a hundred thousand."

Pete walks back over to the window, looks out. "But she dove into that shit. She's gone. We're screwed."

"No we're not. I've got her alternate."

Artie's eyes widen in horror. "No. Please, sir."

"Sorry, Artie. I'm going to need you to get The First Lady."

From: Chip Collins
To: Julie Taylor
Date: November 19, 2017 11:43am
Subject: Re: The Blue Juice, Part Two

Hey Julie,

Believe me. If I had ANY other choice, I would take it. We could go out and try searching through dimensions, looking for another Alternate Chip, or another Alternate ABBA The Cockroach King, or another Bobo, but there's just too much uncertainty. With Gina's Alternate, The First Lady, we've got a *known thing*: a person with verifiable, strong, latent telepathic ability. And we know *exactly* where she is.

"But sir."

"No buts, Artie. Call her."

"But to submerge her into the Blue Juice? Sir… she's… pregnant."

Oh. Shit.

She's carrying Clarence's baby. Three of them! I turn to Tesla. "Nikola. Tell me they'll be okay. In the Juice."

He fidgets with the tube. "I'm not a doctor, Master Chip. The effects of the QUANTUM DISENTANGLER should be minimal, on both mother and children. But the telepathic connection she'll have to make? It drained you completely. I'm not sure what it would do to her… or the babies."

Artie's pacing. "I'm sorry, sir. But I cannot call on the First Lady. We must find another alternative. She's too frail."

Damn. Damn. Damn.

We sit around, staring at each other, for a full minute. Waiting for a miracle, I guess.

The phone rings.

Artie puts it on speaker. "Yes, Terry?"

"Ah, sir. There's been, ah, an issue. Is the President there with you?"

Artie face palms. He knows whatever this is it's not good. "Yes, Terry."

"The, ah First Lady. She's, ah, quite agitated. Quite forceful. Extremely strong."

I put out my hand and stop Artie mid-pace, whisper, "Too frail, huh?"

"Terry. Have the medical staff increase her painkillers."

"Sir. I'm afraid that won't be possible."

"Why?"

"Because she's not in Area 51. She's here. In Washington. Right here in the Oval Office. She's on the line. She wants to speak with you."

The gum falls out of Artie's mouth. I gulp back a little puke.

I lower my voice to a whisper scream. "Terry! Tell her we're not available!"

"Sirs, I don't advise that."

"Tell her we're in a meeting. The Prime Minister of Antarctica or something."

"Sirs..."

I give up. "Shit. Whatever. Everybody fasten your seat belts."

And Julie, Terry puts on the First Lady, and I swear to God I've never heard so many curses in a single breath, and with such barely controlled rage. If she was here, she'd be tearing every single one of our throats out. "I'm coming for you, you fucking impostor!"

"Julie. Shnuggle kitten, listen-"

"It's Shnuggle *BEAR*, you fake! Arthur Ashe, are you there?!"

Artie's motioning frantically for me to say he's anywhere but here, that the Prime Minister of Antarctica kidnapped him or something, but fuck that, I'm not taking this heat alone. "He's right here. Aren't you, Artie?"

Artie shoots me the laser eyes for a second, then goes all

docile, puts his face in his hands, and gives up, too. "Yes, Madame First Lady…"

"Don't Madame First Lady me, Ashe. Do you know who I am? Do you know who my uncle is?"

"Yes, ma'am."

"Yes ma'am is right, Ashe. He's the editor of the *Washington Herald*. If you're not back here, both of you, in two hours, ready to answer questions, you're getting it from every angle. Executive, judicial, congressional, newspaper, TV – you hear me?"

"Yes, ma'am."

I respond absentmindedly. "Yes, Mom."

"What the fuck did you just say?"

Pete actually laughs.

And The First Lady gets even more pissed, if that's possible. "And who the fuck is that? Who else is there with you?"

Pete puts both his hands over his mouth to try to stifle his giggles.

I kick him in the shin as hard as I can. "It's no one. Sorry, I, uh, called you Mom. I didn't mean it. It's just a knee jerk reaction when I get yelled at sometimes. You know, *'sorry, Mom.'* It's automatic. Although, it is kind of ironic actually, considering you're pregnan-"

Artie lunges across the couch and puts his hand across my mouth.

But it's too late.

"I'm *WHAT?!*"

Artie calmly reaches over to the speaker phone with his free hand and hangs up.

Click.

"Sir. The First Lady is waiting. As you requested."

"Shut up, Artie."

Hey Julie,

I can taste blood.

Her first smack was so hard it burst a fucking blood vessel in my cheek.

Ah, my Shnuggle Bear. The First Lady. Right here in the Oval Office, with her sleeves rolled up and two pairs of brass knuckles on her fingers. (I'm kidding about the brass knuckles, but she might as well have them on. I told you she wasn't as sweet as she seemed.)

"So I'm pregnant, huh? Anything else you want to tell me?"

"Um. It's triplets?"

She smacks me again. Wow, she really put her shoulder into that one. I almost black out.

The secret service dudes have left, getting all the other VIPs down to the bunker, leaving The First Lady, Artie, Pete, Tesla and me in the Oval Office. What a crew.

"Ouch. Hey, I thought First Ladies were supposed to be classy."

She gears up for another smack. I flinch. "Okay! I was kidding! You're classy! You're classy!"

The next one lands anyway. *Motherfucking OUCH!* "Hey! You done?"

She actually laughs. "I'm just getting started. Now, who the fuck are you?"

The rest of us look at each other, like "who's going first?"

This is going to take forever.

"Listen, Gina. We don't have time for the full download. There's a serious shitstorm approaching the coast – it could happen at any moment. So I have to make it quick, and you have to keep your mind open."

Her hands clench into fists, I guess to keep her head from exploding. She doesn't even nod. Just stands there like a statue. An extremely tall statue. Waiting.

"Good. I'm a version of Clarence Collins, from another dimension, or parallel universe. Nikola Tesla here – please don't smack him, he's eighty-six – invented a portal to these other dimensions, many of which contain versions of ourselves, or what we call Alternates. Anyway, after we saved my best friend Pete here," Pete steps back, outside her roundhouse kick radius, "your man Artie here intercepted us and begged me to help stop World War Two. Which I did. You're welcome."

She huffs. "You expect me to believe that?"

"Yes."

I must've said that with some conviction, because she unclenches her fists, and looks me over. "Are you the President in your dimension?"

"Not exactly." (Pete snorts. I give him the finger.)

"I didn't think so." She turns to Artie. "Okay, joke's over, Ashe. Tell me the truth."

Artie risks a smack of his own and approaches her. He opens a manila folder with Top Secret stamps all over it and shows her a few paragraphs. She looks back and forth, from me to the folder and back. "What's this C.C.O.B.?"

"Well, officially, ma'am, they don't exist."

"And unofficially?"

"Covert Covert Operations Bureau."

"Let me guess. It's so secret they needed to put the 'covert' in there twice."

"I wouldn't even know who to ask about that, ma'am. I've never met them. But they have been right about everything. And about the threat we face right now. That's why we need you."

"*Me?* Ashe, what the fuck is going on?"

I take her hands – at first she jerks them back and almost

smacks me a fourth time – and sit her down on the couch, and try to be as authentic as possible. "Gina. You need to trust me. And open your mind."

Disarmed by my honesty and strength (or more likely just tired of clenching her fists and thinking about smacking me), she lets out a long breath, and nods.

"First - have you ever guessed someone's phone number?"

"What the hell kind of question is that?"

"Trust me."

"Well, yes. A couple of times. But doesn't everyone?"

"That's nine digits. A one in a billion guess. And you did it twice."

"So?"

"Now close your eyes."

She looks around, seems afraid to be vulnerable, but finally lets her eyes close. I imagine a silver thread running from my mind to hers, and a pulse moving along that thread, a thought, from me to her, me to her.

Please let this work, Chip. Please let me not have lost it completely. Just one thought.

~~*You in there, Gina?*~~

Her eyes bolt open, and yes – she smacks me. Jerks her other hand out of mine and stands up. "Get out of my head, freak!"

I put out my hand. "Please. Gina. Trust me."

It takes her a couple of minutes, but she finally sits back down and closes her eyes.

The telepathy is weak. Barely there. But it's there. I send her memories, and this:

~~*Gina. I know you from another dimension. The version of you I know is also named Gina, Gina Phillips, she's quite a tough one, just like you. And she has powerful latent telepathic ability. But she dove into the Blue Juice, looking for her love, and she's gone. I believe, as her Alternate, you have that same ability, and if so, we need your help. Will you help us?*~~

She opens her eyes. Nods.

~~Good. Now, a being named ABBA distilled his thousands of years of learning into two days for me, and somehow we'll have to compress that even further into an hour or two. So the first thing I want you to do is imagine a silver thread running from your mind into mine, and send a pulse of light along that thread…~~

Suddenly my mind goes white with a flash of thought, raw and powerful. I gasp, throwing my head back, as images and thoughts flood my brain. In an instant, I know this Gina's life story, all her dreams and beliefs, and pain, and love. This is so powerful, too powerful – *but how?* The Gina I knew was nothing like this. How is this Gina's ability so strong?

And that's when I feel it.

Their presence.

The triplets.

Three little unborn minds, so pure and untouched, so powerful with innocence and love. Like Bobo. Their thoughts, united with the torrent of love and protection from their mother, are like a fire hotter and whiter than a million suns. They reach out, the four of them, and envelop me, and they know my life story in an instant. And they say something.

~~We are with you.~~

And the white washes over my mind completely, until there is nothing – no me, no them, no nothing, and once again, I see infinity, and I know: *nothing will stop us.*

I open my eyes slowly, and Gina is looking at me, she's practically glowing, with a soft smile on her face, and a tear on her cheek. She reaches out for my hand.

"Thank you, Chip."

Then she rises, calmly, feeling full the power of her own ability, her infinite love for her unborn children, and their own abilities, growing inside her. She is unstoppable. And she knows it. She looks around, and pushes a thought out to all of us:

~~ Let's go kick some ass, boys. ~~

From: Chip Collins
To: Julie Taylor
Date: November 19, 2017 11:43am
Subject: Re: The Blue Juice, Part Two

Hey Julie,

"Sir. Tell me again why we're not just blowing that sub out of the water?"

The group of us, along with maybe a dozen Navy Seals, are roaring over Delaware Bay, out to the Atlantic, in one of those mammoth twin-engine Chinook helicopters. We're heading out to the latest coordinates we have for the terrorist submarine, about a hundred fifty miles off shore.

Tesla jumps in. "Mister Ashe. Releasing the Blue Juice into the world's oceans would be worse than letting it launch and explode over Washington. It would spread even further, faster, throughout the globe. That is the tipping point. That missile must not be launched. It must be contained at all costs."

My teeth are chattering. I can't tell if it's the chopper turbulence, or if I'm just scared shitless of this stupid tipping point Tesla keeps blabbing about. You know, you'd think by now, after everything me and Pete have seen, I'd be sort of numb to fear like this. But I guess that's not how it works. I'm starting to think the word "fearless" is bullshit. There are going to be times like this, over and over in your life, where your stomach tightens into a knot, and you feel like yakking, and you never get immune to it, but you've got to go ahead and do something terrifying anyway. Like the dad thing, I guess. I'm ashamed to admit how scared I am about that, that it's coming no matter how much I want to hide my head in the sand. I look over at Pete, and damn, I know he knows what I'm thinking, because he leans over and pulls off my headphones and shouts into my ear, "It's going to be okay. You're not alone."

"Yeah. I've got you, dude."

"Fuck that, dude. No, I meant you've got Gina."

But he's grinning, so I know he's kidding, and he's got my back. And they've got him all decked out in Seal gear, wetsuit and waterproof machine guns and shit. Yeah, there's no one I'd rather have my back. I mean, with Pete Turner the Navy Seal covering you, what could possibly go wro-

SKKKKRRRAAAALLLLCCCH!!!

Suddenly up is down, and shit's flying all over the place.

"We're hit! Get into the boat!"

Yes, Julie. As insane as this moment is, I have to stop and take in how awesome the U.S. military is. They built a helicopter so big there's a *boat* inside it. A fucking BOAT. Inside a helicopter. And not just any boat. It's a jet black, covered speedboat with mounted guns all over it. So as soon as up is back to up (and unfortunately some of my insides are now outside, sorry for the mess guys), we frantically clamber into the boat, a dozen of us, and buckle in.

The pilot's screaming at us. "Holding steady! I'll try to get lower, within a foot of surface, for the release! But they've got anti-aircraft, trickier buggers than we thoug-"

SKKKKRRRAAAALLLLCCCH!!!

Oh shit.

This time we're going down. The pilot's using every ounce of strength to control this beast. Smoke everywhere. That sound from the movies, that *yawning-motor-going-into-a-death-dive* sound. *"Gotta go NOW! Hold on!"*

And the next few seconds slip into that strange super-slo-motion thing that I still can't decide if I like or not. The chopper's back ramp opens – oh God, we're still at least thirty feet in the air, holy fuck – and the boat shoots right out, like a goddam bullet, heading straight for the water.

Since there is no way we are surviving this fall, I take this super-slo-mo moment to look around at my companions, and actually chuckle to myself at the absurdity of it: Julie, picture a jet-black mini-waterski gunship diving through the air, with two regular guys from another dimension who didn't ask for any of this, screaming their heads off, and the First Lady, and poor Artie, who I guarantee just swallowed a whole pack of gum, and an eighty-six-year-old genius inventor who's probably saying "I'm getting too old for this shit," and a bunch of Seals trying to look cool even though I'm pretty sure they just made in their pants. It's quite the sight.

The good news, if you can call it that, is that we don't exactly *hit* the water. We're more like an olympic diver, sliding into the water without so much as a ripple.

So far so good.

The bad news, of course, is that we're diving at a million miles an hour, and getting deeper and deeper, and the light is fading we're so deep now, and we're all pinned at the back of this stupid boat, and of course the steering wheel is at the front, and we're all going to die.

But Pete and one of the Seals crawl their way up to the front, and the seal shouts to Pete "Take the wheel! Pull back on it! I'm going to punch it!"

BOOM.

And Julie, I didn't think there was any way we could go faster, but we are. We're like a bullet being shot out of another bullet. Yes, that fast. The G-forces are pushing my cheeks back through my ears. Tesla passes out in Artie's lap. The First Lady pukes. (Hey! You said you were classy!) The whole thing's a mess, but eventually the water gets lighter an lighter, and we slow down, and soon enough – we're bobbing on top of the ocean.

"Cool. Oh, no. Fuck."

I point out to streams of black smoke, where I guess the Chinook went down. I see some parachutes, too, so hopefully the crew made it out. In any case, we're on our own now. Shit.

"Hey, Seal guy. The chopper was supposed to use depth charges to force the sub out of the water so we could get on board. What now?"

Seal Guy steps in some vomit, and says, cool as a cucumber, "How about you worry about holding onto your cookies, and I'll worry about the depth charges." He kneels down into the mini-cabin up front and pulls open a display panel. More space age weapon shit. He taps out a couple of codes, and we hear a couple of whooshes coming from under us. "Seeker charges. Same as up top." And he winks at me. Man, these Seals love their ass-kicking. I guess these charges are smart enough to lock onto a sub, like a torpedo. I wonder how long it'll take to-

BOOM.
BOOM.

Seal guy winks at me again. "Found 'em."

From: Chip Collins
To: Julie Taylor
Date: November 19, 2017 11:43am
Subject: Re: The Blue Juice, Part Two

Hi Julie,

I should have known.

Terrorists aren't exactly in the market for futuristic nuclear submarines, right? So I don't know why I'm surprised when the seeker depth charges from our little gunship force their sub to surface, and I'm like "They're going to fire a missile from that thing?" It's easily World War Two (World War One? I have no idea what the fuck is going on in this dimension) technology, rusty as an old mailbox, you can actually hear it creaking, it's probably leaky as hell. I'm amazed they were able to stay underwater at all. We should just let the terrorists go, they'll probably die of tetanus.

Seal Guy cuts me down a notch. "Hey, those guys shot down a Chinook with that submarine. They're extremely resourceful. Don't underestimate them."

"Right." I nod, and we all stay silent as we approach the hull.

"They'll be coming out the main hatch, probably guns ablaze. We'll take care of them, and neutralize them before then can launch the missile. You three and Seal Five will be heading to that space over there, behind it, see that circular panel? It's a lid. That's the missile silo."

Oh, I forgot to tell you. Me, Pete, the First Lady, and another Seal got a super-amazing, *no-way-this-can-fail* plan on the chopper coming out here:

How to Get Yourself Killed: In Six Easy Steps

Step 1. Climb onto this ancient submarine (which will

probably exceed its weight limit the instant we set foot on it and sink forever, and we die before we even get to Step 2.)

Step 2. Assuming we live through Step 1, pry open the silo lid. I didn't bring a can opener, so I hope this Seal Five Guy has some futuristic weapon thingy.

Step 3. Climb down INTO A FUCKING MISSILE SILO. Yes, you read that right. Climb the smallest ladder you've ever seen twenty feet down into an active missile silo that could launch at any moment. Not scary at all. Pay no attention to the wetness appearing in my pants.

Step 4. Disassemble the warhead, revealing the Blue Juice. Also not scary at all. Just hand me that change of boxers, will you?

Step 5. Gina and me jump into the bathtub-size pool of Blue Juice, send it a telepathic message that it just had an all-you-can-eat-mac-and-cheese-meatloaf buffet, then activate the QUANTUM DISENTANGLER. (Which does whatever Tesla described a chapter back, don't make me explain it again. Not that I could.)

Step 6. Die.

Hopefully, though, in the waning moments of our lives, we'll be able to appreciate the fact that we just saved this dimension, and maybe even the entire multiverse, again. Whoop-de-doo for me. I'd much rather be home eating Doritos on the couch with you and bouncing baby Chuck on my knee.

Peoww! Peoww! Peoww!

Oh shit. The bad guys are coming out of the main hatch on the submarine's central tower. Luckily, sharpshooter Seal Seven is picking them off as they emerge, giving us cover to climb onto the deck of the S.S. Rustbucket, about thirty feet behind the tower. The four of us huddle around the silo lid, a circular steel plate, maybe it's about eight feet in diameter, and I swear to God Julie, I couldn't make this conversation up:

Seal Five: "Ready to cut the hinges. Pete. Hand me the torch."

Pete: "Dude. You were supposed to bring the torch."

Seal Five: "No. I've been doing this for a long time, Turner. I know the plan."

Pete: "Listen, I don't care how long you've been doing this. You heard wrong."

Julie, Seal Five actually takes the time, in the middle of a gun battle on top of a submarine, bullets flying all over the place, to reach into his pocket, pull out his little laminated Operations Plan, and point to the line that says *Silo Torch: Pete Turner*. "See?"

I know this is not the optimal moment for this, but I can't help myself: "Dude. You need to get yourself one of those laminated reminder things."

"Shut up, dude. Whatever. I'll go back and get it."

Seal Five holds him back. "No you won't." Apparently, this is no time for amateurs to run around dodging bullets, so he does it himself. Miraculously, he makes it to out gunship and back to the submarine deck without getting shot, and under fire from the bad guys him and Pete melt off the silo lid hinges, and pry the massive panel open. (Bonus - we get to use it as a shield, giving us a slightly better – though still dismal – chance at survival.)

Pete turns me and Gina over the hole. "Okay dudes. In you go."

The First Lady, clearly offended, punches him in the shoulder. "I'm not a dude."

"Sorry, miss First Lady her highness majesty whatever. In you go."

So there we are, me and Alternate Gina Phillips, staring straight down into what will probably be our death. I turn to her.

"Ladies first!"

From: Chip Collins
To: Julie Taylor
Date: November 19, 2017 11:43am
Subject: Re: The Blue Juice, Part Two

Hi Julie,

We can still hear the small battle raging above us, but it's surprisingly safe-feeling right here, surrounded by the circular wall of the silo, maybe six or seven feet across where I can touch both sides. It feels like a womb. I know, I know, the four of us – me, Pete, the First Lady, and Seal Five – are literally standing on a missile filled with Blue Juice, and above us, any of the hundreds or thousands of bullets flying through the air could kill us in a second. But I feel safe. The top of the missile is nearly flat, with a two-foot-tall protruding column in the middle and a little orange light at the top. We can stand on area around the column, looking in at it like we're standing around a campfire. I reach out the grab Pete's arm. "I feel safe."

"Woah. Don't go weird on me now, dude. We are decidedly not safe. This is the opposite of safe. Here, hold this." He hands me a belt full of tools. A screwdriver falls out and hits the warhead right on the tip. *Clank!*

"Dude. Did you seriously just do that?"

"Sorry." Seal Five points to one of the ratchet wrenches in the belt, and I hand it to him. "Hey, listen, Seal Five Guy, if there's a bunch of wires in there, don't cut the red one. I learned that from the movies."

"Great. Thanks for the heads up. I'll try to remem-" he suddenly grimaces, puts his hand to his stomach, pulling it back to reveal blood. Shit. He *was* shot. He slumps over onto the top of the middle column, blood leaking out of his uniform. I can see his back rising and falling a little, he's still alive – but he is *not* going to be disarming any missiles today.

The First Lady is hyperventilating. "Are you fucking kidding me? What the shit? How the hell are we supposed to–"

And Julie, I don't know what comes over me, there's just so much panic and adrenalin going, I put my hand over the First Lady's mouth. I think that's a no-no.

Her eyes go wide – obviously this is the first time anyone has silenced her in her entire life – and Pete whispers. "Again. Did you seriously just do that?"

The next few moments are a blur: all I remember is getting punched in the face, and a lot of body parts flailing, and poor half-dead defenseless Seal Five getting kicked and elbowed repeatedly and dropping to the floor, and lots of shouting. And in the end, we're right back where we started – except I have a bloody lip.

"You happy, Your First Ladyness?"

"No. You want to go another round?"

Pete shouts at both of us. "Hey! I'm trying to disable this goddam thing! You want to shut the hell up?" His hands are shaking, he's lifting out the part where the little light is, and wires are popping out all over the place.

"Pete. Don't cut the red–"

"Shut the fuck up, dude."

"Got it."

Pete pulls the little laminated Operations Plan out of Seal Five's pocket, looking back and forth between it and the wires. "Damn."

"Don't say Damn dude. Damn is bad. Bad word."

"Shit. How's shit?"

"Not as bad as Damn. But still bad. What is it? Is there a red wire?"

"God, shut up about the wires. The wires aren't the problem. I'm not supposed to cut any wires, okay? It's this input pad."

"Oh. You supposed to type in a code or something?"

"Yeah. But the code they gave me is four letters. X-M-T-K."

"And?"

"And the buttons on this pad are only *numbers*. Zero through nine."

Numbers. Fuck. I hate numbers.

We all take a silent moment (not totally silent, there's still gunfire raging twenty fee above us) to contemplate how truly screwed we are.

And then it hits me.

"Pete! It's zero-zero-zero-zero. It has to be."

"Like the ITA? Come on, man. It can't be that stupid."

"You calling Tesla stupid?"

"Of course not. But…"

"But nothing. Trust me." And I put my hand on his shoulder.

He thinks for a second. Nods. Enters zero… zero… zero…

And the First Lady lunges over and jerks his hand out of the access panel. "Wait!"

Pete waves her hand away. "What, are you suddenly a missile technician now?"

"No. But are you telling me you're just going to slap zeroes in there and hope for the best?"

"Yes."

"Why don't we think about this for a moment. Maybe the numbers correspond to letters… like on a telephone keypad."

Pete rubs his chin. "Hmm. That's actually pretty smart." He goes for the spot he usually keeps his phone. "Whoops. No phone. You?"

Damn. That's right. We're all in Seal gear. They kept our phones back in D.C.

"Shit. Okay, it doesn't matter. We all know this, right?" I tap an imaginary telephone keypad in the air. "Easy peasy. Under the one is A-B-C…"

"No. It starts on two. Under the two is A-B-C."

"What?"

"Two is A-B-C."

"Why would the letters start under the two? That doesn't make any sense."

"I'm not trying to make sense. I'm trying to tell you what letters are on a telephone keypad. For the past hundred years or so."

"Okay, if you're so smart, and it starts on two, how do you get to twenty-six? Two through zero would be nine numbers, with three letters each… that would be twenty seven. There's only twenty-six letters in the alphabet."

"I think the zero only has two: Y and Z."

"Zero has nothing under it. No. Wait. A plus sign I think."

"Well, that makes *absolutely* no sense. What the hell are you guys smoking in this dimension?"

Pete jams his hand back into the recess. "We don't have time for this shit." And he points his finger towards the keypad.

The First Lady tries to grab his hand again, but I'm blocking her. She's shouting, "Zeroes? Really? Are you two a couple of idiots?"

Pete stops short. Then he grins wider than I've seen him grin in a long time. "Yes, ma'am. We are."

And he turns back and presses zero.

From: Chip Collins
To: Julie Taylor
Date: November 19, 2017 11:43am
Subject: Re: The Blue Juice, Part Two

Hey Julie,

So we're standing there, squinting our eyes closed, waiting for the giant missile we're standing on to fire up and shoot us out of the silo towards D.C. at a zillion miles an hour.

"Are we dead?"

"Shhhh!"

"Shhhh what?"

"Shhhh I'll tell you in a second if we're dead!"

Waiting. Waiting. Nothing.

And then the ten or so clamps around the middle column start popping open. *Pop! Pop! Pop!* And I'm like "HOLY SHIT WE'RE GONNA DIE!" and Pete's like "God, really? Still, dude? It's fine. It worked."

What? It worked?

It worked!

The stupid disarm sequence was zero-zero-zero-zero!

And sure enough, as the little light goes out, and Pete hefts the now-released column to the side, he reveals a hole underneath, leading directly into the main compartment of the warhead:

The pool of Blue Juice.

Immediately, peering into the darkness, we can see little tendrils of blue tentatively reaching up to the opening, I guess sensing lunch.

The First Lady gasps.

I take her hand. "Yes. This is the scariest thing you'll probably ever see. But you're not alone. I'm going in with you. We're going to be all right." And against the sure result of getting punched in the face, I put my hand on her belly. "We're *all* going to be all right."

She nods and takes a deep breath. She's shaking.

I turn to Pete. "Okay. Hand me the QUANTUM DISENTANGLER."

"Huh? Dude. You were supposed to bring it."

My heart stops.

The First Lady's grip on my hand cuts off all the feeling to my fingers. "Are you fucking-"

He laughs. "I'm KIDDING, guys. It's right here." He pulls out the metal tube and slaps it in my hand. "Easy. One button. On the top. No red wires. No keypad. Now get in there before you change your mind. I'll take care of Seal Five here."

This is it. I pull Pete in for a hug, and since the First Lady's got a death grip on my hand, she sort of has to come in for it, too. So all three of our foreheads touch, we're all looking down into the blue, and that weird safety feeling suddenly comes over me again. So strange, sometimes in these desperate moments, how much of your fear falls away, to reveal something else. Like maybe how it's really calm right in the eye of the storm.

I pat Pete on the back with my free hand. "Whatever happens, dude, there's just one thing I want you to know."

"What, buddy?"

"I've been subletting your apartment."

He winces. "Do we have to do this now?"

"I just always want to be up front with you. I was going to give you half."

"Half? It's *my* apartment."

"Yeah. But I'm the acting landlord. Ah, whatever. You're right. It's yours. You should get a hundred percent."

"How about seventy-five twenty-five?"

"Deal."

The First Lady smacks both of us. "Hey. Morons. Forgetting something?" And she points down at a couple of blue tendrils trying to sneak up Seal Five's nose.

"Whoops." I let go of Pete, turn, and wrap my arms tight around the First Lady. "Sorry, this is the only way we're fitting into that little hole. Ready?"

"No."

"Me neither."

And we jump in.

27. THE TIPPING POINT

From: Chip Collins
To: Julie Taylor
Date: November 19, 2017 11:43am
Subject: The Tipping Point

Hi Julie,

You remember the first time we kissed? That night at Harper's Tavern? I mean, we were both a couple of beers in, but I remember the exact moment vividly. Our lips touched, and I instantly felt like my entire life up to that moment, every past event, every memory, everything I'd ever done, scrunched down to a single point, that brief contact between our lips, that one small moment, that little paper-thin slice of time, and my mind turned white.

Holy cow. Now that I think of it, ***that*** was the first time I saw infinity.

Everything in a single moment.

I opened my eyes, and I could tell you felt as dizzy as I did, and giddy, and I could see my life explode back out from that single point, in a million different directions, my heart shooting out beams of whatever it shoots out, love I guess, it's too mysterious for me to even think I know, shooting through space and time and forever. And I said, "Wow. That was powerful stuff," and you laughed and whispered in my ear, "It's my lip balm. It's peppermint."

God, I miss you, babe.

Anyway, that infinite, white feeling? Right now I'm feeling that same thing again.

On the edge of the tipping point. The entire past and future of the entire multiverse, balancing on the razor of this single moment.

We're in the Blue Juice, floating, me and The First Lady, assaulted by its thoughts of hunger. *Hunger. Hunger. Hunger.* In my weak telepathic state, I can feel myself folding, breaking. But I can see, through the blue, Gina's face relax, and even form a little smile, and she puts her arms out, as if she's embracing it all.

And everything turns white.
Infinity.

Suddenly I'm standing in a pumpkin patch.

The First Lady taps me on the shoulder from behind. "So this is one of your favorite new places, huh?"

I smile. "Yeah. Me and Julie came here last month. I don't know, something about the cloudless sky, the orange pumpkins, the cool in the air, the smell of the pies, the little trio playing country music at the winery down the road. The quilts on the bed at the B&B we stayed at. It's perfect."

"It's the day you conceived your baby."

My eyes well up immediately. "It's true? Julie's pregnant?"

A little hand tugs at mine. I look down. A little girl.

No. Three little girls. The triplets. Giggling and running around the pumpkin patch, trying to find just that perfect one to bring home and carve into a jack-o-lantern. "Here, Chip! Over here!"

They lead me over to the biggest pumpkin they could possibly find, I could never lift it, and they're squealing in delight watching me exaggerate trying to budge it, and huffing and puffing, and then I start chasing them, and their giggles are like bubbles of joy filling the air around us. They run to the protection of their mom, Alternate Gina, the First Lady of the United States, and hide behind her, still laughing.

She puts her hands out to me. "Well, will you look at that? You're a natural. Nothing to be afraid of. You're going to be just fine." And she embraces me, and I don't know why, the tears start rolling down my cheeks. Then she pulls my head up so our eyes meet. "It's time to go, Chip. The girls and I have done our part. We talked to the Blue Juice. In the end, it was no match for us. "Now it's your turn, Chip. To finish the job."

I hesitate. "This might not work, you know."

She laughs. "Tesla invented it. What could possibly go wrong?"

I laugh too. And I press the red button on top of the QUANTUM DISENTANGLER.

Instantly I feel the Blue Juice scream, as every single electron of every single one of its atoms stops spinning. Our atoms are intermingled with it, too, and I can't tell where it ends and we begin. The feeling of infinity gets cut in half, then half again, and on and on, dividing faster and faster, closing in, as space and time and universes split off and isolate themselves, leaving me, and Alternate Gina and her girls, and the Blue Juice with no connection to other dimensions, or to anything at all. Alone.

I'm not sure I'm even me any more.

Goodbye, Julie.

Wait.

I feel a rumble.

And I know, without knowing, what's happening.

The disarm sequence wasn't zero-zero-zero-zero. That only opened the column.

The disarm sequence was nine-six-eight-five. Corresponding to the letters on a telephone keypad. Of course.

The Blue Juice is neutralized, but the missile is going to fire anyway.

With Pete and Seal Five sitting on top.

And us inside.

With the last of my energy, I take Alternate Gina's hand, and thrust it upward, towards the opening, and pray for a miracle.

Nothing.

I've been granted enough miracles, I guess. I don't blame you, God. You've gotten me out of enough jams for a million lifetimes.

The light goes dim, I can barely see my hand at the end of my arm, desperately reaching for something, anything to hold on to.

Please.

Is anybody up there?

From: Chip Collins
To: Julie Taylor
Date: November 19, 2017 11:43am
Subject: Re: The Tipping Point

Pete!

I feel Pete's hand!

He's feeling around, and grabs the First Lady by the wrist, heaving her out of the blue.

Good. She was the important one. They were the important ones.

The rumble is getting louder. I feel upward movement. The missile's propellant has been ignited. In a few moments, this silo will be filled with five-thousand degree flames, and we'll all be dead.

And my light is getting even dimmer. Pete's hand hasn't come back. It's been forever. Blackness is enveloping me, inviting me to make this my final resting place.

I accept the invitation.

It's over. Well, it was a good run.

I close my eyes.

And suddenly a thought occurs to me.

Actually, it's not my own thought. It's a thought from somewhere else, somewhere very far away, very faint, it sounds a little like the First Lady's voice, but it's not her, and the thought is:

"Collins! Don't you *dare* give up."

28. OPEN YOUR EYES

From: Chip Collins
To: Julie Taylor
Date: November 19, 2017 11:43am
Subject: Open your eyes.

Hi Julie,

"Open your eyes."

I can hear a voice. Is that the same voice I heard in the darkness? No. I don't think so.

"Open your eyes."

It's getting closer. It's a male voice. I feel like I recognize it. "...*dad...?*"

"No, you idiot. It's me."

I can manage one eye I think, and open it, and yeah, it's Pete. He's grinning like he just won the Powerball. "I thought we lost you."

I groan. "Yeah. Because you want your rent money from the apartment."

He laughs. "Yeah. That's it." He's beaming at me.

"Wait! The missile!" I sit up, and my brain feels like an axe just went through it. Dizzy. Almost fading out again. Pete gingerly lays me back down.

"Rest, dude. We got you out last just before the missile launched. And I mean JUST before. Thank God for the Seals."

"But the missile... the Blue Juice..."

I'm frantically looking around, nobody's looking concerned. What the fuck? They're all smiling at me: Pete, the First Lady, Artie, Seal Five and the other Seals, and of course, Tesla.

"Master Chip. We did it." And he reaches over and tousles my hair. "The missile fell harmlessly into the ocean just two miles from here. And the Blue Juice has been neutralized. We have verification from others. It is neutralized, and disentangled, across the planet, across dimensions. The multiverse, once again... is safe."

"So... we did it?"

"Master Chip. We did it."

Wow.
WOW!
WE DID IT!

As my eyes focus, and my brain begins to feel like there's only a bread knife cutting into it, I can see we're still on the super-duper little gunship. There's another chopper hovering above us, sending down winch lines and hooks and shit, getting ready to pull us on board. Artie hands me a piece of gum. "Here. You could use some sugar."

I look past him. "Wait. Who's that?" There's a bunch of ratty looking dudes in the corner back by the motors.

"Prisoners. Al Mofo." At the sound of their name, one of them raises his hand, like he wants to say something. Seal Seven goes to give him a kick in the face, but I wave him off. "Wait. Let him talk."

He stands up, tentatively, and bows. "You send own President and First Lady into dangerous mission to save country? We have saying for that."

I expect him to come out with some ancient religious phrase or something, some psalm from whatever their holy book is, something that sounds like summoning a deity. But he's like, "We call it 'BALLS.' We impressed."

Their little group all bows their heads.

Well, what do you know? This dimension might get a little more peace out of this whole thing than they expected. Good for them.

But me?

I just want to go home. I slap Pete on the knee. "Hey. Next stop home, buddy."

The First Lady coughs. "Um, actually, there's someone that would like to speak with you before you go."

"The President? He's awake?"

"No. Charles Collins. His father."

I spit out my gum.

From: Chip Collins
To: Julie Taylor
Date: November 19, 2017 11:43am
Subject: Re: Open your eyes.

Hi Julie,

I never seriously thought about it: at some point, in one of these dimensions where I meet an Alternate Chip, he was bound to have an Alternate Dad.

Dad.

As I walk down the hallway somewhere deep in the Med Center of Area 51, I have that feeling again. *Run away. Run away. He's not your dad. He's not your dad.*

But a hand takes mine and calms me as we walk. She knows what I'm thinking. Alternate Gina. The First Lady. She literally knows what I'm thinking.

"He's in here, Chip. With Clarence. I'll let you three be alone."

I enter the room and shut the door behind me. Clarence is laying there, in a coma, poor guy, more tubes and wires than you'd think a guy had places to put them, but otherwise he looks like a lot more than a thousand bucks. Probably a billion, with those schnazzy new bionic legs he's sporting. He'll probably be able to run a faster mile than me. Well, that's not saying much, a first grader can run a faster mile than me. But you get the point. He looks good. No bandages, no blood, no bruises, no coughing up a lung. Good.

There's a man sitting at the little chair beside the bed. An older man with thinning, gray hair, one hand on the President's arm. He's got a half-finished *New York Times* crossword puzzle in his lap. And he's letting out this God-awful sound. It's so sad, he must be weeping and wailing or something.

Oh, wait. He's snoring.

Can't blame him. Dude's probably here twenty-four-seven,

looking after his son. Of course he's tuckered out. I cough a little to wake him up.

Nothing, he's still snoring. Man, he sounds like a dying wildebeest. It's inhuman. Somebody get the *Guinness World Record* folks in here, Christ, I need earplugs.

I cough a little louder.

Nothing. (Well, not *nothing*, still a whole lot of super-fucking-loud snoring.)

I can't take it. I poke him on the shoulder. Hard enough to wake up a hibernating bear.

He wheels around like somebody caught him stealing the crown jewels, and stares up at me, eyes wide but unfocused, like he's still in the middle of his dream. "….*clarence…?*"

Holy shit. His face. He looks exactly like he does in the old picture in my wallet, handsome guy, just older – and totally freaked that he's seeing his son's doppleganger in a dream. It takes him a minute, but he wipes his face with his hands, blinks a few times, looks over at Clarence, then back at me, and raises an eyebrow. He asks, "What's my favorite color?"

"Purple."

"What's a five-letter word for the club a golfer uses in the sand?"

"Penis. Of course."

And he leaps to his feet – *careful, old man!* – And grabs my shoulders, grinning. "You rotten kid! It *is* you! I didn't believe them. I had to find out myself. It *is* you!"

"It is me."

"Thank you from the bottom of my heart. You were worthy of standing in for him, Clarence. Um, Alternate Clarence."

"It's Chip. In my dimension, Grandpa took one look at me and said I looked just like you. A Chip off the old block."

He looks off, somewhere far. "Grandpa…" and his eyes fill with tears.

I put my hand on his. "I want to know something, too."

He wipes his eyes. "Yes. Of course. What?"

I pull a ukulele from behind me and hand it to him. "I need to know. Do you remember?"

He looks down at the ukulele. Back up to me. Remembering. Trying.

Then, a little stiff with age, he plays and sings:

When the late afternoon sun
Bends down it means we've won
We've made it through another trying day.
So come along and take my hand
As the twilight coats the land
The sun will rise again, just hours away.

I can't help it, I put my arms around him, and hold him tight, so tight, for fear that this ghost from the past might slip through my fingers. This time I'm never letting go. I'm going to take him home with me, to meet you, Julie, and to be back with Mom, and to make it all just like it was when I was eleven. I let out a pathetic whimper.

"Is everything all right, son?"

Oh God. That word. I know he didn't mean it. *Son*. It's just a word any old man would say to any young man. But… "Dad. You died in my dimension. When I was too young. You didn't even say goodbye."

He takes my face in his hands, and kisses me on the cheek. His eyes dig deep into my own, and we both know everything we need to know: that it was never perfect, and it will never be perfect, and he's not my real father, and I'm not his real son, but for right now, this moment, we *are* father and son. He leans in and whispers.

"Goodbye."

From: Chip Collins
To: Julie Taylor
Date: November 19, 2017 11:43am
Subject: Re: Open your eyes.

Hi Julie,

Here I am again.

Standing at the doorway of dimension #234,698,594,394,683. Home.

Nikola has already stepped back in first, back to 1943. He looked older than usual this time, like all this crazy interdimensional shit is finally catching up with him, he's hunched over even more, breathing with a little more effort. I mean, he is eighty-six, right? The last thing he said to me before leaving and slipping into his robe for a bath and a full reading of *Being and Nothingness* was this: "Master Chip. I am a young man no longer. While I thrill at our adventures, and find great joy and fulfillment in helping other universes in our grand multiverse... I'm afraid this time may truly be... goodbye."

"Goodbye? But Dad– I mean Nikola–"

Now Tesla might be old, but he caught my little slip there, and he grinned. "Chip. You have been like a son to me, it's true. A son I didn't have. And it's been my honor to, perhaps in a way, be a surrogate father for you. But I want you to know something very important."

I sniffed back a tear. "What?"

"The time for looking back, to your own father, or fathers, is over. Now you become father yourself. It is your time."

He pulled his stopwatch from his vest pocket, unhooked it, and handed it to me. He opened the face and pointed to the hands, stopped in time. "Take this. And look, always look now, to the future."

I closed the face of the watch, and looked up to see Tesla amble into his room. (How does he never his his head?) He turned back and smiled and nodded, and I closed the door.

Goodbye, Nikola.

And now, maybe for the last time, I enter zero-zero-zero-zero, pull the latch, and hear the familiar whoosh of another dimension – my own. Before I step in, I look back into the never ending hallway. Pete is safe, and ready to start another chapter of life with Meg. The President will live, and with the First Lady, usher in, hopefully, an era of peace in their dimension. Old Tesla and Young Tesla, and Albert Einstein, have all reached their homes, no worse for the wear of our adventure. And I'm even back in my tuxedo. (If you can still call this mess a tuxedo. Artie said they had strict rules about what goes in and out of the ITA, so even though I saved their asses a dozen times over, they couldn't let me keep the custom-tailored President suit. But he did sneak the little US flag pin onto my tux and winked as I left. Thanks, Artie.)

All is well.

But then I think of Gina. She certainly wasn't my favorite flavor, but I grew to really like her. Admire her. And she's gone. I hope she found T-Rex at least. She deserves that.

And Bobo. God, is there ever a situation where he doesn't get the shit end of the stick? But you know what? I'm not going to be sad about him. He's gone, sure, but he has a strange way of not staying gone.

With that thought, I smile, put the stopwatch in my pocket, and bound back inside.

And hit my fucking head on the door.

29. HOME

From: Chip Collins
To: Reader Person
Date: November 19, 2017 11:43am
Subject: Home.

Dear reader person,

My emails to Julie are all on the FBiPad, which I handed to Fred as soon as I walked in, so they could publish this book. But you've come with me this far – I can't leave you hanging, right?

Anyway, Fred's right there, at the ITA entrance, hands on his hips, smiling wide but trying to look pissed. "You've got some explaining to do, mister."

I drop my backpack and put a hand on Fred's shoulder. "Listen, dude, can we debrief later?"

Fred pats me on the back. He understands. "Of course. You've been through quite the – *something* – today. The bureau has lots of questions, but for the most part, overwhelming thanks. By the way, that little, uh, issue with the ITA lock before, which we'll agree never to discuss, anyway Tesla's fix caused a bit of a ripple, so your trip wasn't instant. You're coming back three hours later. It's almost three in the afternoon local time."

I pull out Tesla's stopwatch. Turn the little dial forward three hours. *Look to the future, Chip.*

"Fred. Is Julie–?"

"Right outside. In the hallway. Waiting for you."

I rush past the guys in the clean suits, who look after me and – yes – shrug, and I'm at the door in seconds, and before I even see her, I can smell her perfume, she doesn't always wear it, but I remember it's still our wedding day, just a few hours later, even though it feels like a million years ago, so of course she has it on.

I look down. She's sitting on the floor. Asleep. In those jeans I love with no knees, and her Captain America t-shirt. Her hair's still made up from this morning, but she's got a baseball cap on.

I sit down, quietly, next to her. God, she looks like an angel. I don't want to disturb her.

Her eyelids slowly open.

But instead of freaking out, jumping up and down, she just smiles. "Wow. What the hell did you do to that tuxedo?"

I lift her chin so our eyes are locked. "I love you, Mrs. Collins."

"Even if I'm pregnant?"

"Especially if you're pregnant. And you *are.*"

"What? How could you possibly…?"

"The First Lady told me."

"The *who?*"

"It's a long story. You'll have to trust me."

"Okay. But… are we ready for this?"

I take off her baseball cap, lay it on the floor of the hotel hallway, noticing the paisley swirls in the carpet design for the first time, and it strikes me: another hallway. Doors on either side, as far as I can see. Like the choices we make, each one leading to a different place, a different ending. And a new beginning. We are forever making choices, opening doors, taking chances. Falling and getting up and moving on. And falling again. But if we keep getting up, and make enough of the right choices, nothing can stop us. *Nothing.*

Wow, what a weird feeling: I actually think I might have my shit together. How about that.

I push the stray hairs away from Julie's eyes, and pull her into my arms.

"We're ready."

And the time for words ends. Our lips touch, and just like our first kiss, the moment stops time, and starts infinity, and all I see is white, and forever.

We must be rolling around on the floor, because I find myself elbowing some random guy's shin. "Whoops."

He looks down at us and frowns. "Get a room. We're in a hotel, for Christ's sake, it shouldn't be too hard."

30. HOW NOT TO RETURN A TUXEDO

From: Chip Collins
To: Reader Person
Date: November 21, 2017 4:06pm
Subject: How not to return a tuxedo.

Dear reader person,

So me and Julie stroll into New York Best Formalwear Rentals, and I put the tuxedo (in the bag - God, I hope he doesn't look inside) on the counter. The guy swipes the bag and walks into the back, like he's done this a cajillion times, and we're giving each other the thumbs up, because clearly we're off the hook.

And then we hear the scream from the back room.

"WHAT FUCK IS THIS?!?"

The guy comes running out, his face looks like it's going to explode, and he points down to the tuxedo. And clearly, what the hell were we thinking? It's torn, battered, there's purple snot on it, yellow anti-radiation paste smeared on the shirt. Jeez, now that I'm really looking I can't believe I was actually wearing that the whole time. Yikes.

"So, before you pay for brand new one, you mind saying what you did to my tuxedo?"

"You wouldn't believe it."

"No. You piss me off. I want to hear. You tell me."

I clear my throat. Julie face-palms. But the guy's asking for it, so here I go:

"Okay. So me and Julie," I point to her, "are getting married, not a single stain on this thing, it's pristine, wrinkle-free. Then the FBI grabs me, and sends me into an interdimensional portal to go get my friend Pete. Because like an idiot he touched this blue goo that can suck you in and keep you in a state of suspended animation forever. Literally. Anyway, It turns out the only thing that can stop this goo is telepathy, which I had to learn from ABBA The Cockroach King. Nikola Tesla – the young version of him, if you're still following – gave us directions to ABBA's dimension, where I undertook the Three Terrible Trials. I passed – of course – and Gina, me, Tesla, and an alien named Bobo met a perception-manipulating being who built us a back door to the Blue Juice. We saved Pete – oh, and Albert Einstein. We saved him too. Then, to make a long story short, I had to act as interim President of the United States stop World War Two – shit's crazy, don't ask – and neutralize the Blue Juice throughout the entire multiverse."

I wait for a reaction. None.

"The End?"

The guy starts shaking a finger at me. "Oh. So you're funny man. I see. Ha ha. Funny man. Not so funny now that you will be giving me your credit card, yes?"

I hand him my Visa card. He's right. That was kind of a douche move trying to return the tux. But it's making Julie struggle to hold back her laughter, and that makes it all worth it, because she can't wait to see his face when I ask.

"So. Sir. Moving on. I, uh, need another tux for this weekend. Can I pick it up on Friday? We're having a do-over."

31. MY DO-OVER CITY HALL WEDDING

From: Chip Collins
To: Reader Person
Date: November 28, 2017 10:31am
Subject: My do-over City Hall wedding.

Dear reader person,

I know, I know, I tend to go over-the-top on this shit, but I can't
help it. I'm a sentimental mush. And if you're going to do a
wedding over, GO BIG, right?

We're back in the little chapel/transaction room at City Hall.
It's raining today, not quite the beautiful day we had last time, but
my mom kissed me on the cheek and assured me that rain on
your wedding day is good luck. (I don't know about that. I mean,
what do you say to all the people who get married on *sunny* days?
Sorry about the shit luck, dude?)

Anyway, the place is PACKED. All our friends. My mom
brought her mahjong friends, too. Mrs. Rosen and her walker are
here. Everybody I know at the FBI, including, of course, Fred.

And Pete. Yes, I've been very protective of Pete since our little
run-in with the Blue Juice, so I made sure he was available. He's

standing right next to me, in fact. My best man. Meg's over on the other side of the aisle (if you can call it an aisle), as maid of honor. Even though she's super scrawny like everyone from her dimension, she's got this cute little baby bump going on, and she's glowing.

I lean back and whisper. "Hey, Pete."

"Sup."

"What are you going to name the baby? *Chip?* I like Chip. Has a good ring to it."

"Yeah. All I need it *two* Chips in my life. No, we're thinking Edmund."

I laugh. "Edmund? Like Edmund's Used Pianos over on Second Avenue?"

"Seriously? No, dude. Edmund like Meg's grandfather's name. Now shut up and pay attention."

Whoops. He's right. It's almost time. The music is starting. I look around. There's a giant cake in the corner, and even a rose arbor above our heads, compliments of the FBI. (Oh, yes. They owe me BIG TIME for getting rid of the Blue Juice. And you can bet I'll be extracting as much payment as possible, dudes! You're *welcome!*) They even went out and got us one of those white throwaway rollup carpets.

Good old Mr. Patel – you'll remember him from Disaster Wedding #1 – enters the room from the back, and does the most hilarious double-take you've ever seen. Like is this room supposed to even hold this many people? He almost backs out, but we've all seen him, so I guess he realizes there's no escape. And when he steps up to the lectern, he sort of changes. Like maybe it dawns on him that this is the culmination of everything he's worked for, a big-ass wedding like this. Or he just let out a satisfying fart. I don't know. Anyway, he smiles broadly. "Welcome, ladies and gentlemen. And now... the bride, please."

Wow. Julie. I might have to do this every month, it's so awesome. Do my wedding over every single month for the rest of my life. I mean, why not? What could be better than your beautiful mate standing across the room in her off-white dress, all your friends, your family, and a big cake? Nothing. Nothing, I tell you.

So anyway, we get right into it, right to the part where Mr. Patel says "… if any party has reason why these two should not be married, speak now or forever hold your peace…" and the place falls dead silent. Everyone looks around, waiting for the other shoe to drop.

Nothing? Good. We're good.

And as Mr. Patel opens his mouth to speak the next words, the doors in the back fly open, and someone shouts "Stop!"

The whole room spins around.

It's Gina. Agent Gina Phillips.

What the fuck?

I run towards her, and she runs to me, and we meet in the middle, and she lifts me up and swings me around (I mean, could you imagine *me* trying to swing *her* around?), and the FBI agents in the room erupt into hooting and hollering and raucous applause.

"Gina! How?"

"Bobo led me through the Blue Juice. It had become its own portal to other dimensions. We almost got trapped, but then you put the nail in the coffin. In that missile."

"Wait! That was *you* I heard in the missile?"

"Yes."

"But… what about…"

She puts me down. "I lost Bobo. I'm sorry, Chip. But…" She points to the open doors.

And T-Rex walks in, grinning like a little kid.

Gina smiles back at him, a tear making its way down her face. She leans down and says, "Chip. I couldn't have done it without you." And – in a moment I'll remember forever because it sure as shit will never happen again – she kisses me gently on the cheek.

I spy Fred out of the corner of my eye, laughing to himself. He winks at me. "Sorry, Chip. We knew for a while. But I know how much you like surprises." And the whole crowd starts laughing and cheering along with him.

So me and Gina, and T-Rex, make our way to the altar (again, not an altar, but close enough). There we are: three couples, three symbols of the power of love, three unions that are creating the next generation. Oh, except for Gina. She's not pregna-… wait… I turn to her. "Gina. Don't tell me you're…"

She nods. Smiles. And T-Rex stands even taller and prouder than he already was.

Holy shit. More babies.

And without anyone having to say a word, the six of us – me, Julie, Pete, Meg, Gina, and T-rex – join hands and form a circle. I look around, at the people I love, and grin.

You know what? Mr. Patel was right:

LOVE WINS.

32. ONE YEAR LATER

From: Chip Collins
To: Reader Person
Date: October 15, 2018 11:43am
Subject: One year later.

Dear reader person,

So me and Julie are walking down Thirty-Fourth Street, to the little kiddie park they put in when they re-did Madison Square Garden.

We had a girl – of course, because this whole time I was calling it Chuck and assuming it was a boy – and we named her Gina. Yeah, I know that's sappy, but we've actually become pretty close friends with Gina and T-Rex, so it felt right. Whatever, like I said I'm sentimental. They, for their part, refused to name their kid Chip, but did name him Collin – pretty cool, right?

Anyway, we're pushing the stroller past the thirty-foot statue of Bobo, and- *oh, shit*, I haven't told you, have I? Well, since the FBI owed me *huge* for saving the multiverse (again), but still refused to officially acknowledge the existence of Bobo, I stuck it to them by making them work with the City of New York to erect a big, giant, obnoxious brass statue of him next to the new Madison Square Garden. They wouldn't put a plaque or anything on it (again, officially being douches about it), but they caved and did the statue, leaving no records at all. So now everyone passes and gawks, and has to figure out for themselves what they think it is. On days like today, sunny and warm with nothing else going on, we like to sit on a bench nearby with baby Gina and listen to the tourists speculate, scratching their heads and taking pictures. It's hilarious.

Well, on this particular day, baby Gina points up to the tippy top of the statue, and giggles. We smile, of course, because nothing's more full of joy than a baby's giggle, and Julie says in her mom voice, "What's that you see up there, Gee-gee? All the pretty birds?"

And she keeps giggling, and I look up, and yeah, there are pigeons up there, shitting all over the statue like responsible New York pigeons should. But...

No, I'm seeing things.

I squint.

Yeah. There's something up there. Not a bird.

Something furry.

Humping the top of the statue.

YOU'VE FINISHED

Please review this book!

One of the best ways for independent authors and small publishers to get exposure for their books is to receive as many honest, thoughtful reviews as possible.

Please take a moment to visit the place you purchased it from and let the world know what you thought!

Thanks in advance!

ALSO BY ROB DIRCKS

Gigi Make Paradox (Where the Hell is Tesla? Book Three)

The Third book in the Where the Hell is Tesla? Trilogy is coming June 2019!

Listen, having kids is great, my little Gigi Collins and Pete's daughter Hannah are sweet little fluffs of cotton candy, spun from the silk of fairy spiders who live in the clouds. But MAN, can they cause trouble. Seriously, you'd think a two-year-old couldn't possibly threaten the very existence of our physical reality, but, well, you know where this is going.

So join me and Pete, and Bobo, and of course the man himself, Nikola Tesla, on another spine-tingling, bowel-loosening thrill ride, and remember: bring your adult diapers.

WARNING: If you haven't read Where the Hell is Tesla? and Don't Touch the Blue Stuff! (Where the Hell is Tesla? Book 2), I apologize in advance, as you might get completely freaking lost. If you do, just call my apartment, if I'm not watching Gigi I'll try to pick up the phone, and I'll fill you in. (Assuming our physical reality still exists.) – Chip

————

Praise for the series:

"★★★★★ An incredible, madcap adventure that only Dircks could deliver. The "Tesla" books are living proof that original stories are still out there waiting to be discovered."

"★★★★★ I love this series! It gets better and better. Love wins! If you haven't read *Where the Hell is a Tesla?*, you must. You'll love both. I promise. Thank you Mr. Dircks!"

"★★★★★ **So damn funny and insanely entertaining!** Loved the first one and this was just as fun."

"★★★★★ There isn't another writer like Rob Dircks in the entire multiverse."

"★★★★★ **The CHIP MASTER IS BACK.** My second favorite of all audiobooks I've ever listened to... only because *Where the Hell is Tesla?* is number one."

ALSO BY ROB DIRCKS

The Wrong Unit

I DON'T KNOW WHAT THE HUMANS ARE SO CRANKY ABOUT. Their enclosures are large, they ingest over a thousand calories per day, and they're allowed to mate. Plus, they have me: an Autonomous Servile Unit, housed in a mobile/bipedal chassis. I do my job well: keep the humans healthy and happy.

"Hey you."

Heyoo. That's my name, I suppose. It's easier for the humans to remember than 413s98-itr8. I guess I've gotten used to it.

———

Rob Dircks, bestselling author of *Where the Hell is Tesla?*, has a "unit" with a problem: how to deliver his package, out in the middle of nowhere, with nothing to guide him. Oh, and with the fate of humanity hanging in the balance. It's a science fiction tale of technology gone haywire, unlikely heroes, and the nature of humanity. (Woah. That last part sounds deep. Don't worry, it's not.)

———

"Rob Dircks manages to bridge the tricky divide between science-fiction and humor so effortlessly that a comparison to Vonnegut is not a hyperbolic stretch." - *Ruth Sinanian, Literature Reviewer*

"★★★★★ The Wrong Unit is the right story for today... it reacquaints us with our human ingenuity and shortcomings, our deepest longings, and, most notably, our great capacity to love."

"★★★★★ FUNNY. HUMAN. A GREAT RIDE! The Wrong Unit is a fun and twist-turning journey that keeps you on the edge of your seat."

"★★★★★ I'm such a fan of this book that I'm going to recommend it for next month's Book Club pick!"

"★★★★★ OUTSTANDING!! With The Wrong Unit, Rob Dircks has established himself with this potentially prophetic view into humanity's future and the consequences of our growing reliability on and appetite for technology."

"★★★★★ The Wrong Unit is such a great ride!! The pace is fast, the dialogue is smart and sarcastic and witty. The sci-fi world created by Dircks is new, imaginative, and so original. No easy feat! I loved the main characters Heyoo and Wah. Laugh out loud funny and sure, I'll admit, I got a little weepy at some spots. Highly recommended!"

ALSO BY ROB DIRCKS

You're Going to Mars!

Living and slaving in Fill City One, you get used to the smell. We call it the Everpresent Stink. But every once in a while, on a spring day with a breeze, it clears away enough to remind us that there is something more out there. Most Fillers' wildest dreams would be just to get past the walls and live in the mainland. But my dream? It's a little bigger.

I'm going to Mars.

Well, I'm only going to Mars if I can find a winning Red Scarab to get on Zach Larson's crazy reality show. And then I'll have to figure out how to escape this hellhole. And then compete on live television for three months. And somehow win a spot on the crew of the very first manned mission to Mars. Oh, and one more slight obstacle? There might be a reason that by 2085 a human still hasn't set foot on the Red Planet. A dangerous reason. A reason worth killing for.

———

In *You're Going to Mars!* Rob Dircks, Audible best-selling author of *Where the Hell Is Tesla?*, creates a near-future filled with family (the good kind and the insufferable kind), pop divas, mobsters, and the world's first trillionaire - and sends them all on a science fiction odyssey/comedy/love story/adventure that will change their world forever.

———

"★★★★★ Reviewers' Choice Award – it's THAT good. Captivating, interesting and creative. I could not put it down. I would love to see it filmed!" — *AudioBookReviewer.com*

"★★★★★ One of my favorites of the year! This book was a pure joy to listen to. One fist-bump moment after another. I enjoyed every minute of it." — *DabOfDarkness Book Reviews*

"★★★★★ A remarkable book. *You're Going to Mars!* was one of the most interesting, entertaining stories I've listened to in quite a while. A fabulously written book with a unique plot, endearing characters, and a richly crafted world, You're Going to Mars is one of those books I just didn't want to put down until I finished it." — *BriansBookBlog.com*

"★★★★★ Mr. Dircks once again hits a home run! I have been a fan of Mr. Dircks' works from his premiere release… you cannot go wrong giving this book a listen if you like science fiction and great writing." — *Quella Book Reviews*

"★★★★★ Fun, Fast-Moving, and Genuinely Funny Sci-Fi. This audiobook was a blast! A comedic sci-fi take on the Charlie and the Chocolate Factory story with a female protagonist. Even though *Ready Player One* was similarly-themed, this book is about as different as you can get, and in many ways a better book." — *Wynne McLaughlin, Author of* The Bone Feud

"★★★★★ Hits it out of the park again! Dircks' unflagging ability to imbue plot-crackling science fiction with a deep vein of humor, heart, and hope reminds me of Ray Bradbury with curses. An incredibly inventive plot of a young woman's journey in a world both similar and very different from ours. Wow, just wow." — *Wendy Mass*, New York Times *bestselling author of* Pi in the Sky *and* The Candymakers

ALSO BY ROB DIRCKS

Listen To The Signal: Short Stories Volume 1

Like episodes of The Twilight Zone or The Outer Limits, the sixteen stories contained in Listen To The Signal, Short Stories Volume 1 ask questions like, "What would happen if an iPhone game was addictive - to everyone?" and "Are we all living inside a simulation? And if so, who's running it?" and "When a pilot has to emergency land in a remote town near Area 51 what does he find?"

Hi, Rob Dircks here. I'm the Audible bestselling author of Where the Hell is Tesla?, and I've been writing and narrating these stories since 2016 on my podcast, Listen To The Signal. But now I've made them available ONLY here in this book. They include: Dakō • Today I Invented Time Travel • End Game • November 8, 2016 • Quick Fix • Horatio Breathed His Last • Purgatory • Out of the Blue • Tick Tick Tick • Rose • Red Parka • Bloop • Their DNA Was No Longer the Same • The Last One • Mister Personality • Christmas in Silver Peak.

"★★★★★ There is no one writing scifi as well as Rob Dircks right now, and this short story collection proves it.
I listened to all of these stories when they originally came out on his podcast, and was blown away every time by the quality of his writing and his mastery of the short story form. He knows the tropes and how to subvert them. He can build a world in a few paragraphs so that you understand it intuitively. He creates characters that are uniquely relatable and gosh darn it, he's funny to boot.
That is when he is not making me tear up. Add to all that the fact that he

does a terrific job narrating his own stories and you have a very appealing package.

But now that I have been able to re-listen to all the stories again via this collection, hearing them all together rather than strung out over a series of months, I perceived something I had not noticed before. Something that unites not only these stories but also his novels. Something special that only Rob Dircks can deliver.

It's a sweetness, a love of life and humanity, that shines through all of his characters and all of his imaginary worlds. I feel instantly better when I finish something he has written, I feel uplifted and hopeful. What a wonderful gift Rob has to allow us to see the good in one another, and how lucky we are that he is sharing it with us through his art.

Can't wait for the next collection."

ABOUT THE AUTHOR

 Rob Dircks is the Audible bestselling author of *Where the Hell is Tesla?*, *The Wrong Unit*, *Don't Touch the Blue Stuff! (Where the Hell is Tesla? Book Two)*, and a member of SFWA (Science Fiction & Fantasy Writers of America). His prior work includes the anti-self-help book *Unleash the Sloth! 75 Ways to Reach Your Maximum Potential By Doing Less*, and a drawerful of screenplays and short stories. Some of these sci-fi short stories appear on Rob's original audio short story podcast *Listen To The Signal*, also narrated by the author. Rob's a big fan of classic science fiction, and sci-fi conspiracy theories (not to believe in them, just for entertainment.) When not writing, he's helping other authors publish their own work with his own little imprint, Goldfinch Publishing. He lives in New York with his wife and two kids. You can get in touch at www.robdircks.com.

facebook.com/robdircksauthor

twitter.com/RobDircks

instagram.com/Rob.Dircks

goodreads.com/robdircks

amazon.com/author/robdircks